Vidocq
and The Lemonade Girl
& Other Plays
of Murder & Vengeance

FROM THE SAME AUTHOR

Vidocq
and The Lemonade Girl
& Other Plays
of Murder & Vengeance

Plays by
**Paul Mahalin & Louis Péricaud,
Louis Péricaud & Ernest Vois,
Xavier de Montépin & Jules Dornay**

Adapted by
Frank J. Morlock

A Black Coat Press Book

ISBN 978-1-61227-944-2. First Printing. February 2020. Published by Black Coat Press, an imprint of Hollywood Comics.com, LLC, P.O. Box 17270, Encino, CA 91416.

TABLE OF CONTENTS

Antoine Paul Mahalin (b. Epinal, 17 January 1828; d. Paris, 20 March 1899) was a popular novelist, and journalist. A number of his novels reused characters created by Alexandre Dumas (D'Artagnan, Porthos, Aramis, Monte-Cristo) and Paul Féval (Lagardère). Vidocq, ou la Belle limonadière *was first a novel which Mahalin published in 1884. It was based on the historical character of Madame Romain, who had already been featured by Balzac in* César Birotteau *(1837). Then it became a 5-acts drama, co-written with Louis Péricaud, and first performed at the Théâtre de l'Ambigu on 20 July 1894. Louis Jean Péricaud (b. La Rochelle, 10 June 1835; d. Paris, 12 November 1909) was a very successful playwright, but also a historian of the theater, a director, and even an actor.*

VIDOCQ AND THE LEMONADE GIRL

by Paul Mahalin & Louis Péricaud.

CHARACTERS

VIDOCQ a.k.a. M. JULES
COCO-LACOUR
YVRIER
M. DE BERGONDE
ROLAND
SABINE
MADAME MAZEROLLES
GEORGES MAZEROLLES
JACQUES LEBRUN
HELENE LEBRUN
M. COURTOIS
MADAME MADOU
NAVET
VAILLANT

BRIGITTE LIEGEOIS
ANNETTE CHEVASSU
AUGUSTE
A RAG PICKER
A LAMPLIGHTER
A CLERK
TWO COPS
AN OLD GENTLEMAN
A DOCTOR
MEN AND WOMEN OF THE PEOPLE, DINERS, SOL-
DIERS, ETC.

The action takes place in Paris in 1823.

ACT I

SCENE I

THE RUE DES MAÇONS-SORBONNE[1]
On one side, the hotel Mazerolles, a huge, lordly lodging with
an immense coach-door and high windows near the audience.
Mid stage, a café.
Near the audience on the opposite side, a cabaret with the sign
"Courtois, wine merchant." Further back, a grocery with win-
dows, boxes of candles, and sugared bread in wooden boxes.
Further still, on the same side, a butcher shop. Adjacent and
usable streets.
AT RISE, it is mid-night. The café alone is lit up. A Lamplight
hangs across the stage. Shops and windows, closed.
Courtois is shutting the blinds of his establishment. Passers-by
cross at the back. Annette arrives from a street near the cabaret, and takes leave of some acquaintances who accompany

---

[1] Later absorbed into the Boulevard Saint-Germain and the
Rue Champollion.

her, and leave in various directions. Annette heads for the hotel.

COURTOIS: Heavens, Mamselle Annette.
ANNETTE: Good evening, neighbor. You're closing up your establishment already?
COURTOIS: Hell, since we are in the year of grace 1823, His Majesty Louis XVIII reigns in the Tuileries, it's only the lemonade vendors who provide consumers with the means of getting drunk after mid-night, while as for us simple wine merchants—but you neighbor, so late in the street?
ANNETTE: Just imagine, I'm coming from the theater. I saw them play *Victor, the Child of the Forest*.[2] Oh, how much fun we had! We wept all the time.
COURTOIS: Truly?
ANNETTE: Now I must rush to go in before M. Jacques Lebrun brings back my mistress from her old friend on the Rue Hautefeuille, where she went, as she does every night, to play Boston.
COURTOIS: M. Jacques Lebrun, the supervisor, the factotum of the house. Ah, it's he who serves as the cavalier to this good Madame Mazerolles. Well, what about Brigitte, her chambermaid who undertakes that duty?
ANNETTE: Brigitte obtained Madame's permission to go to the Calf Sucking Tits to take part in a wedding dance with the niece of Butcher Vaillant, the supplier of our house, and God knows when she'll be back! But I'm gossiping, and my Mistress's table is not set. And then, I'm in a hurry to sleep and dream of Victor.
COURTOIS: You won't have much time to dream—nights are short at the moment.
ANNETTE: Till tomorrow, M. Courtois.
COURTOIS: Till tomorrow!—we are done.

---

[2] *Victor, ou L'Enfant de la Forêt*, 3-act play by René-Charles Guilbert de Pixerécourt (1773-1844) first performed at the Ambigu-Comique theater on 10 June 1798.

(He goes into his house humming. Sabine and Roland enter from the back.)

ROLAND: You see, my dear Sabine that I follow you with confidence—but yet once more: where are you taking me?

SABINE: Where I have business, my dear Roland.

ROLAND: Here? In the Rue des Maçons-Sorbonne? In front of this hotel where I lived like a son, and where I later was cast out, head bowed, read in my face, scolded like a child, and kicked out like a lackey?

SABINE: Yes, for having stolen a hundred crowns from Madame Mazerolles. She's your godmother who since she became a multi-millionaire, no longer understands the appetites of youth.

ROLAND: And why did I commit this first sin? Because I loved you! Because you sing for a living in a dive at the Palais Royal, and I dreamed of taking you away from a precarious existence of running adventures, and creating a situation more worthy of you. Unfortunately, the meager resources that I took from this house were soon exhausted.

SABINE: And it's to put you afloat again that I decided to attempt a trick, which, it's true, I have no great confidence in.

ROLAND: A trick? At this hour? Here?

SABINE: If I succeed, you'll know what I have done.

ROLAND: And if you don't succeed?

SABINE: In that case, my poor friend we'll have to resign ourselves to a necessary separation.

ROLAND: A separation. Ah, you never loved me!

SABINE: You are mistaken; I do love you.

ROLAND: You?

SABINE: I love you to the degree that I'm astonished myself that this feeling was able to revive in a heart I thought dead. I love you without knowing why. Perhaps, because we have the same nature, the same passion, the same thirst for power, for luxury, for pleasure. Perhaps, in the end, because our two stars were destined to shine with the same dazzle. The one that brings fortune or to extinguish in some dark catastrophe.

ROLAND: But, if you love me, why refuse to belong to the man towards whom all joins to carry you away, to the man who, since he met you, asks on his knees to give himself completely to you, to possess you, and would be capable of anything, even crime?

SABINE: My darling, because I don't want our first night of marriage to be framed in a hovel. Because I don't want that worry over the future slip between the intoxication of our kisses. Because a love made of two poverties is quick to change into regret and reproaches. Finally, because I don't wish to give myself today if the necessities of life will oblige me to take myself back the next day.

ROLAND: You are right. It's necessary to be rich. Rich at any price. Rich by any means.

SABINE: Do you have the means?

ROLAND (considering): Hold on—a last hope. See that house? (pointing to the café)

SABINE: That house?

ROLAND: Under the appearance of being moderate and calm, it's a dive, where, when I was living at the Hotel Mazerolles, I turned my first card, and won my first sou. I've got two sous left. I kept them to be able to offer you every morning that bouquet of red carnations with which you love to perfume your corsage.

SABINE: And you want to gamble them?

ROLAND: Luck is smiling on me, I'm sure of it. First of all, I've discovered an infallible plan. Yes—soon a heap of gold will be amassed before me.

SABINE: In that case go, but don't return with a new deception.

ROLAND: You won't go with me?

SABINE: I told you—I've got business that keeps me here. I'll finish it while you are playing.

ROLAND: You'll stay alone, at night, in this deserted neighborhood?

SABINE: I won't be alone since I'm waiting for someone, and you know, I'm not a little girl.

ROLAND: Then, till later, since you wish it—(starting to walk away) But, since you won't be at my side to bring me luck, give me something that will! (He points to her bouquet.) One of those flowers which feels your beating heart.

SABINE: Here. (listening) I think I hear someone coming. Go.

(Roland puts the flower into his buttonhole and goes into the café.)

SABINE(looking): There she is. Ah, the Intendant is accompanying her.

(She goes close to the door of the hotel. Jacques Lebrun and Madame Mazerolles enter. Jacques gives his arm to the old lady, and holds his lantern in his hand.)

JACQUES (grumbling): My sacred word! Madame, you are not reasonable. To go back after curfew. Really you deserve to spend the night at the police station.

MADAME MAZEROLLES: Don't scold me, my good Jacques. Hours pass so quickly when one talks about the past. The time when one was young, gay, carefree, loveable and when my old friend and I start getting deep in memories—

JACQUES: That's it, useless for the clock to tick—by then, you are too tired to go home.

MADAME MAZEROLLES: It's true. I'll have a bad day to-morrow.

JACQUES: By Jove, here you are at home! But, as for me, I live near the Palais du Luxembourg. And what must my beautiful Helene think, not seeing her father come home? You have your key?

MADAME MAZEROLLES (giving it to him): Here it is.

(Jacques goes to the door and bumps into Sabine.)

JACQUES: Who's there? (raising his lantern) A woman?

MADAME MAZEROLLES: A woman? (recognizing Sabine) You!

JACQUES: The boss's daughter-in-law!

(He puts out the lantern and paces it by the coach door)

MADAME MAZEROLLES: What are you doing here in front of my house?

SABINE: I have to wait for you outside, since you refuse to receive me in your home... (leaning) ...Mother.

MADAME MAZEROLLES: I am not your mother! I forbid you to give me that name!

SABINE: Am I not the wife of your eldest son?

MADAME MAZEROLLES: Say rather, the widow of my son, of my poor son, Charles, whom you cheated on with lovers, whom you made very ridiculous, and the most unhappy of men, and who ended by dying of shame because of your disorders. You are no longer anything to me! And I refuse to receive you, I refuse to listen to you.

SABINE: All the same, you must listen to me, and this will be the last time I importune you.

JACQUES (intervening): See here, my little lady, this is neither the time nor the place to hold a conversation. It will soon be tomorrow! What the Devil—my mistress will consent to listen to you.

MADAME MAZEROLLES (excitedly): No! This woman will not cross the sill of my dwelling. She opened the door too much to everybody. And I won't open mine to her.

SABINE: Madame—

MADAME MAZEROLLES: If she really has something to say to me, let her say it and say it quick.

SABINE: So be it. I will be brief. Madame, you are rich and I am poor.

MADAME MAZEROLLES: Ah, I understand. You are coming to demand money from me. As if I hadn't given you enough—which didn't prevent you dragging the name of your husband through the mud with venal favors and high priced tendernesses. But those days are over. To encourage vice with my own money, my God! Strike that out of your papers, my sweet.

SABINE: You are going to let me starve to death?

MADAME MAZEROLLES: That's better than living the way you live!

SABINE: You refuse me the alms of a scrap of bread?

MADAME MAZEROLLES: I don't wish to do harm to true indigents.

SABINE: That's your last word?

MADAME MAZEROLLES: The final and only word. When I play cards, I never take my card back.

SABINE (striding toward her): My sweet mother-in-law, watch out!

JACQUES (getting between them): All in vain! You're forgetting I'm here.

SABINE: M. Jacques Lebrun, I am not speaking to you.

JACQUES: That's possible. But if you threaten my mistress, this old dog growls and shoes his teeth. It's idle for you to glare at me with that set of pistols. Although, I know you and what you are capable of—it was you who ruined the unfortunate Roland.

MADAME MAZEROLLES: Roland, my god-son—it's she who—

JACQUES: Hey, yes, by Jove. She's the one who dug a gulf beneath the feet of that weak lad—into which she pushed his fantasies. She's the one who forced him to pile up debt upon debt, until you were forced to kick him out of the house— where he'd deceived your trust. She turned him into a debauchee, an ingrate, a thief—and perhaps will do worse.

MADAME MAZEROLLES: Oh! The slut! the slut! Get out! Do you hear—and tell your lover to leave, let him leave Paris, let him go to the colonies and repurchase his past with a new life. At that price, he can hope that I will forgive him one day. But, if he resists my orders, beware in your turn. And remember—remember carefully that there is forced labor for thieves, and a penitentiary for prostitutes. Goodnight, Jacques! I no longer need you, because Annette must be waiting for me.

(She goes into the Hotel.)

JACQUES (closing the door and picking up his lamp): Goodnight, my dear Mistress. (passing before Sabine) Madame, I don't bow to you.

(He leaves in a different direction from the way he came.)

SABINE: Rejected! Insulted! Threatened! Decidedly, it's she who's asking for it.

(Roland comes slowly out of the café. A window is lit on the first floor of the Hotel Mazerolles.)

SABINE: My poor friend, I see from your somber air that you were no luckier than I.
ROLAND: Ah, you—
SABINE: Madame Mazerolles saw me without pity—
ROLAND: Madame Mazerolles! You addressed yourself to her.
SABINE: Yes. I attempted to get you back in her good graces. I begged. I wept. But all failed against her bull-headedness. Here's the ultimatum from your sweet god-mother. You must go immediately to some port from which a ship will take you three or four thousand leagues from France, if you don't wear some uniform on your back, if you don't do penitence in the end—
ROLAND: Well?
SABINE: Well—she will have you arrested.
ROLAND: So—it's exile or prison, the camp or the galleys, the cap of a soldier or the helmet of a galley slave!
SABINE: You're in this woman's power. Remember, a word fallen from her mouth can ruin you. At any cost you know how to obtain her pardon.

ROLAND: Me, submit? Leave! Come off it! I'd prefer to break my head on the pavement. The chain gangs aren't as far from Paris—which is my life, because you live here, as the colonies.

SABINE: Oh, as for me, my darling—it's nothing less than a question of locking me up, like you.

ROLAND: Locking you up because of me?

SABINE: In a penitentiary with ruined girls.

ROLAND: They would dare! Why, then we must flee! Both of us must flee!

SABINE: And what will we do for money?

ROLAND: It's true. We are without resources! (enraged) Oh, the means, the means to procure our escape from the will of that woman!

SABINE: The means—there is one. And the money—it's there. (She points to the window.)

ROLAND (shaking): A theft!

SABINE: Didn't you demand of her strong box what your god-mother's avarice refused you? You know the secret of that strong box. Look—the light just went out. Madame Mazerolles has gone to sleep.—You've kept the key to the door?

ROLAND (repeating): A theft!

SABINE (very coaxing): Didn't you say just now that for me you would be capable of a crime? Well—the time has come to prove if you love me! Do you want me?

ROLAND (entwining her): Sabine!

SABINE (releasing herself): Then get going. A bit of courage, and I am yours. Yours, without reserve—forever, for life.!

ROLAND (still hesitating): My God!

SABINE (pushing him towards the hotel): Once again—be a man! Tonight or never!

ROLAND: Well, so be it!

(He goes to the door and opens it with a key that he pulls from his pocket.)

SABINE (leaning on his shoulder): And think that it's your mistress who awaits you!

(Roland goes in and shuts the door behind him.)

SABINE: Finally!

(Looking about she goes to carpet under the roof of the porch of the grocery. A patrol passes. Assured she's alone she goes to the hotel and listens to what is taking place. At this moment a rag-picker appears on one side, lantern in one hand, his pike in the other. He strides forward and picks up several scraps of paper from the pavement, and throws them in his bag. Meanwhile, Sabine crouches against the coach door of the hotel; the Rag-picker picks up a scrap of newspaper, steps under the light hanging in the middle of the stage, and starts reading it. The Lightman comes in. Dawn begins to break.)

RAG-PICKER: "Today, His Majesty heard Mass in his apartments." (spoken) What's that to me?
LIGHTMAN: And what about me?

(He goes to the Hotel Mazerolles to the box on which the light swings and opens the box.)

LIGHTMAN: Lookout below!

(The Light descends on the head of the Rag-Picker.)

RAG-PICKER: Hells Bells! (continues to read) "At the most interesting place…"
LIGHTMAN: Sorry, buddy, but I have to make the Sun agree with Government oil. (He turns his box and places the light back up.)
RAG-PICKER: Satanic Jesuit, begone!
LIGHTMAN: Jesuit! I?
RAG-PICKER: Since you extinguish the Enlightenment!

(He goes off.)

LIGHTMAN: Wise guy!

(Roland emerges from the hotel.)

SABINE (going to him): Well?
ROLAND (very pale): Shut up! Shut up!
SABINE: You've got the money?
ROLAND: Yes, but at what price.
SABINE: What do you mean?
ROLAND: She woke up. And she tried to scream, to have me arrested. I saw a prison—the galleys, separating me from you. Oh, as to that—never! Never!
SABINE: So what did you do?
ROLAND: I grabbed a knife that I used as a letter opener, and I stabbed her with all my strength, until she collapsed in my arms, mute, lifeless. Ah, I am a wretch!
SABINE : We have no time for remorse! Let's go. Come on, come on, quick.

(They disappear on the side opposite that the Lightman left.)

(Vidocq enters, dressed like a man of the *Ancien Régime*, a wadded garment of silk skin, pigeon wings a tricorne hat, large muslin tie, frilled shirt, fancy cuffs, breeches, low stripes, slippers with buckles and a hooked cane. Coco-Lacour is dressed as an old servant, and carries a small dog under his arm. They come from a street at the back.)

COCO: Not so fast, Chevalier. You are devouring the legs of your faithful Jasmine.
VIDOCQ (looking around him): The street's deserted. You can leave off your jargon, my lad, and speak normally.
COCO: Hey! That's not to be refused, boss! (cutting a caper) It's good to stretch one's pins. And I was beginning to have

enough of the role you've made me play since yesterday evening, about which I understand nothing.

VIDOCQ: Now, I can explain. Open your eyes, my faithful Coco. Yesterday, your chief, M. Angles, said to me, "Vidocq, my friend, things cannot go on this way! For the last three months, Yvrier, your colleague in charge of the political brigade, has been vainly trying to obtain for me the names of some Royalist conspirators who meet twice a week in the home of Baron de Saint-Fleurette, one of the most rabid ultras described in our reports. One of those who find His Majesty Louis XVIII to be a revolutionary, the Charter an abomination, and dream of bringing back the monarchy of the good old days, and the good pleasure and the right of the master."

COCO: Be still, my heart!

VIDOCQ: The Prefect continued, "Yvrier hasn't yet been able to infiltrate one of these meetings. Are you the man to succeed where your colleague has failed?"

COCO: Seeing the longstanding rancor between you and this old idiot you accepted?

VIDOCQ: Of course! I got my information, and I learned that the Baroness de Saint-Fleurette adores, has a cult, a religion—

COCO: Of her husband.

VIDOCQ: No, his parakeet. I jawed with the first *valet de chambre* of the house, a Frontin that I commend to you, and by means of six sous, I obtained from him that he would leave open—momentarily—the cage of the interesting bird. Only he'll take before going any further, the precaution of decorating its foot with a little lead weight which I gave him.

COCO: I get it: the cockatoo flew off.

VIDOCQ: But fell down a few meters from the house.

COCO: Where you picked him up.

VIDOCQ: And evening came, when the baron, the baroness, and the whole house are weeping tears of blood over Jacquet. Then I presented myself, bird in hand.

COCO: Freeze frame!

VIDOCQ: The baroness fell in my arms; the baron, who she'd already broken for a thousand francs, called me her savior. We chatted. I slipped in my horror at the deplorable liberalism which is flourishing at the Tuileries. He recognized me for a fellow comrade, and invited me to remain for the meeting of a group which meets twice a week with him—the true, the sole supporters of the throne and the altar. I accepted, you may be sure, and at mid-night, I left the house of this excellent Saint-Fleurette, carrying in my pocket the list that this imbecile of Yvrier was unable to secure in three months, and that I got in two hours.

COCO: Long live the boss!

VIDOCQ: And now, let's go sleep the sleep of the just—with the conscience of a duty fulfilled.

COCO: Let's go.

(Vidocq stops.)

COCO: What's wrong, boss?

VIDOCQ: What's wrong, M. Coco Lacour, is that my stomach wants sugared water to gratify it, and the entire dinner at Saint-Fleurette constituted a thin gruel in comparison—and it groans over a pitiful supper.

COCO: And what about mine, boss? At the office, we only get your leftovers, and you never leave anything. Only a skinny hen like Madame de Saint-Fleurette. That's different at this time of night.

VIDOCQ: Hold on. Here's a little café that, scoffing at the law, the owner who's a friend of mine, keeps open for gambling clandestinely well into the night and sometimes until dawn. (looking back) We are holding a leg of our chicken, Coco.

COCO: Don't let it go, boss, and nice try to nab a wing, too.

VIDOCQ: All the same, I think that my colleague Yvrier's nose will be a bit more out of joint than yesterday evening.

(They go into the café, Enter Vaillant, with Brigitte on his arm, and Navet.)

VAILLANT: Well, here we are at our destination.

NAVET: The marriage party went well?

VAILLANT: Marvelously.

NAVET: You had an enjoyable time, Madame Brigitte?

BRIGITTE: Too good, Monsieur! I feel all done-up.. I don't know if it was the dancing, or maybe the cold.

NAVET: Fact is—it's sharp this morning.

BRIGITTE: I've got to hurry in and try to get a couple hours sleep before my master rings.

VAILLANT: Till later, then.

(She goes into the hotel. Tradesmen begin coming in, setting up for morning market. Suddenly, she comes out running, terrified.)

BRIGITTE: Madame—in her room, stretched on the floor!

NAVET: Fainted?

BRIGITTE: No—dead! A murder!

COURTOIS (coming from his shop): A murder?

(The shopkeepers and tradesmen mill around her.)

BRIGITTE: Madame Mazerolles has been murdered!

ALL: Murdered!

COURTOIS: Quick, Navet—run to the guard post and inform the Commissioner. (to Auguste) You—go wake up M. Jacques Lebrun. You know, rue de Vaugirard.

(The two men leave in different directions.)

VAILLANT (to Brigitte): Here, Mademoiselle Brigitte—have a drink of this. It will set you up.

MADAME MADOU: They say someone was murdered. Who?

COURTOIS: The owner of this hotel.

MADAME MADOU: Madame Mazerolles? My customer since 1813!

NAVET (returning with soldiers): This way, soldiers.

VAILLANT: Ah, here's the armed forces!

MADAME MADOU: And here come the humming birds of the Police.

(Yvrier enters with two cops led by Auguste.)

COURTOIS: Ah, it's old man Yvrier and the hounds of the Police.

MADAME MADOU: Yes, the rival of Vidocq.

YVRIER (importantly, to soldiers and cops): Cordon off the scene of the crime and let none enter before the arrival of the magistrate. (He goes into the house.)

TWO COPS: Come on, folks, move on, move on.

(Murmurs—the crowd slowly disperses.)

BRIGITTE: Yes, M. Jacques, murdered!

JACQUES: Why, I left her barely a few hours ago, healthy and vigorous. Destined to live to a hundred. Ah, I want to see! I want to see!

(He goes into the house and bumps into Yvrier.)

YVRIER: Where do you think you're going?

JACQUES: Why, here, Monsieur, to see my mistress who's been killed. Try to revive her, if I can.

YVRIER: No use, my boy. Your mistress is quite dead, and the character who did it, didn't fail. As for entering the house, it's impossible. No one can enter before the Investigating Judge that we're expecting.

JACQUES: Still, Monsieur…

YVRIER: Useless to persist. I've said what I've said. (to Courtois) Who's this guy?

COURTOIS: That's M. Jacques Lebrun—the intendant and trusted man of Madame Mazerolles. Oh, a very fine man, M Monsieur Yvrier.

YVRIER: So much the better for him.

(Monsieur de Bergonde arrives)

YVRIER: Ah, the Investigating Magistrate is here.

DE BERGONDE: Is it true what they told me? A crime on the person of Madame Mazerolles?

YVRIER: Yes, your honor.

DE BERGONDE: The mother of my friend, Captain Georges Mazerolles.

JACQUES: Ah, that's good, Monsieur. If you are a friend of M. Georges, you'll have the courage to avenge his mother.

DE BERGONDE: Is someone here from Police Headquarters?

YVRIER: Yes, Monsieur, me.

YVRIER: You, Yvrier? Hm. I expected Vidocq because this crime seems to be up his alley.

YVRIER (drily): Vidocq is occupied at the moment in a political matter. I was on duty when the news arrived, and I came immediately. Since Vidocq can meddle in my department, I can meddle in his.

DE BERGONDE: So be it. Come!

JACQUES: Can I accompany you, Monsieur?

YVRIER (to the Magistrate): This is Jacques Lebrun, Madame Mazerolles' intendant, who lives outside the house and has just arrived.

DE BERGONDE: Yes, come with us, friend. You may be able to give us exact information. Let's go, gentlemen.

(Monsieur de Bergonde, Yvrier, Jacques and Brigitte enter the Hotel.)

COURTOIS: Didn't I tell you, old man Yvrier's a nasty one.

NAVET: A nasty one…

COURTOIS: But he's not worth M. Jules.

NAVET: Who's M. Jules?

COURTOIS: Vidocq.

NAVET: The nasty of nasties.

COURTOIS: Vidocq who undertakes to deliver 365 criminals per year.

NAVET: Including leap years!

(Vidocq and Coco enter.)

VIDOCQ: A gathering. Hold on! We have to know what it's about. (aloud, changing voice) Jasmin, be so good as to follow me at a distance, and don't let go of Zephyrine! I'm afraid of misalliances.

COCO: Yes, Chevalier.

NAVET: Oh, these two mummies. I'd like to ask them the address of their embalmer.

VIDOCQ (to Courtois): Monsieur, some information, I beg you. Have they arrested some malefactors?

COURTOIS: What malefactors?

VIDOCQ: Well, Liberals, of course, by Jove. Because this gathering—these rumors... I presume it's a question of a new conspiracy against the throne and the altar?

NAVET: What, venerable has-been, you remain standing there, like a wig head in a wigmaker's shop, and you don't realize it's a crime of blood.

VIDOCQ: Of blood?

COURTOIS: Yes! A brave lady was just found in her home stabbed by a number of dagger blows.

MADAME MADOU: A dozen at least from what they were saying.

NAVET: A dozen! It's no longer a woman, it's a chopping block.

VIDOCQ: Such a crime. It's worth the trouble, Coco. Get rid of the disguise, my boy.

COCO: Let's shed it. (He puts the dog in his pocket.)

COURTOIS: So you are?

NAVET: It's M. Jules, by Jove! Long live M. Jules! What a man.

MADAME MADOU: M. Jules, you will arrest the villain!

24

VIDOCQ: That I promise you, Madame, or I'll lose my name. In a few weeks.

VAILLANT: As long as that?

VIDOCQ: Ah, what do you want? There's the slowness of the investigation, the arguments. Guilty people always make a furor about allowing their heads to be chopped off. (to Coco) To work Coco, to work! (heading toward the house.)

COCO (who has during this time informed himself) But, Boss, someone else is in charge.

VIDOCQ: Someone else? Like who, for instance?

COCO: The other boss. Your *bête-noire*.

VIDOCQ: Yvrier! Ah, the scoundrel! So, while I succeeded in a mission he couldn't fulfill…

COCO: …He's cut the grass under your feet. Ah, that's low, that is!

VIDOCQ: Well, Coco, let's go in all the same. I have orders from the Prefect to deliver to the Magistrate this list my colleague failed to obtain. And while in there, it will be amusing to see what the cook is going to prepare.

THE CROWD: Long live M. Jules!

C U R T A I N

SCENE II

THE ROOM OF THE CRIME

In the rear an alcove with the curtains hermetically sealed. On one side of the alcove a small door, half open. On the same side, a fireplace. A secretary opened containing a safe against the wall between the window and the bed. Near the small door, a table turned over. A candlestick on the ground. An armchair, also turned over.

AT RISE, the clerk is installed at a table. Monsieur de Bergonde is seated near him. Yvrier stands mid-stage. Annette and Brigitte are in front of the fireplace. Jacques Lebrun is seated in front of the chimney, head in his hands apparently paying no attention.

DE BERGONDE: You've described exactly the condition of the place and confirmed that the door to the large stairway was found bolted inside?

CLERK: Yes, your honor.

YVRIER: You've likewise established the existence of this exit (pointing to the small door at the back) which communicates with the service entrance?

CLERK: Yes, Monsieur.

DE BERGONDE: We'll end with the servants. (to Yvrier) Bring forward Brigitte Liégeois and Annette Chevassu.

YVRIER: Let's go. Come forward.

(The women come forward.)

DE BERGONDE: Your mistress had two sons?

ANNETTE: Yes, your honor. M. Charles, the eldest, is separated from his wife.

DE BERGONDE: Ah, M. Charles Mazerolles is separated?

ANNETTE: Seemingly because the young lady didn't conduct herself as she should.

BRIGITTE: Every day, another dog bite in the contract.

ANNETTE: So much so that, to avenge the honor of the family, M. George, the youngest, was obliged to fight one of those men who brought trouble to the household of his brother.

BRIGITTE: And killed him outright.

ANNETTE: M. George—brave as a lion, and good as bread.

DE BERGONDE: This girl is right. I've met the Captain.

ANNETTE: As for me, I raised him—and Mademoiselle Helene.

BERGONDE: Mademoiselle Helene?

ANNETTE (lowering her voice): Helene Lebrun, M. Jacques' daughter.

YVRIER: Ah, M. Jacques has a daughter?

ANNETTE: Who was educated at Madame Mazerolles' expense.

BRIGITTE: Not to mention that she left her a large sum in her will.

YVRIER: In her will. (low to Bergonde) Do you see a trail there?

DE BERGONDE: The direct protégée of the victim—that would be quite unlikely.

YVRIER (going to Annette): No one in the house was unaware that the safe was in this room—which contained the victim's jewels and valuables?

ANNETTE: That's right, Monsieur, we all knew.

YVRIER: But someone besides Madame Mazerolles possessed a key to this apartment? And this safe?

ANNETTE: There was M. Jacques Lebrun.

DE BERGONDE: You are sure of it?

ANNETTE: Ah, everyone will tell you as I do, Monsieur. (a nod from Brigitte)

YVRIER: What do you think?

DE BERGONDE: We must question this man Lebrun. (goes to Jacques, taps him on the shoulder) Monsieur Lebrun?

JACQUES (raising his head): Huh? What? What's wrong?

(The women step back, Jacques comes forward slowly.)

DE BERGONDE (to Yvrier, pointing to Jacques): This distraction, this sorrow…

YVRIER: Bah! I've seen criminals with whom such sorrow was only a mask designed to turn away suspicion.

JACQUES: What do you want with me?

DE BERGONDE: Monsieur Lebrun are you at last disposed to answer Justice?

JACQUES: But I have nothing to tell you. I didn't see anything. I don't know anything. Nothing except that they killed my benefactress, my dear mistress, my old friend. (pointing to the alcove) And that her corpse is there, eyes shut forever, mutilated, all bloody under the sheet that covers her.

DE BERGONDE: You were Madame Mazerolles' confidant? She seemed to depend greatly on you. On your part, you seem to have been very attached to her.

JACQUES (bursting into tears): Yes, she loved me! Yes, I loved her, the poor dear lady!

DE BERGONDE: Are you prepared to furnish us with information which would lead us to discover the identity of the murderer?

JACQUES: Yes, but I don't know anything..

DE BERGONDE: Do you know if the victim had enemies?

JACQUES: None.

DE BERGONDE: This strong box—in her secretary—(pointing with his finger) was opened by the murderer. Someone other than yourself knew the secret of opening it.

JACQUES: No, Monsieur.

BRIGITTE: Ah, pardon, M. Jacques, if I contradict you. There is also M. Roland.

DE BERGONDE: Who is this M. Roland?

BRIGITTE: A relative of Madame Mazerolles—her godson.

JACQUES: Well, yes, you're right. Her godson that she brought from Burgundy to serve as her secretary.

ANNETTE: Happily, this bad actor didn't spend long in the house. Lazy, debauched like the seven sins, and a gambler like the Queen of Spades!

BRIGITTE: Notwithstanding all that, a very cut lad. And so friendly with the ladies.

ANNETTE: Finally, Madame was obliged to pay him off despite the affection she felt for him.

YVRIER: And you suspect that this Roland...?

JACQUES: You can't think it! Roland—the murderer of Madame Mazerolles? It's impossible. His faults are those of his age. He's not a monster! Besides, Roland is no longer here. He left Paris, France... I'm sure of it. I'll answer for that. I affirm it.

YVRIER: From the moment you affirm it...?

JACQUES: On my honor as a soldier! (aside) Heaven will forgive me this lie.

(goes back and sits down.)

YVRIER: Let's take our investigation to another side.

(Vidocq enters, followed by Coco who hangs back.)

VIDOCQ: Pardon, your honor, if I disturb you.
YVRIER: Vidocq!
VIDOCQ: I'm obeying the Prefect's order—to bring you the list you wanted as soon as possible.
DE BERGONDE: Truly? You've got it? (going to Vidocq) I really hoped you would succeed, but I didn't dare hope you would do so so quickly.
VIDOCQ: Oh, your honor, it's the way of the profession. Another would have taken a week. I took two hours. It's the triumph of talent over routine.
YVRIER: What insolence! (aloud) But tell us, Mr. Boaster, what's this masquerade signify?
VIDOCQ: Ah, indeed, Yvrier, these are the secrets of my profession. I have my ways, you have yours. But you only put your finger in your eye.
YVRIER: Bah! Talker! The school of youth!
COCO: Which works better than the old school, venerable Methuselah.
VIDOCQ: I hope yours leads you soon to discover the criminal you are seeking.
YVRIER: The criminal! The criminal! Why not *criminals*, first of all?
VIDOCQ: Because there was only one.
DE BERGONDE (raising his head): In your opinion, a single person committed the crime?
VIDOCQ: Allow me to ask a question of my colleagues. (to the two cops.) Which of you was the first to enter this room?
YVRIER: I was, wise guy.
VIDOCQ: You took care not to disturb anything?
YVRIER (scornfully): Everything is exactly as it was.
VIDOCQ: And you did the right thing. Objects are the most precious witnesses.

YVRIER: True enough. But that doesn't prove that this crime was the work of a single murderer.

VIDOCQ: Patience, Papa, we'll get there. No woman, strong as she may be, can defend herself against a single man.

(Agreement by the Magistrate)

VIDOCQ: Against two men, it would be totally impossible. Yet, here, there was a terrible struggle. These torn curtains, this overturned table, armchair.... The victim defended herself vigorously with energy— (seeing the candle) Ah, that's understandable, since she wasn't yet asleep.

YVRIER: What does that prove to you?

VIDOCQ: She came to snuff the candle. And see—(going to it) The candle had hardly burned. That shows the victim hadn't gone to sleep when the killer came in. (after looking around) From this direction— (pointing to the small door at the head of the alcove on the left.)

YVRIER: Ah, really, that's too much! You know the murderer got in this way?

VIDOCQ: Yes, by this door. Condemned.

YVRIER (ironic): And what's more, you divine, without having come into this room, that this door was condemned?

VIDOCQ: Ask the servants?

ANNETTE: Indeed, it was.

DE BERGONDE: But how can you tell, M. Vidocq?

VIDOCQ: Look at this spider web, over here on the left. It's broken in half, and this half—some candle wax hangs on it. This broke when it was opened. You recall the story of good King David, who, pursued by his enemies, hid in a cavern. A spider hung his web over the opening. His enemies, seeing the web intact, believed no one was there.

YVRIER: So?

VIDOCQ: Well, this is exactly the same in reverse.

DE BERGONDE: Vidocq, you are an acute observer.

VIDOCQ: You flatter me, your honor. With a moment's reflection, a child could do as much.

COCO: That wasn't meant for you, Papa, you're a reasonable man.

DE BERGONDE: Let's proceed now to examine this safe which contains what the servants say were the valuables and cash of the victim.

BRIGITTE: And the jewels, Monsieur. Just the diamonds were worth a fortune! Madame Mazerolles had more than a 100,000 francs worth in diamonds.

YVRIER (who's opened the drawers): You see, your honor, neither the jewels nor the money are there.

VIDOCQ: Yes, it's a nice trick; the guy who did it must be rubbing his hands.

DE BERGONDE (rummaging): Letters. Papers. Ah, a portrait. (showing it to Brigitte)

ANNETTE: Ah, my poor Mistress when she was young.

VIDOCQ: Can I have a look, your Honor?

(De Bergonde gives him the portrait)

VIDOCQ: I wasn't mistaken. It's she. She who in the past— on the frontier in Flanders—saved the life of a proscribed soldier! She was my best friend! (goes to the alcove.)

JACQUES: Where are you going? Leave her in peace. I don't want her looked at.

VIDOCQ: Don't scold, friend. We don't intend to do her harm.

(He goes into the alcove, followed by Coco. Yvrier and de Bergonde continue to examine the secretary. Jacques falls back in his armchair.)

YVRIER: A hidden letter.

DE BERGONDE (reading it): This is her will.

YVRIER: Perhaps we will find some clue in there.

DE BERGONDE (tearing it open and reading): "All my fortune goes to Georges Mazerolles, my son—but I expressly leave to my faithful servant and old friend Jacques Lebrun—

who once saved my life—the sum of 100,000 francs to be used as a dowry for his dear daughter Helene. This sum will be paid to him in cash immediately after my death."

YVRIER: After her death.

DE BERGONDE: To Monsieur Lebrun.

YVRIER: Find the one who profits by the crime.

DE BERGONDE (raising his voice): Jacques Lebrun.

JACQUES (getting up and coming forward): What now?

DE BERGONDE: Did you know the contents of this will?

JACQUES: By Jove, I was present when Madame wrote the article concerning me.

YVRIER: He admits it.

DE BERGONDE: It's a presumption, but not evidence.

COCO: Pardon, your honor—but in this fold of the victim's dress, I just found a knife which—it seems to me—must be the one that was used to commit the crime.

YVRIER (extending his hand): Gimme.

COCO: Pardon, Papa, I was speaking to His Honor, and I don't think that up to now you've achieved that grade.

DE BERGONDE: Let's see. (to the servants) Which of you has seen this knife before?

ANNETTE: I certainly have. For sure.

BRIGITTE: Yes. It belongs to Jacques Lebrun.

YVRIER: To Jacques Lebrun? Well, well.

DE BERGONDE (calling): Monsieur Lebrun.

JACQUES: Yes?

DE BERGONDE: Do you recognize this knife?

JACQUES: By Jove, easily. I took it from a Mameluke at the Battle of the Pyramids.

DE BERGONDE: Why is it no longer in your possession?

JACQUES: Because I loaned it to Madame.

YVRIER: Loaned it? Why?

JACQUES: Very simple. The poor woman adored reading—novels especially, and she recently received one that's all the rage. It's by the Vicomte d'Arlincourt.[3] Right away, she set to devouring it, and not having a paper knife at hand, she asked me if I still had mine.

DE BERGONDE (abruptly changing his tone with Jacques): Ah—that's fine.

(Jacques returns to his seat.)

VIDOCQ (emerging from the alcove): It's she. (turning) Rest in peace, poor woman. You'll be avenged, or may thunder destroy me.

DE BERGONDE (to Yvrier): Decidedly, you are right. This last evidence is crushing.

YVRIER: You no longer hesitate.

DE BERGONDE: Doubt is no longer permissible. All overwhelms this man. (to the clerk) Get the servants out of here.

(The cops leave with Brigitte and Annette.)

DE BERGONDE (sitting): I'm going to prepare an arrest warrant.

VIDOCQ: I need a clue... (looking at his fist) Hey, what's this? A red nosegay. Where'd this flower come from?

YVRIER: Well, M. Dreamer, M. Acute Observer, M. Reformer, there you have it—the mute witness, this strip of material which allows you to put your hand on the guilty.

VIDOCQ (hiding the flower): Maybe.

YVRIER (rubbing his hands): Meanwhile, we're the ones who've caught the murderer.

VIDOCQ (startled): You've caught the murderer of Madame Mazerolles?

YVRIER: Yes, my friend, without having any need of your talents and your science. There he is! (pointing to Jacques)

VIDOCQ: The Intendant!

---

[3] Charles-Victor Prévost d'Arlincourt (b. 26 September 1788-d. 22 January 1856).

COCO: The old dragon.

VIDOCQ: Come on, you're crazy.

COCO: You're trying to fool us, Papa.

YVRIER: Listen to the orders the Magistrate is going to give you.

DE BERGONDE (rising after having signed the warrant): My dear Vidocq, you are going to take this man to the Conciergerie. And you will do it in secret. But first, accompany him to his residence and make a minute inventory and search of it.

VIDOCQ: Why? This man is not—this man cannot be the guilty party.

YVRIER: Everything accuses him.

DE BERGONDE: And my opinion is settled. Execute my orders.

VIDOCQ: I bow, Monsieur. You command and I must obey.

DE BERGONDE: In case of resistance, take as many agents as you need.

VIDOCQ (after having taken the warrants from the Magistrate): When the law's on my side, I don't need anybody to help me do my job. Your man will follow me, will he, even if I have to carry him between my teeth, and you can consider it a done deal.

DE BERGONDE (to Yvrier and the Clerk): Come, gentlemen. We're done here.

(They leave. Vidocq whispers to Coco who then follows the clerk.)

VIDOCQ (looking at Lebrun): The poor fellow... I'll snatch him from the claws of this fool, Yvrier. The saying is true. An imbecile is more dangerous than a bad man! Come, do your duty, Police Officer... Jacques Lebrun... (after a silence) Jacques Lebrun, you must accompany me. (He touches the man's shoulder.)

JACQUES: Accompany you? That's fine—only support me, comrade. (rising with difficulty) Ah, I don't know what's got me beat, but I can barely hold myself up.

VIDOCQ: On your way.

JACQUES: Yes, on my way, but we'll find who did it, right?

VIDOCQ: Alas, my poor fellow, these gentlemen pretend there's no need to look any further.

JACQUES: The wretch has been discovered?

VIDOCQ: They think so, yes.

JACQUES: And we are going to arrest him? I'm with you.

VIDOCQ: Arrest him? No, it's already been done.

JACQUES: Bravo! Ah, bravo, Vidocq! Let me strangle him. Where is he?

VIDOCQ: Here.

JACQUES: Here? But there's only the two of us. (after a terrible outburst) Ah! It's me they accuse!

VIDOCQ: Yes.

JACQUES: Me? Me?

VIDOCQ: The appearances are overwhelming against you, so naturally the Magistrate accuses you.

JACQUES: Why, it's absurd, stupid, senseless. They have no common sense.

VIDOCQ: Oh, you don't need to convince me.

JACQUES: But to accuse someone you must have evidence.

VIDOCQ: There's evidence.

JACQUES: There must be witnesses.

VIDOCQ: There will be witnesses.

JACQUES: So you're ordered to take me to prison?

VIDOCQ: After having gone to your domicile, where I must perform a search and inventory.

JACQUES: To my home? You're taking me home? I'm going to see my daughter again. We shall go when you wish. I no longer need your arm. I am solid, now. Come on, Let's march, M. Vidocq.

VIDOCQ: Let's march.

(They leave.)

CURTAIN

ACT II

SCENE III

THE HOUSE OF JACQUES LEBRUN. HELENE'S ROOM.
Modest but minutely proper interior. Window to the left giving on the street. Entrance door at the back.
Another door on the right. A work table on the left. A wall with two hangings. One encloses a wall of honor, the other a military discharge. A tallboy at the right.
AT RISE, Helene is alone, seated at a table running through letters that she takes from an open box..

HELENE (reading): "Believe me, dear Helene, that this separation is as hard for me as it is for you. Luckily, everything makes me hope that, in the near future, my regiment is going to be garrisoned in Paris. So stop afflicting yourself over an absence that may only be momentary. Soon, we'll be able to declare our relationship to all. I will repay you for all the pain you have had in hiding it so long. Your husband before God will soon be your husband before man." (to herself) My husband, George Mazerolles. (she continues reading) "Burn my letters with care, for your father must never learn how we have deceived him." (a silence) Two months ago, his last words were: "Helene, my adored Helene, I swear to you that you will be my wife."

(George half opens the door at the rear. He wears the uniform of a Hussar. He tiptoes behind her.)

GEORGE: Helen, my adored Helen, I swear you will be my wife.
HELENE: George! You! You! (she falls in his arms.)
GEORGE: You were thinking of me?

HELENE: Always! I've reread this letter many times. Why did you leave me so long without news?

GEORGE: I was stuck in Verdun. As soon as I was able, I escaped. I haven't even been to see my mother yet.

HELENE: That's bad. That's very bad. I could have waited a little longer. (pointing to the letters) Am I not with you?

GEORGE: Those letters! You didn't destroy them? It was very imprudent—if your father—

HELENE: You know he's gone all day—with your mother.

GEORGE: Dear Jacques.

HELENE: Oh, if you knew how I suffer! How I reproach myself for having hidden our love from him.

GEORGE: Don't alarm yourself, dear child. It will soon be over. I will ask my mother to consent to our marriage.

HELENE: Her consent! My god, suppose she refuses?

GEORGE: Refuses? Why? She brought you up.

HELENE: I am poor.

GEORGE: She's never forgotten that she was, too.

HELENE: I am only the daughter of a servant.

GEORGE: Your father is part of the family. Besides, she'll do anything I want.

HELENE: I hope so.

(violent noises outside)

GEORGE: What's going on?

HELENE: I don't know.

GEORGE: It sounds like a riot.

HELENE (looking through the window): Yes—it is a riot. A mob is pursuing a carriage, throwing stones.

GEORGE: Stones?

HELENE: Don't come near the window, you might be seen. A man's getting out. It's my father.

GEORGE: Your father?

HELENE: People are cursing him. I don't understand.

GEORGE: They're coming upstairs.

HELENE: Hide in there. You mustn't be discovered here.

GEORGE: What? Do you want me to hide?

HELENE (pushing him into the room on the right): I beg you. Go!

(He disappears. Jacques followed by Vidocq enters.)

JACQUES: Helene, my child.

HELENE: Father, father, what's going on?

JACQUES: I'm going to tell you. (to Vidocq) Here's my judge, my only judge, M. Vidocq.

HELENE: Vidocq?

JACQUES: Listen, child. I've been arrested.

HELENE: Arrested? Why?

JACQUES: For my alleged involvement in a shocking crime.

HELENE: You! A criminal! That's ridiculous! That's impossible!

JACQUES: Thank you! Now, let them take me to court. Let them condemn me, let them execute me, my daughter knows that I'm not guilty. I don't care about the rest.

VIDOCQ: You may talk while I make a search. But don't waste time. It will be dangerous for us to dally here.

HELENE: Dangerous?

JACQUES: It seems so.

HELENE: But what exactly are you accused of.

JACQUES: The most infamous, imaginable crime!

HELENE: Oh!

JACQUES: I've spent forty years proving I was brave and honest. But now, they pretend, nay, they affirm that I treacherously murdered—

HELENE: Who pretends, my God?

JACQUES: Just about everybody. The police, the magistrates, the mob...

HELENE: But who is the victim?

JACQUES: Ah, that's the most monstrous part! Your benefactress—and mine, Madame Mazerolles.

HELENE: Madame Mazerolles!

(George comes out.)

GEORGE: My mother! My mother, murdered!
JACQUES: George! George!
VIDOCQ: The son! He is here!
GEORGE (pointing to Lebrun): Look, Jacques, did I misunderstand—or is my reason abandoning me?
JACQUES (weeping): No. She's dead.
GEORGE: Dead?
VIDOCQ: She was murdered, last night.
GEORGE (tearfully): Dead—my mother! (he sits down)
HELENE: George, my friend, courage!
VIDOCQ (low to Jacques): This is the younger son? Captain of a Regiment at Verdun?
JACQUES: At Verdun—yes, Monsieur.
VIDOCQ: In that case, why are we meeting him here?
JACQUES: Here—why? I don't know. I don't understand.
VIDOCQ (aside): I think I do. (aloud) Allow me to remind you, Monsieur, that your place is at the bedside of the deceased.
GEORGE: Yes, you're right, Monsieur. But I've lost my head. Ah, Jacques, rest assured that nothing will make me believe that you are guilty, and whatever I can do to prove your innocence, I will do.
JACQUES: Thank you, Monsieur!
VIDOCQ: I'd better go with you so the crowd will let you pass.

(They go out by the rear.)

JACQUES (slowly, after a silence): What was Monsieur George doing here?
HELENE: Father?
JACQUES: Well, answer me.
HELENE: Father, let's talk about this horrible accusation. (yelling in the street) And those men shouting for your death.

JACQUES: Forget that! I want you to tell me what George was doing here—in my home—when we arrived!

HELENE (helplessly): Captain Mazerolles?

JACQUES: Yes, him! Why did I find him here at an hour when he'd be certain not to meet me? What was he hiding in that room for?

HELENE: Father, George loves me.

JACQUES: Wretched girl—you've seduced the son of our benefactress?

HELENE: He's sworn I will be his wife.

JACQUES: And you've become his mistress? (raising his hand to her)

HELENE: Father, forgive me!

JACQUES: So both of you have deceived me! You, my hope, my pride—and the boy I used to dangle on my knee!

HELENE: George didn't fail in honesty or honor. He'll keep the oath he made.

JACQUES: And he'll marry the daughter of the man accused of having killed his mother?

HELENE: Why not? You are innocent!

JACQUES: What'll prove that?

HELENE: He will.

JACQUES: He who took what was most dear to me! He who stole you from me!

HELENE: Or I'll do it. It's my duty.

JACQUES: Duty! How dare you invoke that word! Ah, she's clever and tricky—the daughter of a servant who knew how to spread her web, and catch the son of the house in it. And the father? The father and daughter must be accomplices. And because Madame Mazerolles refused to consent to this shameful marriage he killed her. That's what they'll say.

HELENE: Father, don't talk like that. You're breaking my heart.

JACQUES: Well, let death come. I want it, I desire it. I bless it—for delivering me from this torment.

HELENE: No! I don't want that! I don't want that!

JACQUES: Get away from me, I tell you! You are no longer my daughter. I no longer know you.

VIDOCQ (at the back): Quick! Quick! Let's get out of here or we'll be outflanked.

(Coco runs in)

COCO: Boss, they're on my heels.

(The crowd erupts on the stage. Navet is in the lead. Courtois, Vaillant and Madame Madou are in their midst.)

NAVET (pointing to Jacques): Ah, there he is, the old scoundrel!

MOB: Death! Death!

JACQUES (in a paroxysm of rage): Kill me! Kill me quick to prevent me from cursing her. I confess everything. Yes, I was the one who butchered my benefactress. And it was only justice because the son of that woman slid into my house like a robber and stole my honor, and so struck me in what I hold most dear in the world. He stole my daughter, I killed his mother. We're even.

HELENE: Don't believe him.

JACQUES: Shut up, you! You have no right to defend my honor. You didn't protect yours. I'm the murderer! It's me.

NAVET: We've got to put his head in the river.

(All talk together.)

MOB: Yes—to the river with the murderer. To the water!

VAILLANT: Like a dog—with a stone around his neck.

VIDOCQ (to Helen who tries to shield her father with her body): Let him go. I'll answer for him.

NAVET: Great! Now, M. Jules is protecting him! To the Seine! To the Seine!

ALL: To the water! To the Water!

VIDOCQ (with one hand on Jacques' shoulder, and laying about furiously with the other): Get back! And respect the law! The accused, this man, belongs to Justice. Convicted—to the executioner!

C U R T A I N

SCENE IV

THE RESTAURANT OF THE GUILLOTINE
A hall on the first floor (above street level) on the Place de Grève.[4] At the back, a large window giving on the square. A side door leading to the office. An entrance door. Opposite, a small door. Tables with clothe coverings. Two o'clock in the evening.

COURTOIS (to the waiters arranging tables): Come on, speed it up, speed it up, gang! Remember today's the day of the big pay. They don't execute murderers every day. Not the one from the rue des Maçons-Sorbonne. (scornfully) My old street. (to the Sommelier) Don't forget to have enough wine. (to Brigitte) And you, what are you doing there, looking at me like a dummy?
BRIGITTE: I wasn't doing that, Mr. Courtois—on the contrary. But you used to be more polite to me when I worked for Madame Mazerolles.
COURTOIS: Now you work for me—so why should I be polite to you? Did you prepare the sign?
BRIGITTE: Yes, Boss, in letters as big as my arm. "Places to let."
COURTOIS (admiring them): By the hand of a public writer at my dictation. Yes, it attracts the eye. Well, go hang it up, my wench.

(Brigitte hangs it out the window. Vaillant and Madame Madou enter.)

VAILLANT: To your health, Papa Courtois.

---

[4] Today Place de l'Hôtel de Ville.

COURTOIS: Ah, my old neighbors from the other side of the Seine.

MADAME MADOU (looking around): Gosh! This is posh!

COURTOIS: Nothing to what I'm planning in the future. A huge café in the autocratic neighborhood. I am ambitious. I aspire to pull myself up.

VAILLANT (laughing): Is that why you are on the first floor above the street level?

COURTOIS: Ah, it's nice of you to come say Hello to me.

VAILLANT: You know it's a bit interesting.

COURTOIS: You wouldn't be sorry to get a glimpse, right?

MADAME MADOU: We owe her that—and that man, a neighbor, an old acquaintance.

COURTOIS: It's true—all three of us were witnesses at the trial. But you have time. M. Sanson, and his helpers are still below having a drink.

VAILLANT: All the same, Papa Courtois, who would have thought that M. Lebrun was a murderer.

COURTOIS (deep) Well, believe me if you like, or not—but as for me, I suspected him.

MADAME MADOU: Not possible! Well, me, too… An old soldier.

BRIGITTE: Captain Mazerolles did all he could to save him during the trial.

VAILLANT: Yes, he didn't believe in his guilt. But M. Yvrier proved to the jurors that there could be no doubt.

MADAME MADOU: Say—where will you put us so we can get a good look—here?

COURTOIS: That depends on how many customers I have—because this room is reserved. It's on his account that this establishment got its name.

VAILLANT: The Restaurant of the Guillotine.

COURTOIS: Because of its location.

VAILLANT: Facing City Hall.

COURTOIS: So that, from this window, folks who don't care to mix with the crowd, can, after dinner, not lose any detail of the ceremony.

VAILLANT: You were shrewd to give up your pot-house for a place where you could make your fortune.

COURTOIS (with satisfaction): Yes, a dozen executions like this and I can but a bailiff for my daughter.

NAVET (in the street): Ask for what's about to happen. The story, the trial and the conviction of Jacques Lebrun. Ten centimes.

VAILLANT: Goodness—that scoundrel Navet.

NAVET: With the portrait of this homicidal murderer and his dying words.

(Navet enters.)

COURTOIS: You cannot come in to this establishment to hawk your merchandise.

NAVET: Suppose I bring you customers?

COURTOIS: That's another matter.

BRIGITTE: Boss—it's already full downstairs.

COURTOIS (to Madame Madou): Have a little glass while waiting.

MADAME MADOU: That's not to be refused. I don't know if it's my corset or my emotion, but I feel a weight on this side.

(They leave. Brigitte approaches Navet.)

NAVET: So, Mademoiselle Brigitte, you work here now?

BRIGITTE: Yes, I had to find a new place.

(Courtois returns)

COURTOIS: The place is hopping. (to Navet) What—you're still here?

NAVET: I wanted to ask you? Will you give me a commission if I bring you customers?

COURTOIS: Customers? Sure! 30 sous per person.

NAVET: That'll work.

BRIGITTE: Boss, here are customers coming.

COURTOIS: Bring them up.

NAVET (below): See the execution from here!

BRIGITTE: This way, Monsieur, and Madame, this way.

(Roland and Sabine enter.)

SABINE (to Courtois): They told us we could get a good look at what's taking place on the square from here.

COURTOIS: As if you were on the scaffold itself.

ROLAND (recoiling): Huh?

SABINE (low): Careful.

COURTOIS: Would you like lunch?

ROLAND: Absinthe, absinthe first.

BRIGITTE: That voice...

COURTOIS: Two cups?

SABINE: No, only one.

BRIGITTE: It's Monsieur Roland!

ROLAND (turning): My name!

SABINE (to Roland, getting between them): Silence! (to Brigitte) What do you mean, Monsieur Roland? My husband is the Marquis de Grand Champ. You are mistaken, Mademoiselle.

BRIGITTE: A Marquis!

COURTOIS (pulling Brigitte) : Silly girl! Me, too. I, too, recognized him. He's the god-son of Madame Mazerolles. But when customers don't want to be recognized—act like you don't recognize them.

(They leave together.)

SABINE: Be calm, for God's sake, be calm! Your mania for guilt will end by betraying us.

ROLAND: What do you want? I confronted the dead, and I'm not intimidated by the living. But the Devil if you'll make me enter a cemetery by moonlight.

SABINE: Hey, who's talking about going to a cemetery? Are we in a place populated by bloody apparitions? Are there ghosts beneath the windows?

ROLAND: No, but it's beneath this window that a drama in which we are involved is going to end.

SABINE: A drama that we are involved in? Are you crazy? Are we accused of the crime in the Rue des Maçons-Sorbonne? Were we dragged before the court? Did a jury declare us guilty of a crime? No—it's someone named Lebrun—who silently bowed his head under the sentence, and whose head will be cut off by the blade that represents the justice of men.

ROLAND: Oh—but you know quite well this poor fellow is innocent.

SABINE: As for me, I know nothing! What I do know is the old axiom: A thing adjudged has the force of truth.

ROLAND (to himself): That's infamous.

SABINE: Besides, if you know the real murderer, what prevents you from denouncing him publicly? Go ahead—open the window and toss the name of the bandit to the curses of the crowd. The scaffold is indifferent and it's always ready for work.

ROLAND (shivering): The scaffold with its bloody tentacles. The Widow whose kiss kills. Oh, no, no!

SABINE: Then stop grieving and get this idea in your head: The law doesn't care who pays for the crime only that someone pays.

COURTOIS (entering with a platter): Your absinth, Monsieur, Madame.

(Navet comes in.)

NAVET: Ah, Papa Courtois. Two Milords for you. The Papa and the Kid.

ROLAND: What—we won't be alone at this window?

COURTOIS: Oh, no. Today even inches are valuable.

ROLAND: Ah!

SABINE: Can't you find us a private room?

COURTOIS (pointing to a door): That one there. But a private room will cost more.

SABINE: Who cares?

COURTOIS: In that case, I'll carry your absinth, Monsieur. Madame. (to Navet): Bring in your Milords.

(Roland and Sabine enter the private room followed by Brigitte. Navet returns with Vidocq, dressed as a fat Englishman, hat with sideband, jacket with a café-au-lait collar, riding breeches, etc. Coco as a boy of 18, long blonde hair—laird boots.)

NAVET: This way, Milord, this way.

VIDOCQ (looking around him): All right! This pub appears quite agreeable to me!

COURTOIS: You won't find a better. Your Ambassador paid twenty-five crowns the day Louvel was executed.[5]

VIDOCQ: Ah, that's not for me. I have a horror of blood. I prefer hanging. (pointing to Coco) This is for the amusement of the little one. Right, James?

COCO: Yes, Papa.

NAVET (to Courtois): How about my commission?

COURTOIS (giving him a few coins): Here you go.

NAVET: The bill is paid. I evaporate.

VIDOCQ: Innkeeper!

COURTOIS: Milord?

VIDOCQ: Have them give me a beefsteak, a big one—with potatoes. Right, James?

COCO: Yes, Papa. And for me, too, innkeeper. Potatoes—big ones—with lots of little beefsteaks around them.

COURTOIS: Yes, Milord. And what will the gentlemen have to drink?

VIDOCQ: Two bottles of Claret.

COURTOIS: From Bordeaux, right?

---

[5] Louis Pierre Louvel, born October 7, 17831 in Versailles and guillotined June 7, 1820, on the Place de Grève in Paris. Louvel was a fierce Bonapartist who murdered the Duc de Berry on the night of February 13 to 14 1820, a crime for which he was sentenced to death on June 6.

COCO. Yes. And some gin. A bottle of Gin. Because my papa drinks gin only in two circumstances: when he eats beefsteak and when he doesn't.

VIDOCQ: Indeed.

COURTOIS: Very well, Milord, and this is your table.

VIDOCQ: Thank you. (looking at the window) So that's the guillotine.

BRIGITTE: Yes, Milord.

VIDOCQ: Very ugly and not very imposing.

COCO: You'd say it was a kind of peephole.

VIDOCQ: Yes—a kind of peephole. And one would never suspect what vistas it gives on eternity.

BRIGITTE: The gentlemen are served.

VIDOCQ: Oh, thank you. (sitting down) Say, Mademoiselle, they told me I'd lunch with Mr. Whatzizname, the Public Executioner.

BRIGITTE: Monsieur Sanson?[6] He ate downstairs and left to fetch the condemned.

VIDOCQ: Ah!

BRIGITTE: He'll be back soon.

VIDOCQ: Are there any others here?

BRIGITTE: In the private room.

(Brigitte leaves. As soon as she does, Coco goes to the keyhole and peeps.)

VIDOCQ: Nice girl, that. (in a natural voice) Who's in there?

COCO (also natural): A gentlemen and a lady. Their backs are to me. Impossible to see them.

VIDOCQ (looking at his watch): Three-thirty. The woman I'm waiting for cannot be late. That is—if she has the strength to come.

(knocking at one of the doors)

---

[6] The Sanson family is a famous family of Normand executioners who worked in Paris from 1688 to 1847.

VIDOCQ: There she is. (to Coco) See that no one disturbs us.
COCO: Don't worry, I'll; stand guard on the stairway.

(He goes out the door. Vidocq goes to the side door and admits Helene who is heavily veiled.)

HELENE (to Vidocq): M. Vidocq—it's you who wrote me?
VIDOCQ: Yes, it's me.
HELENE (after a moment): Ah, then all hope is not lost.
VIDOCQ: Alas, yes, all hope is lost, Helene. Be resigned and be valiant.
HELENE: My God! But then, why did you make me come?
VIDOCQ: Because if no human power is capable of saving your father, at least one can avenge his death, and rehabilitate his name.
HELENE: Ah, the real culprit was clever. But where to find him?
VIDOCQ: Here!
HELENE: Here?
VIDOCQ: If not in this very restaurant, at least in the midst of the crowd, at some window, on a bench—in a tree, on a roof! I'm sure of it.
HELENE: Such imprudence!
VIDOCQ: It is imprudent as you say, but the culprit considers it a final guarantee of his security. That's why I'm sure the assassin of Madame Mazerolles will be present at your father's execution. That's why I'm here. Why my men are exploring, sampling, sounding the crowd. The murderer is rich now. Why not get a good seat at this terrible spectacle?
HELENE: But how can I be of use to you?
VIDOCQ: You can avenge your father. I am going to consecrate all my ability, all my energy to this task. I need your help. Will you do it?
HELENE: Me?
VIDOCQ: More than once Heaven has chosen the frail hand of a woman to defeat triumphant crime.

(Coco returns.)

COCO: Alert, Boss! The cart's coming down the Quai.
VIDOCQ (to Helene): Well?
HELENE: My father will dictate my response.
VIDOCQ: Your father?
HELENE: Can't I see him from the window?
VIDOCQ: You would—?
HELENE: Have his last look, as I will have his last thought, and that look will tell me what remains to be done.
VIDOCQ: But, unhappy child, such a sight—
HELENE: I will extract from its horror the strength that I need to second you. I won't weaken. I'm a soldier's daughter, a martyr's daughter.

(She veils herself and goes toward the balcony with Vidocq. Courtois, Brigitte, Vaillant, Madame MADOU appear.)

VAILLANT: Now's the time.
COURTOIS: Come. Install yourselves there in the rear. Climb on chairs so you won't miss a thing.
VIDOCQ (as Englishman): Take care, Madame, you will prevent my boy from seeing.

(Roland and Sabine emerge from the private room.)

ROLAND: Ah, I cannot watch this!
SABINE: Roland—look—be strong!
ROLAND: To stay alone there with you, with you who made me commit the crime, when this wretch is going to pay for it with his life! I want people around me—near me.
SABINE: Well—in here! At least, perhaps before these folks you will control yourself.
MADAME MADOU (low to Courtois): Look at that, neighbor—It's Roland, Madame Mazerolles' godson.
COURTOIS: Yes, but we mustn't say anything.

VIDOCQ (who's heard): The godson of Madame Mazerolles! Here!

VAILLANT: Doubtless he wanted to see them chop off the head of the murderer of his poor godmother.

MADAME MADOU: Yet they say they never got on well—after she kicked him out.

SCREAMS (outside): There he is! There he is!

BRIGITTE: There's the condemned getting out of the cart.

MADAME MADOU: Oh—how straight he walks. He has no fear.

VAILLANT: Who's that beside him? Behind the priest?

COURTOIS: It's M. Yvrier. And to his right—it's Sanson.

VIDOCQ (to Coco): The Godson kicked out by his godmother. And he's come to be present at the execution of the man accused of killing her…

VOICE (outside): Sabers out!

(The noise of sabers being pulled from their scabbards. A great silence. All heads are bared.)

JACQUES' VOICE (outside in the distance): Yes. I am going to speak. I want to tell my daughter, if she is here and hears me, that my last thought is for her! May God pardon me now for all my sins, as I forgive now those who have condemned me. My friends, you who surround me—behold the death of an innocent man.

(Four o'clock strikes slowly. We hear the sound of the blade falling. Long, choked murmurs from the crowd.)

ROLAND: Ah, I can't take any more! I can't take any more!

(in his distraction he causes Sabine's mantle to fall, allowing a bouquet of carnations to be seen in her corsage.)

SABINE (giving him a drink): Here! Drink!

VIDOCQ: Red carnations. I believe we're getting hot, Coco. Follow these individuals when they leave.

COCO: Yes, Papa.

VAILLANT (moping his face): All the same, it gives you the willies.

MADAME MADOU: Poor man Let's get out of here, huh—neighbor.

(They leave. Helene appears, staggering on the balcony and faints into Brigitte's arms. They place her in a chair.)

ROLAND (seeing her): Helene Lebrun!

VIDOCQ (to himself): He knows her!

SABINE (pulling him): Come on—there's nothing more for us to do here.

ROLAND: Helene Lebrun…

(He leaves, dragged by Sabine and followed by Coco.)

VIDOCQ (to Coco): Be real careful not to lose that man.

COCO: Don't worry, Boss, I'll eat his dust.

BRIGITTE: Why, it's Mademoiselle Helene!

VIDOCQ: Shut up! And get out of here.

BRIGITTE: Heavens! He's lost his accent. (looking) And his kid!

VIDOCQ (with an imperious gesture): Go!

BRIGITTE (terrified): I'm going, Monsieur.

(She literally runs away.)

HELENE (coming to): My father—

VIDOCQ: Your father no longer suffers, Helene. But you, have you decided to avenge him?

HELENE (forcefully): Yes! I will!

VIDOCQ: Are you ready to do whatever is necessary to succeed?

HELENE (rising): Everything necessary?

VIDOCQ: Even to endure the scorn of the crowd, even to choke off your tenderness, your beliefs, your modesty? Even to plunge into the mud and shame to bring the culprit out of it?
HELENE: Even that.
VIDOCQ: That's fine.

(Yvrier enters.)

VIDOCQ: Yvrier! What have you come here to do?
YVRIER (very upset): Listen, Vidocq. I was the one who escorted Jacques Lebrun to the Guillotine. He walked by my side! It was I who received his last glance—before Sanson tapped him on the shoulder and cut off his head. He addressed his last words to me.
VIDOCQ: Well?
YVRIER: I watched him. As I listened to him, I became convinced he was innocent. And I am his killer. And when the blade fell, I felt as if his blood were spattering on my head.
VIDOCQ: So?
YVRIER: So—I sought you out. I'm the one who through jealousy, through hate of your success, did my best to convict the man. Help me, I beg you, to repair the crime I've committed. Use me as the most humble of your agents; hand in hand, foreswearing our rancor—let's work together to find the real culprit. But pardon, Vidocq, pardon me.
VIDOCQ: I'm not the one you need to ask pardon of—it's her. (pointing to Helene)
YVRIER: Her?
VIDOCQ: Helene Lebrun, the daughter of the condemned! The daughter of the martyr!
YVRIER: You! You!
HELENE (standing straight up): I forgive you, Monsieur, as my father forgave you just now.
YVRIER: Ah, thank you, thank you!
VIDOCQ: And now, Yvrier, you are right. The only way of atoning for your mistake—is to have no rest, no truce, until

we've made the head of the real murderer fall. There were two of us! Now we will be three!

CURTAIN

ACT III
SCENE V

THE CAFÉ BEAUJOLAIS
A huge hall richly decorated in the style of the time; golden columns reflected by mirrors, floor decorated with allegorical paintings, divans, tables, etc. Brilliant lighting, hanging candelabra. A counter raised on one side between two doors. At the back a door with glass squares that pens on the street, another door near it. Midstage, the door of the Beautiful Lemonade Girl on one side.
AT RISE, most of the tables are occupied. Waiters come and go as do customers. Courtois strides in the midst of them with importance.

1st CUSTOMER: Waiter, a lemonade.
AN OLD GENTLEMAN: Waiter, a warm milk.
2nd CUSTOMER: Waiter, a Gloria![7]

(Vaillant and Madame Madou enter by the back.)

COURTOIS: Heavens, Papa Vaillant and Mama Madou. This way, this way… Here's a free table.
VAILLANT: What, it's you, Papa Courtois. You're the owner of the Café Beaujolais that all of Paris is talking about.
COURTOIS: I'm ambitious. I told you that the last time we saw each other.
MADAME MADOU: The day that wretch Jacques Lebrun got what was coming to him.
COURTOIS: Don't speak ill of him.
VAILLANT: Why's that?

---

[7] Coffee with brandy.

COURTOIS: Because he's by way of helping me make a fortune—indirectly.

MADAME MADOU: You would profit by his crime? Shame!

COURTOIS: Calm your indignation, virtuous milk-lady. That's not the question.

VAILLANT: Then what is it about?

COURTOIS: Don't you folks in the Latin-quarter hear what's going on in Paris?

VAILLANT (annoyed): Yes, Monsieur. We know that His Majesty Louis XVIII is still in the Tuileries.

COURTOIS: And that Napoleon is dead. But, apart from that—haven't you heard of the Beautiful Lemonade Girl?

MADAME MADOU: Sure we did! That's who we came to see.

VAILLANT: It seems you installed her behind your counter.

MADAME MADOU: And that she attracts all Paris to your establishment.

COURTOIS: And that's all you know? Ah, country bumpkins of Paris. It's not just her beauty that attracts, it's her lineage.

MADAME MADOU: She's the daughter of Napoleon or something?

COURTOIS: No! Of a guillotined man.

MADAME MADOU: Jesus Marie!

COURTOIS: And this criminal is none other than Jacques Lebrun—that's all.

VAILLANT: Helene Lebrun—to take such a job.

MADAME MADOU: A girl everyone said was so sweet, so virtuous—to coin money from the blood of her father.

COURTOIS: Bah! These days one makes one's fortune as one can. Helene is making hers—and mine. I cannot criticize her for it.

MADAME MADOU: Oh, this can't be happening.

COURTOIS: It's not her fault that they tried to corrupt her.

MADAME MADOU: Bah! Who did that?

COURTOIS: Captain Mazerolles, by God!

VAILLANT: Monsieur George!

COURTOIS: Yes, Monsieur George. He couldn't leave his garrison—so he sent old Annette to see Helene, to get her to come to Verdun to be his wife.

VAILLANT: And she refused?

COURTOIS: Good God! Could that situation rival that which she has with me?

OLD GENTLEMAN: Hey, waiter, my hot milk!

COURTOIS: They're preparing it, Monsieur.

(He goes away. Navet enters, carrying newspapers.)

NAVET: Ask for the *Daily Mirror*.

MADAME MADOU: What do I want with your mirror?

NAVET: Oh, I understand, old girl, yours is quite enough.

(She turns towards him furious.)

NAVET: Hey, if it isn't Mama Madou!

VAILLANT: Navet!

NAVET: And Papa Vaillant, too! So, it's true—you're living together?

MADAME MADOU (threatening him with her umbrella): Scumbag!

(Brigitte enters, all dressed up.)

NAVET: Heavens! Mademoiselle Brigitte turned hooker!

BRIGITTE: Waiter, serve me what the most fashionable ladies from the Faubourg Saint-Germain have when they come here.

NAVET: Take china-china. It's very bad, but expensive.

BRIGITTE: Some china-china then, waiter. (going to sit at the old man's table, friendly) I'm not disturbing you, Monsieur?

(The old man bows respectfully, then takes his hot milk to another table.)

BRIGITTE: What—he doesn't respect me? Cad—get out!

NAVET: So—the ill famed business is going well?

BRIGITTE: Don't talk to me about it, Navet! I have to be careful of my money. It seems I look too virtuous, and that discourages the gentlemen. (sighing) Ah, if I could find a good situation again.

NAVET: Would you like one in my heart?

BRIGITTE: Your heart? It's a barracks!

NAVET: I'll remodel it.

(Noisy music. Vidocq, Yvrier and Coco appear in the rear, dressed as street singers.)

COURTOIS: The virtuous of the pavement! Here! In a nice place like this!

VIDOCQ (with a provincial accent): That'll make your customers patient—while waiting for your princess!

(Vidocq plays the violin, Yvrier the clarinette, Coco, the guitar.)

ALL: Ah! Singers! Bravo!

VIDOCQ (after a glance around): Our birds are not yet here. We have to wait, gang. Let's sing.

YVRIER: To make me play a clarinette in the cafés! Me, an officer of the peace! If the Prefect saw this!

COCO: Let's tune up the orchestra, gentlemen.

(comic tuning of instruments)

VIDOCQ: *Listen to the touching story.*
Of an attractive young girl,
That was completely innocent—
But isn't any more.
Dance! Dance! Dance, the jig!
Dance! Dance!
Let's not give a fig!
When fresh grass sprouts
The poor little one's scream.
Oh, Mama. Oh, Mama Oh Mama!
There's the sprout!

(All three dance a jig.)

YVRIER: *The little girl was sleeping—*
Her window, open—over lilacs.
When she felt herself attacked
By she knew not what.
Dance! Dance! Dance the jig!
COCO: *A little later, on waking*
The Doctor told her like this:
Child, if you are inflated—
In nine months you'll be deflated.
Dance! Dance! Dance the jig.
VIDOCQ: *The one who did this work*
Doesn't want anyone to know who he is.
Fearing a reaction—
If they knew what he'd done.
Dance! Dance! Dance the jig!
When the sprout springs out
The poor kid yells
Oh, Mama—it's the sprout!

VIDOCQ: And now, let's sit down.
COURTOIS: Excuse me. Singing is fine—because it renders me a service. But to eat here—street singers! Impossible!
VIDOCQ: When I bring my instrument this way, my dear friend, I'm only a vulgar street actor, but when I put it on my back, I'm a French citizen again. The artist vanishes, but the customer remains. Serve us three glasses of your best.
(They sit.)
COURTOIS: All right. So long as you pay. Serve these gentlemen.
(The waiter pours.)
YVRIER: And you know, my lad, a footbath up to the ankles.
COCO: As for me, up to my ass.

(The waiter leaves. The Old Man gets up furious and finds another table at the back.)

YVRIER: Ah, really, will you explain to me now, why you are forcing me to do a job like this?

VIDOCQ: Because, my old Yvrier, one doesn't merely do police work with one's arms, legs and eyes. You need to employ the passion of others. Men are puppets whose desires are strings. It's only a question of keeping them in hand to maneuver their owners.

COCO: Bravo, boss!

YVRIER: General, I bow. You are great like the world.

VIDOCQ: Remember, gang—that wherever there's a woman, there's a ruined man. And we've got two of 'em.

YVRIER: Two women! Where's that?

VIDOCQ: The first one will install herself behind the counter at 9 o'clock. The other one will prowl around the tables in a few minutes. (pointing to Sabine, dressed as a flower girl) Hold on, If I'm not greatly mistaken—there she is.

YVRIER: That shop girl?

VIDOCQ: Holding in her perfumed fan the head of one man and the honor of a soldier. You'd never think it. Let me chat with her for a moment and watch.

COCO: Don't worry.

(Sabine offers flower bouquets at the table)

SABINE (aside): He's not here yet.

VIDOCQ: Hey, pretty little girl. A flower to spark up my buttonhole, please. (Sabine passes.) Hey! Didn't you hear me?

SABINE (disdainful): I don't sell flowers to street singers.

VIDOCQ: You are wrong, my charmer. For sometimes, appearances are deceiving. And the one who asks for a rose of you may be no more than a street singer than you are a flower girl.

SABINE (after thinking about it): Ah—you want a rose?

VIDOCQ: No. A nose-gay.

SABINE: A red nose gay?

VIDOCQ: Isn't that the favorite flower of the Marquise de Grand-Champs?

SABINE: I don't know what you mean?

VIDOCQ: Oh—you are wrong to be wary of me. We are both here for the same end.

SABINE: Truly? And what end is that?

VIDOCQ: To observe tonight, as last night, and like the days preceding. To see a nice looking cavalier come sit—who's in love with the beautiful lemonade girl.

SABINE: Ah!

VIDOCQ: Here. That's his usual seat. Next to her. But he hasn't got here yet. Because she's not here.

SABINE: Who are you, really?

VIDOCQ: A friend. (reaction by Sabine) Or-to put it better, a servant.

SABINE: A servant?

VIDOCQ: At Rue Cloche-Puce No. 2, there's a little house with an unusual sign, *Tomb of Secrets*. Safety speed, discretion. The house belongs to a poor devil of a cop who, when he's not working for the government sells his services to private persons—who pay him. His name's Vidocq.

SABINE (frightened): And that's you?

VIDOCQ: To be of use to you as I was saying just now.

SABINE: And how can you help me?

VIDOCQ: The beautiful lemonade girl has ravaged many customers. One of them a Spanish minister colossally rich who recoils at no expense to know the progress of his rivals. I am here to inform him.

SABINE: And what are you offering me?

VIDOCQ: To give you, at the same time, the details you are seeking, without risking exposing yourself—as you are.

SABINE (after hesitating): I don't know what you are trying to say.

VIDOCQ: As you please. But you will come to it all the same.

(impatient reaction from Sabine who moves on)

VIDOCQ: Come on Come on! Say what she will—I winged her.

61

YVRIER: Here's news. The King's prosecutor's here.

VIDOCQ: Monsieur de Bergonde.

COCO: With the son of Mazerolles.

VIDOCQ: The Captain! Here! Ah, as you say, Yvrier, he may indeed have news. Let's keep to the side and keep an eye on them.

(They move to a less conspicuous table.)

VAILLANT: Look, Madame Madou. Isn't that Captain Mazerolles? They told us was in Verdun?

MADAME MADOU: Yes, indeed. Oh, how pale and sad he looks.

COURTOIS: What would you like, my officer?

GEORGE: Punch!

COURTOIS: Right away!

DE BERGONDE: My dear George, if I followed you to this place, it's to try to calm you down. I understand how the rumors surrounding the girl remind you of her father's crime.

GEORGE: No, my friend, you don't understand. You don't understand that I doubt, that I still doubt. Helene, this humble child, prostituting herself to the insolent curiosity of idlers, draping herself in a bloody popularity. No! She's making a mockery of all dignity, of all modesty, all prior oaths, of our past love.

DE BERGONDE: Ah! You love her?

GEORGE: Yes, despite the certainty of her degradation, despite the command of my conscience to flee the daughter of Jacques Lebrun, I still love her. Judge my passion. I offered to snatch her from this bucket of mud and to be my wife. She refused!

DE BERGONDE: She did?

GEORGE: Desperate, I left my regiment, and I've come to see her, to talk to her, to know if it's really true she's the most wretched of women, and I am the most unlucky of men.

DE BERGONDE: My poor friend.

MADAME MADOU: It's past nine o'clock

OLE MAN: But the beautiful lemonade girl—

VAILLANT: She's late.

MADAME MADOU: Isn't she coming? That'd be outright theft!

COCO: A scheme to increase the price to customers, I say!

NAVET: Increase! And you suffered it? (standing on a stool) Citizens! To arms!

ALL: The Boss! The Boss!

COURTOIS: Ladies, gentlemen—Mademoiselle Helene Lebrun is indisposed.

(murmurs of protest, sympathy.)

NAVET: She's sick?

COURTOIS: Yes, but only momentarily; she's feeling better by the moment, and shortly—

ALL: Bravo! Bravo!

(Roland enters by the back, and sits at a distant table.)

ROLAND: Waiter, absinthe!

VIDOCQ (to Sabine): You saw him?

SABINE: Him? Yes, it's really him. Ah! I don't want him to notice me.

VIDOCQ: Well? Have you decided to accept my services?

SABINE: Yes.

VIDOCQ: I'll bring you what you want to know at your domicile, Madame la Marquise.

SABINE: You know where I live?

VIDOCQ: 38 Avenue du Roule. Don't I know everything?

SABINE: Oh—I'll get my revenge!

(She leaves by the back.)

VIDOCQ: I'm counting on that.

GEORGE (to M. de Bergonde): You heard. She's going to come.

DE BERGONDE: George, let's get out of here!

GEORGE: No! Leave me alone! I intend to stay. (emptying a glass and slamming it violently on the table)

COURTOIS (coming in from the side): Gentlemen! Gentlemen!

(Helene, very pale, in black satin with décolleté and a red necklace about her neck, stops for a moment, then comes forward slowly.)

GEORGE: Her!

ROLAND: Her!

MADAME MADOU: She's still wearing mourning for her father.

VAILLANT: That red band around her neck. You'd say a sliced off head was resting on her shoulders.

NAVET: She's really chic all the same.

HELENE (heading towards the counter and noticing Vidocq): You!

VIDOCQ (low to her): Not a word! Not a gesture! Only one man knows the secret of the Rue des Maçons-Sorbonne. That man loves you. He's here. Listen to him. Smile at him. Courage!

HELENE: I've got it.

(She takes a few steps and finds herself face to face with Roland.)

ROLAND: Helene—Mademoiselle. I'm the one who, every evening, sends you—

HELENE: Flowers and letters—I know.

ROLAND: Flowers that you refuse, letters that you toss without reading. Several times I've wanted to speak to you. You haven't answered me. Why this cruelty, Helene?

HELENE (looking him in the face): Perhaps because I was expecting something else from you, Monsieur.

GEORGE (rising): That man who's talking to her—it's Roland.

DE BERGONDE: Roland?

GEORGE: My mother's godson. Ah, I'm going to find out what he has in common with that woman. (rushing to Helene) Helene!

HELENE: George.

ROLAND: Captain Mazerolles.

GEORGE: Since everyone here has the right to speak to you, you will listen to me.

HELENE: No, no—I don't want to. (trying to move away)

GEORGE (barring her passage): It's necessary. I want to know why you are making a pedestal of your father's passage.

HELENE (putting her hand over her heart): My God! My hand's going to break.

GEORGE (violently): Speak! Speak, will you!

(Everyone has risen and formed a circle around them.)

HELENE: Captain Mazerolles, I have nothing to say to you.

GEORGE: Still, it's impossible that your heart has changed so quickly. That you've become what you seem to be. You keep silent? Ah, I no longer demand—I beg, I implore, I weep— me, a soldier!

VIDOCQ (behind Helene): Think of your father, Helene!

GEORGE: From pity—a word to tell me you are not a ruined woman—something that proves to me you are not infamous.

HELENE: I repeat to you that I have nothing to say to you.

(He tries to retain her.)

ROLAND (stopping him): Monsieur—one doesn't do violence to a lady.

DE BERGONDE: George, one more time—come!

GEORGE (to Roland): By what right do you meddle in this discussion?

ROLAND: The right of every man to protect a woman against the outrages of a stranger.

DE BERGONDE: You forget, perhaps, Monsieur, that this woman is the daughter of the one who struck down your benefactor.

ROLAND: What do I care? All men who insult a woman are—

GEORGE: Be careful—

HELENE: Ah, this is too much!

(She collapses in the arms of Vidocq. Sensation, Tumult.)

VOICES: She's ill! Help! Get a doctor!

GEORGE (rushing to her): Helene!

ROLAND (jumping in front of him and seizing his arm): In my turn, I forbid you to approach her.

GEORGE: That woman is mine. I love her.

ROLAND: A man in love doesn't behave like a coward.

GEORGE: Wretch!

(He strikes him with his glove. New tumult. They separate them.)

ROLAND: Captain Mazerolles, I will kill you tomorrow.

VIDOCQ (to his acolytes): That remains to be seen.

C U R T A I N

SCENE VI

THE FOREST OF VINCENNES

A clearing. In the midst a secular oak. In the back, a path through which one perceives the Fort and Dungeon in the distance. Yvrier and Helene arrive.

YVRIER (to Helene, who follows him): This way, my dear Mademoiselle. We've reached the end of our voyage.

HELENE (looking around her): Where are we, really? And why after this feverish night of sleeplessness did you come to find me?

YVRIER: To obey Vidocq. It's in this place where the quarrel you witnessed last night will have its ending.

HELENE: The quarrel I am the cause of.

YVRIER: Look child, calm down! That's Vidocq's order.

HELENE: It's vain for me to try to hide my anguish. What I'm suffering is beyond human strength. George, my George!

YVRIER: Don't worry. The Captain knows about swordsmanship and his adversary can barely hold one.

HELENE: His adversary. This Roland. But if Roland doesn't survive the duel, what becomes of the task I've sworn to accomplish?

YVRIER: Vidocq knows what he's doing. He's the strongest of us all. I've been forced to recognize that.

HELENE: But—what to do?

YVRIER: The only way to prevent the duel is by having you here.

HELENE: Me?

YVRIER: It's on you that Vidocq is counting to achieve this result. You've got to coax Roland and make him hope.

HELENE: To feign feelings I'm far from experiencing—and that I actually feel for another.

YVRIER: Correct! What would the use be of woman's wit, if there was no one to deceive in this world? You have only to will it. What the lady wants, God wants—sometimes—and the Devil—always.

HELENE: That man scares me.

YVRIER: Damn it! Go desert the battle when the trumpet sounds. We made a solemn oath to your father, Remember?

HELENE: Well—so be it! I will obey!

YVRIER: Finally! The carriage. It's Roland. Come!

(They vanish into the trees. Roland enters.)

ROLAND: The witnesses will meet me here. Ah, Fate weighs on me! George once treated me like a brother. Now the blood of the son may mix on this hand with that of his mother. Why is he disputing this girl with me.

(He remains absorbed. Helene and Yvrier appear.)

YVRIER: Go without fear, Mademoiselle. I'm watching you.

HELENE (going towards Roland): Monsieur Roland!

ROLAND: You! You here!

HELENE: Isn't this the place you are going to fight with Captain Mazerolles?

ROLAND: Ah, you know. (bitterly) And you've come, I wager, to beg me to spare him.

HELENE: You are mistaken. Didn't you tell me yesterday that you loved me?

ROLAND: I believe I've never loved anyone but you. (reaction by Helene) I'd be lying odiously if I tried to persuade you that you're the first person that I've loved. But what I can declare before Heaven is that the passion that used to draw me towards others in no way resembles that which possesses me today. Yes—because I find you a hundred times more beautiful, more seductive, like in those days when we met as children in the Hotel Mazerolles. I cannot snatch from my heart or my mind this fire that drags me, burns me, devours me.

HELENE: So that if I've understood you correctly, the Beautiful Lemonade Girl will be a conquest that flatters your pride—and you won't hesitate to promise that she become your mistress.

ROLAND: No, not my mistress, my respected and happy wife.

HELENE: You aren't thinking of it; there's an abyss between us.

ROLAND: An abyss?

HELENE: Yes. I'm the daughter of an executed man.

ROLAND: Eh! who cares?

HELENE: Ask yourself this question. How is the daughter of a man just guillotined become so quickly the Beautiful Lemonade Girl of the Café Beaujolais.

ROLAND (embarrassed): My God!

HELENE: You see, I have a plan.

ROLAND: A plan?

HELENE: Yes, since you pretend to love me—it's about my father.

ROLAND (shivering): About your father—Jacques Lebrun?

HELENE: Yes. My father was innocent. Don't bother telling me the evidence against him was overwhelming and convinced judge and jurors. They have their opinion and I have mine. I'm seeking the true culprit—and I intend to find him.

ROLAND: The true culprit—

HELENE: Not to punish him, but to clear my father's name.

ROLAND: Is it possible?

HELENE: I've weighed my duty. It's long and hard. I need someone to help me, support me. That someone must be strong, valiant, and must love me distractedly. To the point of self sacrifice. Are you that man?

ROLAND: Me? You are asking if I want to? Well, yes, I will help you. We will look together. We will discover the wretch. I will raise you up, crushed under the horror of his crime, if you promise me as a reward the caress of your smiles, and the intoxication of your kisses.

HELENE: And if you succumb in this duel that is to take place.

ROLAND: This duel—

HELENE: Now do you understand why I'm trembling and why I'm here?

ROLAND: Helene—!

HELENE: This duel cannot take place. Your life no longer belongs to you, and I forbid you to fight.

ROLAND: Not fight! Can you imagine that? How to decline this meeting?

HELENE: Your love will inspire you.

ROLAND: My God!

HELENE: You hesitate before my prayer? So all these promises of devotion—

ROLAND: I'll keep them, but—

HELENE: So you refuse me the first proof of your devotion when I beg you—

ROLAND: So be it! I will obey.

HELENE: You swear on honor?

ROLAND: Whatever it costs me.

HELENE: Fine. I'm counting on you not to fail. Someone's coming.

ROLAND: Yes, my witnesses.

HELENE: I'm leaving.

ROLAND: Will I see you soon?

HELENE: Once I'm sure I haven't implored you in vain.

(She disappears to the right.)

ROLAND: What she demands is terrible! But since she doesn't reject my love—and George appears to no longer occupy a place in her heart –there's no reason to hate him.

(Enter Vidocq and Coco dressed as officers of the army.)

VIDOCQ (to Coco who follows him): March in step with me, Lieutenant. (seeing Roland) Ah, there's our young man.

ROLAND: Thank you, gentlemen, for the urgency with which you've come to assist me.

VIDOCQ: Yes, a quarrel in an establishment over a woman. Common place! Common place!

ROLAND: Commandant, I told you—

COCO (low): He seems very agitated. Helene must have succeeded.

ROLAND (to himself): Well, I have to do it, I promised. (aloud, with resolution) Gentlemen, there won't be any fight.

VIDOCQ: What? You astonish, me, Monsieur—and that's a hard thing to do.

ROLAND: My God, commandant, it's very simply. We were reciprocally wrong, and I frankly recognize my wrong. I expect Captain Mazerolles won't hesitate to do the same.

VIDOCQ: Ah, superb! The way gentlemen amuse themselves these days!

ROLAND: I need to get this over with.

(Georges, M. de Bergonde and a witness come in as Roland chats with Vidocq.)

DE BERGONDE: I repeat to you: one doesn't fight with men like this Roland. He's a sort of *chevalier d'industrie*, who wastes his money gambling—if he doesn't get money by means less admissible still.

GEORGE: These considerations might stop me if it was a case of an insult received. But I gave the provocation and the insult and I must stand behind the consequences of my acts.

DE BERGONDE: There's another matter between you and the woman you cling to when the crimes of her father ought to raise an insurmountable barrier between you.

GEORGE: Well, yes. I cannot bear the thought that this woman ever belongs to another. You see plainly, I have to kill this man.

ROLAND (coming forward with Vidocq): Then you don't blame me for what I'm going to do?

VIDOCQ: Not at all, Monsieur. No more than I did Beaufond, who refused to fight with me on the fallacious pretext that he was Cavalry, and I was Infantry. Killed at Waterloo. Nasty fellow. (raising his hat) To his memory.

COCO (removing his hat): To his glorious memory.

WITNESS: Gentlemen, I greatly fear that we've been followed by the Forest Warden—in which case it would be suitable to shorten the formalities.

(He chats with Vidocq and Coco who stand near the oak.)

GEORGE: Come on, gentlemen, make it quick!

(He removes his jacket and takes a sword from the hand of a witness.)

ROLAND (coming forward): Excuse me, I have a few words to address to the Captain.
GEORGE: To me?

(The Witnesses make a move to keep them apart.)

ROLAND: Oh—don't worry, Gentlemen, I want you all to hear what I have to say. (to George) Captain, the scene of yesterday was but a misunderstanding from which there is yet time to withdraw. I have for my part no motive of animosity against you; I have not forgotten that I'm obliged to your family. And if on your side you have no reason to wish me ill, it will be easy for us to agree that we brought into the dispute a mutual excitability.
GEORGE (ironically): Truly!
ROLAND: An excitability, in what concerns me, that I deeply deplore.
GEORGE (haughtily): I don't accept the expression of your regrets, Monsieur! (coming forward in a rage) It's not merely a quarrel in a cabaret. There's a woman in it that you've stolen from me.
ROLAND: Monsieur?
GEORGE: A woman that you love.
ROLAND: And that I love more than you, since the promise that I gave her gives me the strength to ignore your insults.
GEORGE: Ah, she's the one who advised this moderation, this prudence.
VIDOCQ (to Coco): This is annoying.
ROLAND (aside): Oh, my oath, my oath… (aloud) Ah, Captain, don't force me to forget I grew up under your roof.
GEORGE: To cross swords with you, I was forgetting that you have neither name, nor family.
ROLAND: Captain Mazerolles, my patience has its limits.

GEORGE (beside himself): Does he truly threaten me? He threatens me, the vagabond. He who to emerge from his cowardice awaits a blow from the flat of my sword before which he cowers.

ROLAND: Ah, that's too much! (He rapidly removes his coat.) A weapon! A weapon! (to Coco who is his second) Give me a sword, give it to me, will you? (to George) I'm waiting for you, Monsieur!

(They fight. George is wounded. M. de Bergonde, Vidocq and the witnesses rush to his side.)

COCO: Look, boss—you who know everything—Ah, Boss—what a shame! You had foreseen everything so perfectly.

VIDOCQ: With lovers, you can be sure of nothing.

ROLAND: He insisted on it.

COCO (to Roland): But you are wounded, too!

ROLAND: Nothing—a mere scratch!

(Coco bandages his hand. He's at the right and doesn't see Helene approach.)

HELENE: George—wounded! (She takes a step towards him.)

GEORGE: You! You! (rising) I forbid you to approach me. Stay with this man, Beautiful Lemonade Girl. Ah, I know you now, you and your father. The one killed my mother, and the other had the son killed. Family of murderers—murderers! Assassins! (falls back)

HELENE: Ah, I don't know what you believe.

VIDOCQ (stopping her): Stop, Helene.

HELENE (low): But this is horrible.

VIDOCQ: You asked me yesterday for the murderer of your father. (pointing to Roland) That's him.

HELENE (low): Great God!

VIDOCQ: One word and our vengeance escapes us.

HELENE: Don't worry—I'll shut up.

GEORGE (standing up): Ah, you're still here. But don't think of it. If I die, the consequences of this meeting may be fatal to your love. Take him away. Take him away, quickly.

ROLAND (coming forward) Monsieur—

HELENE (stopping him with a gesture): Go, Roland.

ROLAND: I did what I could to keep my word, Helene. But, as for you—remember yours!

HELENE: My promise—yes. (eyes to heaven) Yes, I'll remember it, O father.

CURTAIN

ACT IV
SCENE VII

A SMALL HOTEL ON THE AVENUE DU ROULE
An English Garden. On one side a hotel open on the ground floor, allowing a view of an elegant office with a secretary, round table, arm chair, etc. At the back, a window. A door on the same side. A second door allows the office to communicate with the garden. At the rear, in shrubbery—a small gate. Tress, bunches of flowers, seats and rustic benches.
AT RISE, inside, Navet in the livery of a groom, and Brigitte as a soubrette half stretched on a chair. The other, on a divan. Both seem to sleep. Loud ringing at the gate.

NAVET (lazily): Mademoiselle Brigitte—
BRIGITTE (lazily): What?
NAVET: Somebody's ringing.
BRIGITTE: You think so?

(another ring)

NAVET: By Jove—listen.
BRIGITTE: Well—you go open.
NAVET (considering): The Boss has the key and the lady's in her room. Who can it be?
BRIGITTE: Some beggar or nosey person.
NAVET: Besides, it was to have nothing to do that I became a servant.

(They yawn. The ringing gets louder.)

BRIGITTE: What a mad man. Do you hear that?
NAVET: It's like the tocsin.

(Vidocq's voice coming from the other side of the gate.)

VIDOCQ: C'mon, idiots! Are you going to leave me out here forever?

(Navet and Brigitte jump up, rush to the gate and take a peek.)

NAVET: It's a foreigner.
BRIGITTE: With a black servant.
COCO'S VOICE: Open both sides of the gate for my master!

(Navet opens the gate. Vidocq, dressed as a Spanish diplomat, with a black beard and gold rings in his ears, enters with dignity, followed by Coco, dressed in a rich livery. Navet and Brigitte bow deeply.)

COCO: Hello, my little friends, hello, hello, hello.
BRIGITTE: Keep your hands off me.
VIDOCQ (with a strong Spanish accent): Where is the Señor Marquis de Grand-Champs?
NAVET: The Marquis is absent, your lordship.
VIDOCQ: And the Señora?
BRIGITTE: I don't know if she's visible.
VIDOCQ: A seat.
COCO: Right here, good master—let me…

(He pulls up a garden chair.)

VIDOCQ: Bamboula?
COCO: Yes, master?
VIDOCQ: Give my card to this girl.
COCO: Right away, good master.

(Coco goes to Brigitte and gives her a card.)

COCO: Little, señorita—pretty little señorita. (pinches her)
BRIGITTE: Quit it! You're going to bruise me black and blue.

COCO: With pleasure, señorita. Ah, that's all I ask for.

BRIGITTE (reading the card): Don Ramon Charadobal, minister plenipotentiary of His Catholic Majesty.

COCO (trying to kiss her): A little kiss for Bamboula, señorita?

BRIGITTE: Get lost, you creep.

COCO (changing tone, dropping the fake accent): Sonofabitch! you're awfully proud for a hooker, my sweet.

VIDOCQ (rising, to Navet): And you, model of dandified fashion, don't you recognize your place is in this house?

BRIGITTE: Coco-Lacour!

NAVET: M. Jules!

VIDOCQ: Kids, if I placed you in this house where this interesting person lives, it's so you could listen at the doors, and watch through keyholes. You have not, I hope, failed in this delicate mission. Well—your report. (to Brigitte) The so-called Marquise?

BRIGITTE: She cries all day, and gets angry.

VIDOCQ: I see. In the past, she crushed her lover by disdaining his protection. And now that Roland is trying to break his chains, she feels wounded—in her pride as much as in her love. (to Brigitte) Go and tell her that a noble hidalgo desires to communicate things to her of the greatest importance.

BRIGITTE: She's coming now, M. Jules.

(Sabine appears. Brigitte gives her Vidocq's card. Navet walks away.)

SABINE (reading the card): I don't know him. What does he want with me. (seeing Vidocq) Ah! Leave us!

COCO: And to us the amours!

(He disappears with Brigitte into the trees. Vidocq bows to Sabine. She indicates a chair. They sit facing each other.)

VIDOCQ (abruptly): Madame, I'm a foreign diplomat. That's why I won't be diplomatic, but instead, get straight to the point—like a cannon ball. Your husband is cheating on you.

SABINE: Monsieur?

VIDOCQ: As for the rest, you must be informed. I'm told that a rogue who calls himself Vidocq, who's not content to be a Police Officer, has given you some information in this regard.

SABINE: Who told you?

VIDOCQ: Vidocq. He must have told you he was also working for me in this matter.

SABINE: For you?

VIDOCQ: As for me, I guessed you were jealous.

SABINE: Jealous! Come on! You are mistaken.

VIDOCQ: You are jealous, don't deny it. And you are helpless before the one who's causing it.

SABINE: Monsieur, what gives you the right to talk to me this way?

VIDOCQ: Because, I too, am jealous.

SABINE You!

VIDOCQ: Yes! What you are feeling, I am feeling! What you are suffering, I am suffering. But while you French burn, we Spaniards act! You weep, I strike! That's why I've sworn to kill your husband.

SABINE: Kill him? But why?

VIDOCQ: Because he's stolen from me the woman who is my life. The same woman he is leaving you for: the Beautiful Lemonade Girl of the Café Beaujolais.

SABINE: That woman! You love that woman, too! And you believe that this Helene Lebrun—

VIDOCQ: …Loves him. By God, yes! She's running away with him. This very night.

SABINE: They're running off—tonight? (She staggers, and holds onto the chair so as not to fall.)

VIDOCQ: No fainting, please. This is not the time.

SABINE: No—you're lying, they aren't leaving! Roland knows me—he wouldn't dare!

VIDOCQ: Well, read this letter.

SABINE: What letter?

VIDOCQ (handing her a letter): It's a word for word copy of the letter your Roland received last night. Read it!

(Sabine sits and reads.)

VIDOCQ: Vidocq procured a copy for me. Ah, that Vidocq is a clever rogue.

SABINE: The wretch! He won't leave!

(Vidocq takes back the letter.)

SABINE: I know how to prevent him.

VIDOCQ (aside, in his own voice): Sure, you do. (aloud) With prayers and tears? no good!

SABINE: Me, weep and cry? Never! A word from me to Helene is all it will take to make your Helene spurn him in horror.

VIDOCQ: What is it, pray tell me?

SABINE: No—I'll only say it to her.

VIDOCQ: Her passion will prevail.

SABINE: In that case, I'll set the sword of justice after him.

VIDOCQ: The sword of justice? What could he have done?

SABINE: What? Plenty! You are driving me crazy, Monsieur. I need to be alone.

VIDOCQ: But—

SABINE: Don't worry. If he comes home, he won't leave with that girl.

(Sabine leaves, concerned.)

VIDOCQ: She's not ready to talk yet. But—it's only a delay. (going into the garden.) Come to me—the rest of you.

(They all come and gather around him.)

VIDOCQ (to Navet): Your master won't be late. As soon as he returns, give him this letter. Be careful to say it was an errand boy who brought it.

NAVET: It will be done, M. Jules.

VIDOCQ: Now carry out my orders, exactly. Some strange things may take place here tonight. Hear nothing, see nothing, intervene in nothing. And be calm. I won't be far off.

COCO: I hear a key's turning in the lock.

NAVET: It's him! He's coming home.

VIDOCQ: Let's vanish, Bamboula.

COCO: Right, right.

(They leave by the gate. Navet quickly shuts it as Brigitte vanishes to the left. Roland enters furtively by the small door at the back, which he shuts behind him. He heads towards the office then stops, seeing Navet.)

ROLAND (roughly): What are you doing here?

NAVET: Waiting to give you a letter brought by an errand boy—about an hour ago.

ROLAND: That's fine.

(He dismisses Navet with a gesture. Night comes on slowly.)

ROLAND: Helene—Helene is writing to me. "As I promised. I consent to follow you, But before we leave, there's something I must do. You'll find me at the Hotel Mazerolles, this evening." No, never! Never! (a silence) And yet, if Helene is the reward— (another silence) Ah, am I a child? I don't advise the dead to emerge from their tombs—I'm in the mood to send them back. (voice rising) Come on! It's decided, I'll go to the Hotel Mazerolles.

(He goes into the pavilion and rings. Night has now fallen.)

BRIGITTE (entering with a candelabra): You rang, Monsieur?

ROLAND: Put that light down. Where is Madame?

BRIGITTE: She's ill—and went to her room.
ROLAND: I am in to no one—no one, you hear! Go!

(Brigitte leaves.)

ROLAND: Sabine's ill. There's an explanation avoided. Let's not waste a minute.

(going to the secretary, he pulls out bills which he begins to count into two piles. Sabine enters, looks around but doesn't see him at first.)

ROLAND: Two piles. Mine and hers.
SABINE: There he is!
ROLAND: Sabine will have as much as I do, and she's a resourceful woman.
SABINE (watching Roland, who doesn't see her): So it's true…
ROLAND: Now, let's move.
SABINE (leaping in front of him): Where do you think you are going?
ROLAND: Sabine!
SABINE: You weren't expecting to meet me on your way out?
ROLAND: They told me you were ill—the night air might aggravate your cold.
SABINE: Why do you care for me?
ROLAND: Go back and lie down
SABINE (exploding): So you really love that girl!
ROLAND: What girl?
SABINE: The one who's taking you away from me!
ROLAND: You're crazy!
SABINE: No, only jealous.
ROLAND: You, jealous?
SABINE: Why not? Before, it was you. Now it's my turn.
ROLAND: Look, I swear to you…
SABINE: Don't swear or I'll whack you with her name.

ROLAND: Her name? What name?

SABINE: Helene! The Beautiful Lemonade Girl!

ROLAND: So you know?

SABINE: I know everything! Even that you intend to run off with her.

ROLAND: All right. Cards on the table. Well, yes, I do love her. And yes, we're leaving together. I'm leaving you because you've made me hate you.

SABINE: You hate me?

ROLAND: Yes, because you represent a past I want to forget. So, let's end it. I've left you half of what I have—that's fair, I think.

SABINE: I see. A sort of liquidation. But, you forget, we're not just partners, we're accomplices. If you leave me, we'll die together. It matters little to me if they chop both our heads off, so long as they land in the same basket.

ROLAND: Sabine, don't push me beyond my limits.

(He twists to get by her and prepares to leave.)

SABINE: You shall not pass!

ROLAND (stepping back): Beware!

SABINE (pulling a dagger): If you try to leave, I'll kill you.

ROLAND: Ah, you viper! Come on, get out of my way!

SABINE: No. Never!

ROLAND: Let me leave.

SABINE: No, no, no!

ROLAND: So much the worse for you then!

(They fight. Sabine is soon beaten.)

SABINE (still struggling): Coward! Coward! Coward!

ROLAND (covering her mouth to prevent her from screaming): Don't you bite, you slut!

SABINE: Didn't you dare call me a viper!

ROLAND (taking her dagger): Well, you're disarmed all the same. I've pulled out your fangs!

(He pushes her away violently and she rolls on the ground. He heads towards the door at the back, but Sabine gets up and hangs on to him.)

SABINE: You shall not leave! They'll hear my screams! Help! Help! Help!
ROLAND: Damnation! She's going to ruin me.
SABINE: Yes, they'll come. You'll be arrested and I'll tell them everything.
ROLAND: Shut up!
SABINE: Help me! Help me! Murder!
ROLAND: Will you shut up?
SABINE: Murder! Murder!
ROLAND: Ah—enough!

(He strikes her with the dagger. She releases him and staggers away.)

VIDOCQ (from behind the door at the back): Hang on! I'm here.
ROLAND: Someone's coming.

(He tries to disappear by the back but find himself locked in the garden. Vidocq enters by the small door at the rear, locking it after him.)

VIDOCQ: Sabine, where are you?
SABINE: Here!
VIDOCQ (running to her): Are you wounded?
SABINE: Mortally!
VIDOCQ: And the murderer?
SABINE: There—in the garden!
ROLAND (to himself): No way to flee.
VIDOCQ: That exit is guarded. As for this door, I just locked it.
SABINE: I want to name the murderer! Get the Police.

VIDOCQ: In five minutes, the investigating magistrate will be here. But we need evidence.... Do you have any?

SABINE: Yes, there's a billfold. The one he stole from Madame Mazerolles.

ROLAND (to himself): The slut!

SABINE: Go fetch it, quick. I have time to confess to everything. Death is in me. I feel it. Ah, the one who struck me knows how to kill women.

ROLAND (to himself): I am lost.

VIDOCQ: That billfold—where is it?

SABINE: There—in my secretary.

VIDOCQ: Good.

ROLAND (to himself): I'm saved!

(Vidocq goes into the pavilion. Roland follows him on tiptoe. Then he runs to the door at the back and escapes.)

SABINE: Ah, there—there—

(She rises, tries to grab him, but falls. Vidocq hears her. He runs to the door but finds it locked.)

VIDOCQ: Ah, the bandit! He's escaped!

SABINE: Too late! He's gone!

VIDOCQ: Never mind that! I know where to nab him.

SABINE: At the Hotel Mazerolles, right? Ah, I'm dying.

VIDOCQ: The Devil! Not before confessing! (calling) Navet! Brigitte!

THE TWO OF THEM: M. Jules!

VIDOCQ: Help me to raise up your mistress. Let's place her on this bench. Some light now.

(Brigitte brings back the candelabra. Coco follows her.)

SABINE: Water! Water! I'm choking.

COCO: Here we are, boss. Here we are!

VIDOCQ: About time!

(M. de Bergonde, Yvrier, a clerk and a doctor as well as several cops arrive. They head rapidly towards Sabine.)

DE BERGONDE (to Yvrier): This is the woman you spoke to me about?

(affirmative gesture by Yvrier.)

DE BERGONDE (to the Doctor): Doctor, be sure she's in a condition to answer my questions.

(The Doctor examines her as the others watch.)

YVRIER: Ah, the poor woman—but what about her killer?
VIDOCQ: I had him, but he slipped through my fingers. But you won't miss him. Rush to the Hotel Mazerolles—that's where he is.
YVRIER: The Hotel Mazerolles.
VIDOCQ (pulling him aside): Yes. Listen— (they talk low.)
SABINE: Justice! I want to be heard by the Law.
DE BERGONDE: I'm the King's Investigating Magistrate, Madame.
SABINE: Well, then, listen to me. I swear that the crime at the Hotel Mazerolles had for its sole author a man who's known as the Marquis de Grand-Champs, but who is in reality Roland, the godson of the victim.
DE BERGONDE: What about Jacques Lebrun?
SABINE: Jacques Lebrun was not guilty. You guillotined an innocent man. Roland got in with an old key. He pillaged the strong box.
VIDOCQ (to Yvrier): You've understood me?
YVRIER: Yes. Don't worry. The scoundrel won't escape me.

(Yvrier leaves.)

DE BERGONDE: Madame, have you any evidence to support your allegation?

SABINE: Yes! Look! (opening her gown to show her wound) He killed me because I was his accomplice—to stop me from denouncing him.

(She collapses.)

DOCTOR: Quick. Let's transport her to her bed.

VIDOCQ (pointing to the billfold): And here's the billfold which contains the papers and the fortune he stole.

DE BERGONDE: M. Vidocq, you will proceed to inventory the portfolio and place it with the other evidence.

VIDOCQ: Instantly, Your Honor.

DE BERGONDE (writing): I'm counting on you to catch this wretch. Here's the arrest warrant.

VIDOCQ (after consulting his watch): I'll have the honor of delivering him to you within the hour.

DE BERGONDE (to the Doctor and the police): Come, gentlemen.

(They leave by the gate.)

VIDOCQ (going into the pavilion and beginning the inventory): Bank notes, papers. And a declaration signed by Madame Mazerolles herself! (reading) "*The child raised in my house under the name of Roland, is not my godson. He's my bastard son, born in Brussels from a sin I've tried to hide from all eyes. The birth certificate and all pertinent documents are attached hereto.*" (Vidocq goes through the documents.) Why, this sin—I'm the one who made her commit it. These documents and dates allow no doubt. (exploding) Ah, mercy of Heaven!

COCO: What's wrong, Boss?

VIDOCQ: Leave me alone! Don't come near. Go away!

(Coco steps back and goes to chat with the cops at the other end of the garden.)

VIDOCQ: This Roland is my son. And this son murdered his own mother! And I'm the one that the law charges with turning him in! Oh, this is monstrous! But they haven't got him yet. He might still flee—escape them...

(he prepares to go out.)

COCO: Boss—don't forget they're waiting for you.
VIDOCQ (distracted): Waiting for me? Where?
COCO: At the Hotel Mazerolles.
VIDOCQ: Yes. Right. At the Hotel Mazerolles.

(He rushes out, followed by Coco and the cops.)

CURTAIN.

ACT V

SCENE VIII

THE CHAMBER OF THE DEAD
(Same set as Scene II . The Room of the Crime. Same furniture in the same place. A lit lamp on the table.)
AT RISE, Helene is alone, when Yvrier enters.

HELENE (turning): M. Yvrier?
YVRIER: Good news, Mademoiselle, good news!
HELENE: George—?
YVRIER: The doctors are answering for him; and the news—
HELENE: The news?
YVRIER: We've got our man!
HELENE: Is it possible?
YVRIER: We've got evidence of his crime—and the evidence of his accomplice—who's dead.
HELENE (delighted): So my father—?
YVRIER: His honor will be restored. And that lifts a heavy weight from my conscience.
HELENE: Ah, Mr. Yvrier— (taking his hand) Be blessed.
YVRIER: I'm not the one who did it. It's Providence, and after that Vidocq—our great Vidocq—but hush! Don't you hear?
HELENE: Steps!
YVRIER: It's our game come to get his bait. Disappear. Now's not the moment top reveal ourselves. Don't budge until you're called.

(Helene goes into the alcove. Yvrier leaves by the right. Roland opens the door at the left at the head of the alcove and stops.)

ROLAND: Each step on that stair was like a Calvary. (coming into the middle of the room) It seems I'm here early. So much the better. I am free and I can still be happy. Yes—we'll go to America. I'll put the ocean between me and the long arm of the law, long as it is, cannot seize me.

(Yvrier comes out.)

YVRIER: Do you think so, dear Roland?

ROLAND (recoiling): Who are you?

YVRIER: You cannot place me? I'm Yvrier, officer of the Sûreté and deputy of M. Jules.

ROLAND: M. Jules?

YVRIER: Otherwise known as Vidocq. (pulling out his pistol and pointing it at Roland.) Be so good as to sit down.

ROLAND (collapsing in chair): Ah! I'm lost!

YVRIER: That's my opinion, too. The house is surrounded. I've got ten officers at the stairway ready to kill you like a dog if you show your teeth. Damn, you aren't going alone. After the mistress of this house, you sent your own mistress to the next world.

ROLAND: Sabine is dead?

YVRIER: Yes, but she confessed. Told us everything. Women are such tattle-tales.

ROLAND: Ah—to be imprisoned, judged, condemned.

YVRIER: Vidocq swore you'd end up on the scaffold.

(Vidocq enters.)

ROLAND: Vidocq .But why's he in such a tearing hurry to ruin me? T don't know him. What have I done to him?

VIDOCQ: What have you done to me? That's what I'm going to tell you.

ROLAND: You!

VIDOCQ: I was a soldier. I was young. Chance caused me to meet a French woman in Brussels. Between the two battles, we loved each other. The whirlwind of war separated us, and I

didn't find her again until I saw her stretched on this bed—
(pointing to the alcove) Her breast pierced by the knife of a
wretch.

ROLAND: My God!

VIDOCQ: That's not all. I was unaware that a child was born
of this ephemeral liaison. Now, Monsieur Roland, would you
care to know what became of this child?

ROLAND: What became of him?

VIDOCQ: Well, he murdered his mother. And here he is—it's
you!

ROLAND: Me, your son! I, the son of Vidocq! Lord have
mercy. I killed my mother!

YVRIER (going to Vidocq): My poor comrade!

VIDOCQ (to Roland who heads towards the door): Where are
you going?

ROLAND: By God, I was going to do your work, father. I'm
going to deliver myself to your agents.

VIDOCQ: You are?

ROLAND: Yes! I'm going to tell them: Here I am! You were
merely seeking a murderer. Here's something better, a matri-
cide! You must cut off my hand before chopping off my head.

VIDOCQ: You won't do that.

ROLAND: If I don't, you will, right? I'll spare you the trouble.

VIDOCQ: No, it's impossible.

ROLAND: Then—what shall I do?

VIDOCQ: You've got to flee.

ROLAND: What? You want me to do that?

VIDOCQ: Ah, I am committing a crime, but I cannot, no, I
cannot deliver my son to the executioner. Escape!

ROLAND: Will that save me? I've judged and condemned
myself. Let them execute me.

VIDOCQ: But you are my son, wretch! I don't want you to die
in front of the crowd. No, no—I don't want that. Listen, you
are going to slip out this exit. (Pointing to a door.)

YVRIER: Vidocq, you cannot do that. What about your duty?

VIDOCQ: They cannot ask me to take his life after having given it to him. Listen, Yvrier, we've been enemies, rivals, now we've become friends, almost brothers. Well, I beg you—bend—don't force me to dash my brains out against this wall...

YVRIER (after a silence): Fine. I see nothing. But be quick about it.

VIDOCQ: Take this card. You can use it to get through the Police Cordon. Hurry.

(He pushes Roland towards the door. Helene emerges from the alcove.)

ROLAND (recoiling before her): Helene!

VIDOCQ: Helene! I'd forgotten her.

HELENE: I understand, M. Vidocq, that your family affairs have made you forget mine. But, if you forget, I remember. This man shall not flee.

VIDOCQ: What are you saying?

HELENE: I'm saying human justice shall run its course, while divine Justice takes its. I say the innocent must be rehabilitated, by the punishment of the guilty.

VIDOCQ: Bit the culprit is my son.

HELENE: But the innocent was my father.

VIDOCQ: I beg you.

HELENE: M. Vidocq, I understand your sorrow. I even excuse your momentary distraction. But if it makes you forget your duty it's impossible for me to forget mine. (She strides towards Roland) I summon you, the representatives of authority—(grabbing his shoulder) To put him under the law.

(Noises off. The door at the right opens. George appears, shaking, very pale.)

HELENE (running to him): George!

VIDOCQ: Yes, George that I had warned, undeceived—while you are breaking my heart.

GEORGE: So then—this is the murderer; it was you, wretch!

HELENE: George, don't touch that man!

ROLAND: I'm lost!

VIDOCQ: Yes, quite lost! But I don't want you to die on the scaffold. (pulling his pistol from his pocket) Here, take it!

ROLAND: No, no! I'm afraid.

VIDOCQ: Ah, coward, coward! you only have courage to kill women!

YVRIER: The agents are here! The magistrate, too!

(Cops appear in the doorway.)

VIDOCQ: Well! Then, I'm the one who's going to kill you.

(He kills Roland. Excited emotions from the characters present.)

YVRIER: Vidocq!

VIDOCQ (standing up after having kissed Roland's face) I promised justice would be done! (pointing to Roland's body) Justice is done!

CURTAIN

Polichinelle *was a 5-acts drama first performed at the Bouffes Bordelais theater in Bordeaux on 9 June 1887. The play was written by Louis Péricaud with contributions by Ernest Vois (b. Le Blanc, 11 May 1846; d. Beaulieu-sur-Mer, 28 January 1902), another playwright, but also a composer and an actor. The story was based on* Les Mansardes de Paris *[The Garrets of Paris], a popular 1880 novel by Pierre Zaccone (b. Douai, 2 April 1818; d. Morlaix, 21 April 1895). Zaccone was a famous author of crime novels and thrillers, who often collaborated with Paul Féval.*

POLICHINELLE

by Louis Péricaud & Ernest Vois

CHARACTERS

POLICHINELLE
STEEL-THROAT
ROUGEOT THE YOUNGER
GEORGE DIDIER
CLOTILDE DIDIER a.k.a. COUNTESS DES AIGLADES
COUNT DES AIGLADES D'ORVADO
JULIETTE D'ORVADO
GONTRAN DE KERDREL
DOCTOR ROBERT
CHARMETTE
SAC-À-PLÂTRE
MAMA DUMONT.
PAPA MISÈRE
BRIN D'AMOUR.
WILLIAM
JEAN
GERVAISE

A BOURGEOIS.
A WORKER.
GALLEY SLAVES, GUARDS, SOLDIERS, WORKERS, COPS, MALE AND FEMALE GAMBLERS, HUNCH-BACKS.

The action takes place in 1834.

ACT I

SCENE I

A CORNER IN THE PORT OF BREST

All the galley slaves are working. Some work on ropes, others on a ship. Others are seen carrying planks or pushing barrels full of stone or earth. The clock strikes. All the slaves stop working and go find their bowls. They disperse on every side to eat.

AT RISE, Polichinelle and Didier are seated on the left on a plank; Rougeot the Younger and Steel-Throat are seated on the side of a boat, eating.

ROUGEOT: Say there, you are eating too fast.

STEEL-THROAT: Pardon. I'm really hungry.

ROUGEOT: I'm really hungry, too. But I don't want to be seen not eating my share of food.

STEEL-THROAT: I'm not preventing you from hurrying.

ROUGEOT: But I don't want you to finish before me. The shares are already small enough.

STEEL-THROAT: Have you finished? Why don't you ask for some pheasant—delicately?

ROUGEOT: Goodness—it hasn't been so long that I've eaten pheasant.

STEEL-THROAT: Yes, but now, old chum, it's over. The hunt is over!

ROUGEOT: You never know. I still want to eat it, and I will eat it!

STEEL-THROAT: Whereabouts?

ROUGEOT: Not here. They don't know how to treat you! But I know where there are some and good stuff, too.

STEEL-THROAT: You'll take me along with you, won't you?

ROUGEOT: You—come on, you're too much of a coward. All the same, if I hunt, I'll do your business before I go.

STEEL-THROAT (choking as he eats): Say, there—you are going to give me bad digestion.

ROUGEOT: Shut up, will you! The hound is watching us.

POLICHINELLE (to Didier): You're not eating?

DIDIER (darkly): No.

POLICHINELLE: The gentleman is indisposed?

DIDIER: Go away, leave me alone.

POLICHINELLE: Well, that's fine. One shuts up, so many swanks. All these old honest men: They make my head spin. As for me, I eat. You never know what might happen. You might need your strength, so you must eat—if you want to escape. (Didier raises his head) Ah, now you are listening, huh? Ah, these pigeons, when one talks to them of flying off—that agitates their wings in a flutter, right away.

DIDIER: Shut up, you are making me shiver.

POLICHINELLE: There, there—calm down! I'm not yet proposing your vacation itinerary. Go on, you've got time to wait.

DIDIER: Wait! Forever. Here it's been fifteen years, I've been waiting.

POLICHINELLE: You lack patience. In this quarter one must not be in a rush. Look at me. Here's it's been two years I've been bathing in the sea. Am I saying something? And I've already been here twice. I have my season—it's a cure. And besides—I'll escape later. One cannot always remain in the same place. There are temperaments that require change of air. But one mustn't be in a rush. There's a time for everything.

DIDIER: So you still have hope of getting away?

95

POLICHINELLE: Goodness, why not? But for the idea one might escape one day—what would one do here? I ask myself. So—eat up. The soup is good. Ah, heck—it's the butter that chokes you—but still they don't intend to change the chef.

DIDIER: Shut up! You're making me crazy. I'd like to die.

POLICHINELLE: Oh, really? That's not difficult. Swallow your spoon. Ah, you want to die.

DIDIER: Yes—but I would like to avenge myself first.

POLICHINELLE: Not satisfied! Now there's the exigency—Avenge yourself –on whom?

DIDIER: You know very well: on *him*!

POLICHINELLE: On *him*? Ah, yes, the Count des Aiglades.

DIDIER: Yes, and her, too.

POLICHINELLE: Her? Yes, your wife. By Jove—if one were free. There's not a man or woman who would not be fearful. Heck! Heck! and that's it.—But you don't have enough philosophy. You get carried away. Because the Count slept with your wife. That's not enough reason to kill a man. If all husbands—sorry! That would cause the extinction of society. He did wrong, that's all.

DIDIER (reflecting): Free!

POLICHINELLE: I know quite well how he got rid of you. He had the idea of killing someone—Count de Kerdrel—and then said it was you. Indeed, that's not bad. Because that casts a bit of disfavor on the one who was caught. The work was well done. (aside) I know something about it. (aloud) And when one performs these actions, one must always have the courage of one's opinion. But you're always feeling sorry for yourself. You have food, a place to sleep, and the government takes care of you—it watches over us with solicitude. You are an ingrate. Goodness—that one one's serving–the second helping. Come on—maybe there's some left.

(He goes and meets Rougeot the Younger)

ROUGEOT: Well?

POLICHINELLE: In three days I will be ready.

ROUGEOT: And Didier?

POLICHINELLE: Shut up, will you! We need to rid ourselves of him first. He has to die! I am tempting him. Today, it will be over.

A GUARD (to a galley slave): Well—down there. Number 413—whenever you like.

SLAVE #413: Is he sweet! (to Guard) Here I am, my Prince.

GUARD: Come on, no wise remarks.

SLAVE#413: About what? Don't we all love the nobility—democrat?

GUARD: Two days in irons! (He gestures to another guard.)

SLAVE#413: What a way of taking coffee! (aside) Ah, if I were boss here.

(They resume their places.)

STEEL-THROAT: All the same, it's no pheasant.

ROUGEOT: So what—we can pretend.

STEEL-THROAT: Would you like a wing?

ROUGEOT: Yes, and lots of relish.

STEEL-THROAT (to Polichinelle): This is my place.

POLICHINELLE: What's done is done, Vicomte, take mine.

STEEL-THROAT: I really want that place.

POLICHINELLE: It's nice here. You would have done better to keep your place before coming here. Here's an old bird. He didn't have a chance. He put his boss in a storage box—in place of gold coins. He escaped on the stage-coach. Two hours late. A visit to prison was foreseeable. No passport. Sent to Brest. Ah, misfortune. (gets up) There, my prince. Condolences!

GUARD: Silence!

POLICHINELLE: Oh—you. Got to muzzle you. You howl too much! I'll take charge of it. (Sits down with Didier.)

STEEL-THROAT: Say there, what are they plotting together, Polichinelle and Didier? One would say they want to release the establishment. I'm with them if they escape.

ROUGEOT: Shut up, will you! Yes, there's a plan. But first we must rid ourselves of Didier.

STEEL-THROAT: Why?

ROUGEOT: So you don't know the story? It's quite simple. There was Didier, right. He was married, I suppose. And rich, very rich. His wife was cheating on him. That happens, things like that. They wanted to be rid of him. So the lover, a count, sought out Polichinelle. They croaked a gentleman. They put that on the back of Didier—and here he is. A while later, Polichinelle was caught. He was head of an association that worked in a funny way. They were all hunchbacks, there, the boss called himself Polichinelle. When one risks, one separates, you understand. After that he found Didier here. Polichinelle, wanted to leave, to reconstruct his association, but he wants to be sure Didier will never leave. Once Didier is dead, Polichinelle will escape and go in search of the lover—the Count—to consume a few snails.

(A galley slave comes to join them.)

ROUGEOT: Enough for now. Attention to this one—he's a snitch.

DIDIER (after consideration): Polichinelle, I intend to flee.

POLICHINELLE: Do you want me to go find a cab?

DIDIER: I want to leave here or die.

POLICHINELLE: You are not gay this morning. Let me blow on my beans.

DIDIER: Listen, it's really decided, well considered?

POLICHINELLE: You've been speaking to the Director of the Casino?

DIDIER: You told me that you, too, had decided to risk everything to escape .

POLICHINELLE: Damn, that's so. Couldn't be refused. If you have a safe-conduct, think of me. Only, you know, I don't travel except first class. (mysteriously) Soon, we are going in broad daylight to the ship that docked here yesterday. Our

number is the last. When we return, we must push the guard into the water. You know, I always have my file. After that—
Wait—I'm going to finish the story. Five minutes later we miss the call. The alarm is given. The ship guard catches us as easily as I take my snail. Break of the ban, we've croaked a guard. The King's attorney makes a speech He proves that we are swine. Our attorney says we win the prize. The judges know it—and if you've never seen an honest man guillotined, you can pay yourself if I go first. Would you like some beans?

DIDIER: Never mind! In that case we will die!

POLICHINELLE: Say there, you know I prefer dying peaceably. If you have nothing more gay to tell me, I'm going to ask to change my comrade.

DIDIER: Coward!

POLICHINELLE: Ah, you know, no big words. Here one must be polite. (silence) After all, if you are determined—there might be another way. One more sure.

DIDIER: Speak, will you! don't you see I am ready for anything?

POLICHINELLE (aside) Come on. (aloud) Well—listen up. I have some business to propose to you. One might leave one's skin. But if it succeeds, it's freedom forever.

DIDIER: Freedom—speak quickly.

POLICHINELLE: Number 514 is here. The one who eats down there. He's an old pharmacist-very expert in the preparation of poisons. I think it's actually to this cleverness which he owes the pleasure of setting foot in Brest. Not to mention the honor of being with us.

DIDIER: Well?

POLICHINELLE: Well—he works on the boats where he varnishes and treats them with pitch. He's found a way to make a brew he wants to try. Three or four drops of his liquor and one falls thunderstruck.

DIDIER: Dead?

POLICHINELLE: Don't be stupid. In appearance. It's a trick. One becomes livid, hands very sweaty, heart mute for 24 hours. One is a cadaver.

DIDIER: And you are proposing I take this brew?

POLICHINELLE: Hell—it's up to you. In the guise of coffee.

DIDIER (considering): Why not take it yourself?

POLICHINELLE: Ah, decidedly you will never be anything by a nail. Because if the experiment is dangerous, I prefer it be tested on someone else. It's as simple as that.

DIDIER: And you assure me—

POLICHINELLE: Oh—I assure you of nothing. All I can tell you is that if you take the brew in 24 hours you will either be dead or you will be free. And since that's what you want—give it a try.

DIDIER (after a moment): Gimme—

POLICHINELLE (aside): Damnation! I think this is it. (he gives him a flask) Say—aren't you going to say thanks?

DIDIER (hesitating): Death or Liberty. Liberty!

(As Didier hesitates, some visitors, among whom are the Count des Aiglades and Clotilde, promenade with guards in the midst of the slaves. Didier watches them.)

COUNT: What crimes joined together! This is the Kingdom of vice.

CLOTILDE: I feel myself ill at ease. This visit unnerves me. Let's get out of here.—come on, will you!

COUNT: No—I want to be sure—

CLOTILDE: Of what?

COUNT: That they are still alive.

CLOTILDE: Shut up! I gave in to your insistence on coming here, but I want to leave these parts.

COUNT: In a minute.

POLICHINELLE: Ah, it's visitor's day. To think there are people who amuse themselves coming here. Bad luck! If the gate closes again maybe there'd be more than one who would be in the right place. (He turns and comes face to face with the Count and Clotilde.) Damnation, what was I telling you! Here's one that's a very bad case. (He bows.) Madame. Now here are two who come to inspect the apartment before moving in. Don't be afraid my turtle-doves. The house is cared for. Air, water food and heat in the pension. A real paradise, what! Only the government that believes in tranquility puts the husbands on one side, and wives on the other. That prevents discussions. There's no more need for divorce. (bowing) Till soon, Count des Aiglades.

(The Count looks at him with a haughty air.)

POLICHINELLE: We make our mark. Go, my gallant, you will pay for the two of you. All the same if Didier returns to himself it's going to get hot.

COUNT (to Clotilde): Polichinelle is alive—but I don't see Didier. If only he were dead.

CLOTILDE: Shut up and let's leave.

DIDIER (seated, reflecting) : Who cares about death? It's still freedom.

(Clotilde recognizes Didier and utters a scream.)

COUNT: What's the matter with you?

(Didier hears her scream and observes the Count and Clotilde.)

DIDIER: Heavens! It's a vision. She! Here! Oh, the cowards! They are coming to insult my shame.

COUNT (low to Clotilde): Be careful.

POLICHINELLE (to Didier): Be calm or you are lost. If you say a word it's no escape, no vengeance.

DIDIER: If I could just kill them.

POLICHINELLE: You are dumb! How? Leave them alone. We'll catch them later.

DIDIER (barely containing himself): Cowards! Cowards! Cowards!

CLOTILDE: Let's flee!

DIDIER: You are right. I want to get out of here, and avenge myself. We will see indeed if there's a God on high! (He drinks the flask.)
POLICHINELLE: You are there, my good fellow.

(Didier screams and collapses.)

GUARD: What's wrong?
POLICHINELLE: Number 217 is ill.

(Guards surround Didier and carry him to a bench.)

GUARD (to another guard): Call a doctor!

(The Count has seen the action and holds Clotilde back.)

ROUGEOT (to Polichinelle): Say—is this it?
POLICHINELLE: Yes—it's in the bag. Now the Count des Aiglades no longer needs worry about Didier. He can marry his widow.
ROUGEOT: He'll need to think of us now.
POLICHINELLE: Don't be in such a hurry. I intend to be at the wedding.
ROUGEOT: We'll be there.
COUNT: I am not sorry we came today. We are at ease.
DOCTOR (who has examined Didier): He's dead.

(Didier is carried out. The clock strikes. The galley slaves go back to work. The Count and Clotilde disappear.)

CURTAIN

SCENE II

THE TALKING CORPSE
Doctor Robert's Office. At the back a door opening on a platform. Doors left and right. A large desk on one side, a chimney on the other.
AT RISE, the room is dimly lit. Doctor Robert and Gontran de Kerdrel are seated near the chimney.

ROBERT: Trust me, my dear Gontran—all the prejudices that religion imposes on you are weaknesses which ought to be left to women and children.
GONTRAN: My dear doctor, all men who believe have scruples that cannot be destroyed, and my conscience is revolted at the idea of snatching from the tomb secrets that God alone can know.
ROBERT: My friend, it's 1834. All this is out of the question now.
GONTRAN: What do you want, doctor—there are circumstances in life that decide the future of each individual. I never knew my mother. My father, the victim of a horrible snare, died, murdered when I reached my twelfth year. I was raised by an old Breton soldier who taught me only two things: The use of weapons and prayer. After four years, I received each month from an unknown hand money needed to live—and to march straight in life. I am unaware what feeling motivated this mysterious affection. Each payment is accompanied by these unhappy words, "Pray for criminals and assuage the unfortunate. A friend, Juliette." Within the limits of my means I accomplish these two inscriptions that are sacred to me. Attracted by your glory, I've come to ask you how your science might make use of me. You greeted me with kindness and I thank you for it. But on the side of this science, there's a strange philosophy about you that I respect but that I don't know how to share. Allow me then, as your pupil to separate from you.

ROBERT: My friend, science is also a religion, and in my opinion, it's the best.

GONTRAN: I respect your ideas, dear doctor, but in short, the tomb is the soul refuge of the unfortunate. Let's not discuss this terrible secret called death.

ROBERT: Suppose, by penetrating this secret we could prolong the lives of those who remain?

GONTRAN: You would be equal to God, and that's impossible.

ROBERT: We will destroy this word that science cannot admit.

GONTRAN: You won't destroy death and you can only profane it.

ROBERT (rising): I hear some noise—it's our men.

GONTRAN: Allow me to withdraw.

ROBERT: You've decided?

GONTRAN: I've decided. I neither judge nor condemn what you are doing, but I don't want to associate myself with it.

(Knocking. Robert opens. William and Jean appear carrying a shroud. Robert points to a door. They enter with their burden. Robert follows them.)

GONTRAN (alone): Does the doctor speak the truth? I don't know. The man who just died no longer belongs to humanity, and is it not a theft that robs the tomb of a prey that God gave it? No—I won't associate myself with this profanation! Goodbye, Doctor! Nothing can revolt me against death. I bow when it passes, and I believe, decidedly, that Science offers to its adepts more humane means of progressing than troubling the repose of beings who, having slipped down here, have the right at least to the repose that death gives.

(He leaves. Robert returns with William and Jean.)

WILLIAM: It's as I tell you, Doctor Robert. This one is worth a good 60 francs. He's not an ordinary subject.

JEAN: Ah, hell! We would risk the galleys if someone noticed the fraud.

WILLIAM: We would be seized and we would go in his place.

ROBERT: His place?

JEAN: He was a galley slave.

WILLIAM: Who was poisoned.

ROBERT: I actually saw it. There was a congestion. His lips were bluish.

JEAN: He was a strange case. And he didn't have a long time to wait.

WILLIAM: I should say so. Twenty-four hours ago, he was as alive as you and me.

ROBERT: What—so suddenly?

JEAN: Heck—you understand. At the prison they don't waste time. They don't guard them for long, guys like this. I tell you, you will be satisfied.

WILLIAM: That's why we say—60 francs.

ROBERT: Here.

JEAN: Till next time, Doctor Robert.

ROBERT: Be careful of the platform in the garden.

WILLIAM: Yes, don't worry. I don't like to break my head. Jean would have to bring me here, in my turn. But I have my lantern. Bye, doctor Robert.

(They leave.)

ROBERT (alone): Gontran is no longer here. Ah, these young men. Death frightens them. Come on—let's get to work. Work, knowing one knows nothing. And tomorrow, if this cadaver teaches a bit more of what I don't know who could blame me for having forced death to render a service to those who are living? Profanation! Come off it! Human skull , you who cannot know that when you no longer think—show me what is going through my mind. And thus you will give me the science necessary to save one of my peers tomorrow! Let's get to work!

(He takes his instruments, and heads towards his office. Didier appears, scantily clad in his galley slave clothes, pale and barely able to stand.)

DIDIER: Alive! Alive!

ROBERT: What do I see? It's a hallucination!

DIDIER: No, I am alive.

ROBERT: But just now, I saw—

DIDIER: Just now, you saw a cadaver and now you see a man.

ROBERT: But my scalpel already opened—

DIDIER (pointing to his breast): Yes, my breast. And the pain awakened the strength in me to live.

ROBERT: But those men who brought you?

DIDIER: They thought I was dead, as did the Doctor at the Galleys, as did everyone. They buried me!

ROBERT: You were buried?

DIDIER: Yes. For a few moments. The men who brought me here wasted no time and that's what saved me. After the beginning of my lethargy, I understood everything the Doctor said. "He's dead" said he. The room in the hospital, then the shroud! The hammer! Silence! It's horrible, isn't it? Finally, the cemetery. I heard the grave digger say: "Let's bring him to the Doctor, he will pay handsomely." And so here I am. You purchase cadavers. I am yours.

ROBERT: You are a galley slave?

DIDIER: It's true. I am a galley slave.

ROBERT: A great criminal?

DIDIER: A great one? Yes, a great criminal. Murder, theft. It seems I did all that. You are a doctor. My presence in your home sufficiently explains that you seek from death the science of life. Your subject speaks, that's all. Science obeys Nature, it is Nature's slave! And before this sinister and inviolable thing—Death!—it screams, "Stop! One cannot pass!" Well, I did pass, and I can tell you what death is since I am leaving the shroud. Let's get to work, doctor.

ROBERT: All this is strange!

DIDIER: You wanted to know the secrets of my skull. I'm going to give you those of my heart. And more terrible still.

ROBERT: Speak.

DIDIER: Nature gave me all I needed to be happy, and I'm free of the galley. The antithesis is odd. I possessed a great fortune. At twenty-five my father made me travel. Chance led me to America. I spent a year in Havana. I fell in love with a young Creole, Clotilde d'Orvado, whose father granted me her hand. And our marriage was, in appearances, that of two spouses that nothing could disunite.

ROBERT: You believed you were happy?

DIDIER: Why shouldn't I have believed it? All good things are believed in. Six months after my marriage, I received a letter telling me of my father's death. I left, leaving my wife in America. She was soon to join me. The months unfolded. I had decided to return to Havana, when I heard of her arrival. I went to wait for her at Havre. Oh, what a wait. After the first effusions of tenderness she presented me with a character who accompanied her: The Count des Aiglades, "a friend of my family," she said, "and who will become yours if you like that." For a year I was the happiest of men; my fortune was considerable, my love was immense, and no woman was more coddled, more adored than mine. But one night a stranger brought me a letter saying, "Your wife is cheating on you with the Count des Aiglades, whose wife she became before becoming yours." Three days later, the shocking truth was known to me. I am choking!

(Robert goes to his desk, pours a drink for Didier and gives it to him.)

DIDIER: Thanks! I provoked my wife's lover and wounded him. I vanished from my house and threw myself into the Parisian whirlpool demanding intoxication from the uproar and its pleasures—if not consolation at least its forgetfulness. In the midst of this dissipated life I met a pure child—ignorant of the danger of life—and we loved each other. Her name's Helene, and every night a garret sheltered our amours. A child was the result of this reciprocal tenderness. Then, one night, we heard a noise on the landing of our room. I went to see, The door opposite was open. I noticed a strange disorder. I entered, slipped on the floor which was covered with blood, and I bumped into the body of a man who was killed with three knife wounds. I tried to recall life to the unfortunate victim. At this moment, the Police arrived—I was covered with blood—and despite my denials tried and condemned.

ROBERT: Condemned!

DIDIER: During the investigation an anonymous letter arrived containing these words, "In the Garret of the Rue Soly inhabited by the accused"—the one where I came every night—"there's a small oak furniture in the corner on the left—the furniture has a double back. Search it." They searched it and they found 20,000 franc notes stained with blood together with a letter signed by the victim. How did these bank notes and letter get there? I swear to you before God who has just returned me to life that I wasn't aware until this moment.

ROBERT: So now you know?

DIDIER: Yes. The murdered man was called the Count de Kerdrel. A galley slave condemned some time later informed me of everything. At the slave depot, the guilty boast their misdeeds. This individual, who unknowingly had been the instrument of the Count des Aiglades and my wife, informed me that that, during my amours with Helene, I'd been spied on, followed. That the horrible murder had been knowingly planned and that was the only way they had found of ridding themselves of me. A child—a girl was born of this monstrous assemblage. Then the horrible drama beneath which my happiness and my honor succumbed—was the work of these two beings. The one broke my life by mocking my profound love, the other withered my honor by making me a galley slave. Now, it's my turn to avenge myself.

ROBERT (after a silence): All this is very moving—but I don't believe a word of it.

DIDIER: What?

ROBERT: What galley slave is there who doesn't have a story all made up that proves his innocence?

DIDIER: What do you mean?

ROBERT: I mean that if chance caused you to leave the slave depot, my will can and must put you back in it. Because my conscience doesn't allow me to return to society a reprehensible person that society has banished.

DIDIER: You want to give me up, you say? Don't you see in my words, in my tears, the accent of truth? The quaking of my hand doesn't tell you that I am sincere? Well go ahead, denounce me. The two of us will be in the Depot together.

ROBERT: The two of us?

DIDIER: Am I the first cadaver missing from the cemetery at Brest?

ROBERT: What do you mean?

DIDIER: You too, are a criminal. Society condemns the profession you perform. You cannot give me up without ruining yourself. How will you explain my presence in your home?

ROBERT: That would be treachery!

(Gontran enters and listens.)

DIDIER: I don't know if before God it's a crime to snatch cadavers mysteriously from the tomb and deliver them for experiments, but before the law it's a sacrilege. And you cannot denounce me without betraying yourself. (He takes a ruler from the desk and breaks it in two and forms a cross.) Here's the image of truth and redemption. I swear to you on this cross that I haven't told you a word that is untrue. I'm an honest man.

GONTRAN (advancing towards Didier): I don't know who you are, or what you've done. And I don't want to know. But a man who takes an oath on the cross cannot lie. Here—this is all I possess. (Gives him money) Your tone convinced me. You'll find fifty francs in this purse. Clothes in this room. (he points) And, I hope, justice and freedom.

DIDIER: Thanks. Here's my name. (writing at the desk) You have faith in me, I have faith in you.

GONTRAN (pointing to Robert): Think that you must forget the name of the man in whose home you are.

DIDIER: I no longer remember it.

(Didier goes into the room pointed out by Gontran.)

ROBERT: I still don't know if I'm dreaming. All this is staggering. Are you sure you've done the right thing?

GONTRAN: Yes, doctor—my heart tells me so.

ROBERT: The heart is not always a good counselor.

GONTRAN: We never regret the enthusiasms of conscience. That man is innocent. I am sure of it.

ROBERT: Because he invoked God! Fanatic! With that word they can make you believe anything.

GONTRAN: Anything except evil. I'm sure I did the right thing.

ROBERT: Child! Maybe you'll never see that man again.

GONTRAN: Here's his name. (looks at the paper) Good god! It's the murderer of my father!

(Rushing into the next room)

GONTRAN: Gone! He's gone!

ROBERT: What! Your father—

GONTRAN: Yes, my father, the Count de Kerdrel—murdered by that man!

ROBERT: And you just declared him innocent. Do you believe in your God now?

GONTRAN: Oh—I'll find that wretch!

CURTAIN

ACT II
SCENE III

THE REVIEW OF JULY 28, 1835.
The Boulevard du Temple. On one side old theatres. On the other the Café Turk.
AT RISE, the mob is massed on stage. Soldiers line up on one side facing the audience. Sac-a-Plâtre has climbed a tree. People are at the windows.

BOURGEOIS (running in): Heavens! Now this is a nice place!
WORKER: That's no reason to push me!
A WOMAN: Say—can't you stand still?
WORKER: Push me—I push back!
COP: Come on, come on—calm down!
WORKER: Ah, naturally—it's always the same thing. These cops. Always, provocateurs!
BOURGEOIS: Say rather, guardians of our security.
WORKER: They would like to overthrow the barricade of Saint Merry.
BOURGEOIS: That's not a bad idea. To profit by the burial of the brave General Lamarque,[8] to shed the blood of brave National Guards.
WORKER: Excuse me. It was one of the Republicans who shed that blood.

---

[8] Jean Maximilien Lamarque (22 July 1770 – 1 June 1832) was a distinguished commander during the Napoleonic Wars and later became a member of Parliament. Lamarque was an outspoken opponent of the return of the Ancien Régime and an ardent critic of Louis Philippe. His views made him popular and his death from cholera was the catalyst of the Parisian June Rebellion of 1832, which provided the background for events depicted in Hugo's *Les Misérables*.

111

BOURGEOIS: They didn't steal it.

WORKER: If you want to get yourself carried off, just keep talking.

BOURGEOIS: I beg you—who's going to carry me off?

WORKER: I am—and all those who work. Men who only demand peace and freedom.

BOURGEOIS: Yes—freedom for themselves.

WORKER: And for the whole world. Do you even know what freedom is?

BOURGEOIS: Yes—it's the right I have for you to leave me alone—and the will to stay here if I please. (He takes a step forward.)

WORKER: Granted. On the condition you don't annoy me.

SAC-A-PLÂTRE: That's the thing. To each his own.

WOMAN: Nothing will come of it.

SAC-A-PLÂTRE (in the trees, watching): They are funny, these two birds. Ah, here comes the National Guard!

(The Guard marches past and forms up at the rear. The Count and Clotilde, now Countess des Aiglades, as well as Juliette and Charmette, stroll in.)

CHARMETTE: Now what a crowd there is! Look, will you, Juliette. It's amusing to see all these people.

JULIETTE: I don't like it, Noise, people moving about—all this is unnerving.

CHARMETTE: It's so funny to see all these folks elbowing each other. And then these uniforms—soldiers—music. Oh, how much fun it is.

JULIETTE: Child!

CHARMETTE: Hold on, Juliette—see down there—all those officers.

JULIETTE: Why you are going to get yourself crushed.

(Enter Rougeot the Younger and Steel-Throat.)

STEEL-THROAT: So—you say it's for tonight?

ROUGEOT: Yes. Be at the Cabaret of the Place Maubert. Polichinelle has rebuilt the company of hunchbacks. They're back in business again. You understand he's tracked down the Count des Aiglades, and he intends to make him pay for his stay in the Casino, as he calls it. Only the miser doesn't want to release a large sum. He'd prefer to rid himself of Polichinelle.

STEEL-THROAT: Goodness—not a bad idea, that.

ROUGEOT: Yes, but the old boy is nasty—and he has an idea. He wants to live on his income, like a bourgeois, in a corner. He intends to go straight.

STEEL-THROAT: Ah, bad luck.

ROUGEOT: He's right. As for me, I'm like him. He has remorse.

STEEL-THROAT: What will become of us?

(A bourgeois pulls out his handkerchief and with it, his wallet. Steel-Throat sees it.)

STEEL-THROAT: See that!

(Rougeot picks up the wallet, empties to contents into his pocket and politely returns it to its owner.)

BOURGEOIS: Oh—thanks.

ROUGEOT: Think nothing of it.

STEEL-THROAT (to Rougeot): Let's get out of here.

ROUGEOT: Calmly, as if nothing happened. Like honest men.

(They saunter off into the crowd.)

BOURGEOIS (opening his wallet): Why, I've been robbed!

GONTRAN (who is next to him): You must make a complaint, Monsieur.

BOURGEOIS: Oh, that's quite useless, I'm sure. For sure, it's the guy who had the audacity to return it to me so politely. But empty.

GONTRAN: Never mind. But if you have need of me as a witness, here's my card. M. Gontran de Kerdrel.

JULIETTE (having heard—she cries out): Ah!

CHARMETTE: What's the matter, Juliette?

JULIETTE: Nothing. Someone pushed me. I was afraid. But, it's nothing. (aside) Gontran here. It's Gontran.

GONTRAN (coming forward): Would you allow me, Mademoiselle? (He offers her his arm)

JULIETTE: Thank you, Monsieur, but here's my mother.

(The Count and the Countess return.)

GONTRAN: Would you allow me to get you a chair?

JULIETTE: Thank you, Monsieur, but I feel better. It's over.

CLOTILDE: Would you like us to go back home, Juliette?

JULIETTE: Yes—I'm a bit tired.

(Gontran bows. The Count and the Countess bow. They separate.)

JULIETTE: Don't fail to come tomorrow. I need to talk to you. Or better, no—I'll come to your place.

CHARMETTE: You know that young man?

JULIETTE: I'll explain everything to you tomorrow.

(They disappear.)

WOMAN (to Worker): Don't push like that!

WORKER (pointing to the Bourgeois): He's the one who elbowed you.

COP: Ah, indeed. I'm going to fine you.

BOURGEOIS (pointing to the Worker): It wouldn't be bad to rid us of this gentleman. All these Revolutionaries will ruin France.

WORKER: Aristo!

BOURGEOIS: Revolutionary!

(They shove each other.)

A WOMAN: They're going to fight now.

2nd BOURGEOIS: Have you finished with your politics?

1st BOURGEOIS: It was the Revolution that ruined everything.

WORKER: We've been eating better since that time.

SAC-A-PLÂTRE: I think it's going to get hot.

(People separate them.)

SAC-A-PLÂTRE: Leave them alone, will you? If there's a duel—we'll have lunch. As for me, I'm for explanations.

(Two more cops arrive attracted by the noise.)

A COP: Come on, Beat it or you'll do your explanations at the station.

1st BOURGEOIS: But I didn't say anything.

WORKER: He's the one that provoked me.

COP: Come on, no explanations. Tell it to the Judge.

SAC-A-PLÂTRE: Well, they were speaking of liberty, that's it—equality before the law. Ah, bad luck!

(Polichinelle enters as the two men are led away by the Cops.)

POLICHINELLE: Now that's pleasing, so long as one isn't one of them. (Seeing Sac-a-Plâtre) What are you doing here?

SAC-A-PLÂTRE: Me? I'm contemplating Nature. Counting the National Guard.

POLICHINELLE: Come down to earth. I need to talk to you.

SAC-A-PLÂTRE (descending from his tree): Let them whittle my armchair.

POLICHINELLE: This evening, at ten o'clock, at the home of Papa Misere, Place Maubert—reunion of the Hunchbacks—

and if you want to be a member, you must present yourself. There's going to be a soiree.

SAC-A-PLÂTRE: With music?

POLICHINELLE (giving gold): Yes.

(Sac-a-Plâtre reaches for the gold)

POLICHINELLE: Hands off! Got to earn it first. Have you seen the des Aiglades?

SAC-A-PLÂTRE: No.

POLICHINELLE: I'm expecting him. Get back in your perch. When you see him—whistle.

(Sac-a-Plâtre climbs back up his tree. Polichinelle turns and sees Didier in the crowd.)

POLICHINELLE: Damnation! What do I see? Him! It's not possible.

(Shouting. The crowd reacts and Didier is pushed back; as he turns he comes face to race with Polichinelle.)

DIDIER: Polichinelle!

. POLICHINELLE (altered): Didier!

DIDIER: Yes—Didier, and free!

POLICHINELLE: Ah, indeed. Why, the dead return to life!

DIDIER: So it seems. But yourself—how are you doing?

POLICHINELLE: Pretty good! I had enough of the place and left. It's not like they'll miss me. Plenty of replacements. (low) So then, it seems my famous brew worked after all, eh?

DIDIER: Listen, since chance brings us together—would you work for me, with me? There's money to be had.

POLICHINELLE: You've got some?

DIDIER: More than you could dream of.

POLICHINELLE: That's a lot.

DIDIER: No matter. I am on the trail of Count des Aiglades. For the last year I've spied on him. I've got to get into his home. A last proof is lacking. Will you help me?

POLICHINELLE (aside): Here I am, stuck between the two of them. (aloud) If there's money to be had.

(Didier shows him a purse, then a billfold.)

POLICHINELLE (offering his hand): Whatever I can do. I've always loved you. From day one.

DIDIER: This evening, at my house.

POLICHINELLE: Where?

DIDIER: No. 86, Champs-Elysées.

POLICHINELLE: What did you just say? Fancy residence! Are you a Minister? Not of Justice, I bet! That said, I'm going to come and see you.

DIDIER: Don't fail!

POLICHINELLE: There's no danger of that! It's not my way. I was born to live in High Society.

DIDIER: At 9 o'clock.

POLICHINELLE: Ah, I cannot. I have a conflict.

DIDIER: Tomorrow then.

POLICHINELLE: I'll be there. You won't have to send a search party to find me.

(Didier gives him gold.)

POLICHINELLE: If I were King, I'd give you a medal. Who shall I ask for when I arrive?

DIDIER: Baron de Lorsay.

POLICHINELLE: A Baron. Decidedly, you are a sorcerer.

DIDIER: I have no need to tell you that my precautions are taken.

POLICHINELLE: Don't make bad jokes. You used to be nice. Bye.

(Didier starts to leave. Suddenly, Sac-a-Plâtre whistles.)

POLICHINELLE: Now for the other one. (calling after Didier who vanishes into the crowd) Till tomorrow, my Prince.

WOMAN: Here's an Aide-de Camp passing.

2nd BOURGEOIS: The Headquarters staff cannot be far behind.

POLICHINELLE: I'm in a nice place. On one side, a swine; on the other, a victim. Which one will I work for? Maybe both. The one who pays me best will be served best.

(The Count des Aiglades reappears.)

POLICHINELLE: Get here, will you! If you had come here five minutes earlier, I would have presented you to an old friend.

COUNT: Who?

POLICHINELLE: Didier.

COUNT (laughing): Didier!

POLICHINELLE: You can laugh.

COUNT: You're joking, old boy. I saw him die before my eyes.

POLICHINELLE: Well—he's been resuscitated, that's all.

COUNT: You've gone mad.

POLICHINELLE: No, I am not mad. I saw him. I spoke to him—here—two minutes ago. It's not to be believed—but it's so.

COUNT: But the slave depot! There, before my eyes!

POLICHINELLE: If you are going to make speeches, you are done for. Now is the time for action, not gestures. And I warn you—there's not much time. He's on your track—he told me so.

COUNT: And what of it? What have I to fear from him?

POLICHINELLE: There you go again! Decidedly, you don't see things clearly.

COUNT (cautioning): Polichinelle…

POLICHINELLE: Oh—no great airs. You know that I don't fear you. You would do well to listen to me, since I work for you. (aside) And for your money.

COUNT: So what needs to be done?

POLICHINELLE: Didier needs to be feared only if he has proof of his innocence—and your crime.

COUNT (correcting him): *Our* crime.

POLICHINELLE: So be it! That doesn't change anything. If there's proof against one, there's proof against both. And evidence exists.

COUNT: Yes—Clotilde has it.

POLICHINELLE: That's exactly what worries me.

COUNT: What—you think that Clotilde would—?

POLICHINELLE: I think that instead of getting your back up, you should reflect a moment. If you did, you would think as I do: that a woman who made her husband pass for a murderer so as to live with her lover, very well might betray that lover—if she took another.

COUNT: Oh—to say that after nearly twenty years my life hangs under such threats. Yes, that evidence exists. She has it, because I wrote her—

POLICHINELLE: Ah—there we go again—love birds. Love birds write stupidities that—one day or the next could send him at the very least to eat beans with the old chums at the Casino. Did I write? They caught me—but not because I left a paper trail. I'd be kicking myself for that. I never wanted to learn to write, I've always been afraid of learning—it's always brought me misfortunes.

COUNT: So—what to do?

POLICHINELLE: First of all—let's think. First of the most pressing thing—Didier. Let's worry about him.

COUNT: What do you mean?

POLICHINELLE: By Jove—Denounce him!

COUNT: To the King's Prosecutor?

POLICHINELLE: I've already told you. Don't speak to me of those clowns. They've often frosted my vanity. Come—we are going to fix this. Caught like a hare. I know a trick.

(They go off together.)

WORKER: Here comes the parade!

(The crowd presses. Charmette is jostled by two or three persons.)

CHARMETTE: Now there's a brute!
GONTRAN (near her): Goodness—that little kid from a while ago. Little Mademoiselle, you are going to get yourself hurt. Look, if you will permit me, I will protect you.
CHARMETTE: Thank you, Monsieur. But the wisest thing is to leave.
GONTRAN: What! At such a nice moment! See, the parade is coming this way.
CHARMETTE: Ah, those uniforms are so pretty.
GONTRAN: Stand there. In front of me. Don't be afraid.
CHARMETTE: Thank you, Monsieur, but—oh, I'd really like to see.
GONTRAN: Stand there, I tell you. Hold on—here comes the parade.
CHARMETTE: It's annoying—all these people!
GONTRAN: Lean on my shoulder. There—like that!
CHARMETTE: Thank you, Monsieur!

(She stands on tiptoe. Gontran finds a chair and helps her stand on it.)

SAC-A-PLÂTRE: There's the King!
SHOUTS: There he is! There he is!

(Reaction by the crowd. Drumbeats. Trumpets. Shouted orders. The cortege passes. Acclamations.)

BOURGEOIS: He still seems well, eh?
WORKER: By Jove—he's got a cushy job!

WOMAN: All the same, he's a good king.
WORKER: He's the one who feeds us.
SHOUTS: Long live the King!
SAC-A-PLÂTRE: Those uniforms are really pretty.

(Suddenly, an explosion, detonations. Shouting. Confusion, reaction by the crowd. Soldiers run in, weapons out. The stage fills.)

MAN: Someone shot at the King!
ANOTHER: An infernal device. This is childishness.
ANOTHER: Four generals have been killed.
ANOTHER: And some soldiers.

(Firing)

ANOTHER: They're firing on the people.
ANOTHER: Imbeciles!
ANOTHER: Was the King killed?
ANOTHER: No—he wasn't hurt.
A WOMAN: So much the better.
SHOUTS: Long live the King! Long live Liberty!
A MAN (to his wife): Let's get out of here. They're shouting Long Live Liberty. There are going to be arrests.
ANOTHER: This cannot be the end!
ANOTHER: The troops are going to charge!
SHOUTS: Here come the soldiers! Save yourself, if you can.

(General uproar. Charmette who is near Gontran is knocked over.)

CHARMETTE: Ah! (She falls down.)
MAN (the one who knocked her over): Sorry—but I don't want to be caught.

(He vanishes.)

GONTRAN: Are you hurt, Mademoiselle?
CHARMETTE: I don't know—but I cannot walk.
GONTRAN: Take my arm, and let me escort you.
CHARMETTE: But, Monsieur—
GONTRAN: Let's hurry. The crowd is coming this way.

(They disappear. Clotilde and Juliette pass by.)

JULIETTE: Gontran. Does he know Charmette?
SAC-A-PLÂTRE (in his tree): Now that's a strange parade. What do I see down there? Charmette on the arm of a young man.

(The crowd invades the stage. Soldiers lead prisoners. Shouts. Tumult. Cops make arrests.)

POLICHINELLE (to the Count): Now there are the ducks. They are sure of diversity and I am sure they didn't do anything. It's always like that!
A COP (pointing to Polichinelle): Get that one!
POLICHINELLE (vanishing): Delicate. You're going to get it.
DIDIER (who finds himself behind Polichinelle notices the Count des Aiglades): Him!

(The Cop grabs him taking him for Polichinelle.)

DIDIER: This is infamous! I haven't done anything.

(Cops drag him off.)

POLICHINELLE (to the Count): There! This is working for us! You saw him this time. No luck for Didier. Let's get out of here. So much the worse for him. I give him up. Politics is unhealthy.

(The Count and Polichinelle disappear)

CURTAIN

ACT III
SCENE IV

POLICHINELLE'S GARRET
The stage is divided into three parts. On the right, Charmette's room. To the left, that of Mama Dumont. There's a door of communication. Above, there's a garret. The garret belongs to Polichinelle. Rooftops and skyline can be seen.
AT RISE, Mama Dumont is on stage. Sac-a-Plâtre enters.

SAC-A-PLÂTRE: Morning, Mama.
MAMA DUMONT: Ah, there you are. Where are you coming from? You've been gone two days.
SAC-A-PLÂTRE: I'm going to tell you, Mama, it's that—
MAMA DUMONT: It's that, it's that—always the same thing! Never any work. Always outside, you vagabond. You abandon me without even knowing if I have something to eat. You are a bad son!
SAC-A-PLÂTRE: A bad son! Ah, Mama, don't ever say that. I am lazy, I am a bully—but instead of quarreling with me, you should scold me—gently—That might make me better. And I might change. You always bug me—you call me a bad son. That makes me furious! I go cry in a corner and I begin to absent myself all over again. That's wrong of me. But you are my mother—you know very well that I love you. Give me your hand. I won't let it go. Come on, you will save me.
MAMA DUMONT: From what?
SAC-A-PLÂTRE: Well—from everything. That's what leads me nowhere. Give me a hug, and I swear to you that from now on—
MAMA DUMONT: You've been saying that for the last three years—and you don't straighten out.
SAC-A-PLÂTRE: That's your fault, too –because you ridicule me. I never find anything but reasons here—or slaps. Then, I

go out. That's wrong, I know it. The more I go there, the more bad I get. If you still want it, I have it in me to be a good son! Isn't a mother supposed to forgive?

MAMA DUMONT: Forgive you? Haven't I done that for the last three years, since your poor father died? Every day, you leave me. Do I know where you are going? Or what you are doing? No—you will turn out bad—if you haven't already. I repeat to you, you are simply a bad son!

SAC-A-PLÂTRE: Goodness, Mama, you've said that twice to me this morning. You're wrong to do it. You'll repent of it, and me, too.

MAMA DUMONT: There you go, threatening me now. It's not enough to let me die of hunger. Well, kill me then—that's all that's lacking.

SAC-A-PLÂTRE (gently): I only ask you to tell me that you love me. I will kiss you! That will give me happiness and courage. Just one time, every evening. At the end of three good years I will have repaired the three bad ones. Come on, Mom—give me your cheek. A son's kiss is really worth more than a crust of bread. Come on!

MAMA DUMONT: No! I no longer love you.

SAC-A-PLÂTRE: That's a bad thing to say, Mom, you aren't thinking, or you would regret it. You know very well that at bottom, I love you. I am not bad. Only I lack the courage to do good. Besides, bad things are so easy to do.

MAMA DUMONT: Ah, shut up, shut up! Evil child! No, no, I no longer love you.

(She leaves.)

SAC-A-PLÂTRE (alone): It's all over. (falling into a chair) All I've got left in the world is Charmette.

(At this moment, Charmette enters her room with a basket of provisions and a box of milk.)

SAC-A-PLATE: There's Charmette. Decidedly, she doesn't love me! (rising) It's my fault, too, if Mother doesn't love me. Why do I play the vagabond? She's suffered, poor old lady. Father wasn't tender. All the more reason to love her. I ought to make her forget. Ah, the rich are happy. When one has money, it's really easy to be good. And it's not evil to be honest. The rest of us were born for poverty. Ah, misfortune. If I was rich, I would make two—one for my old lady, and one for Charmette and me. And there would be happiness in it.

CHARMETTE (in her room): There—there. My provisions are ready. I'm going to make lunch.

SAC-A-PLÂTRE: Ah, I'm going out. I will never come back. Charmette is there. I'm going to tell her goodbye.

CHARMETTE: What along while I've been lunching alone! There are houses where there are several at table. In houses like that, there's a family. While here, just me and my flowers. These are the only tenants. Ah, my flowers. I forgot to water those plants. That's bad luck. A sprinkling is what they need.

SAC-A-PLÂTRE (coming up): Hello, Charmette.

CHARMETTE: Heavens! Hello, Sac-a-Plâtre. What's wrong with you? Your eyes are all red.

SAC-A-PLÂTRE: Oh, that's nothing. I was rubbing them.

CHARMETTE: Yes—until they wept.

SAC-A-PLÂTRE: Ah, damn it, my mother is always after me. She never wants to kiss me—and then—

CHARMETTE: And then?

SAC-A-PLÂTRE: And then—I rub my eyes and that brings on tears. That's not my fault.

CHARMETTE: It is—if you cause her so much pain.

SAC-A-PLÂTRE: She causes me more. She doesn't love me. That's pretty hard, go on. To have a mother who doesn't love you. It's like—it's like not having one at all. Ah, forgive me, Charmette—I'm causing you pain. I was forgetting that you don't have any, any more. –I've had no luck today. I am causing harm to those I love—because you and my old lady— Well! That's all. And of the two there's one who doesn't love

125

me at all. And the other one doesn't love me enough. That's the score. Still, I'm not too bad.

CHARMETTE: As for me, I love you well enough.

SAC-A-PLÂTRE: For true? Yes, I don't say no. Ah, if you hadn't consoled me sometimes, I would have gone away. I wanted to tell you that. Till we meet again, Charmette.

CHARMETTE: Till we meet again, Sac-a-Plâtre.

SAC-A-PLÂTRE: Say, would you give this to my mother? I didn't dare to—she would have rejected it.

CHARMETTE: Indeed. What's this?

SAC-A-PLÂTRE: It's three francs.

CHARMETTE: Ah, that's nice—to still think of her when— Thanks.

SAC-A-PLÂTRE: But I want my reward. You told me that for every twenty sous I gave my mother, you would give me a kiss.

CHARMETTE: Gladly. (She kisses him on both cheeks.)

SAC-A-PLÂTRE: That makes two. Would you let me take the last myself?

CHARMETTE: Why not?

SAC-A-PLÂTRE (embracing her): That's nice. You are lucky I don't have more money.

CHARMETTE: Never mind. I'll pay in advance. (She offers her cheek.)

SAC-A-PLÂTRE: Ah, if Mother would do as much. (at his mother's door.) Naughty. Go—goodbye, Charmette. I owe you a dozen sous.

(He leaves.)

CHARMETTE: Funny lad! He's like good bread. He weeps because his mother refuses to kiss him—he loves like an honest man—and he's just a little bully. Ah, if God wanted one day to save all those who are ready to fall—how many brave folks less in prison. Ah, indeed. Let's have lunch. It will give me strength and courage.

(She sits at her table and eats. Knocking)

CHARMETTE: Come in.

(Juliette enters.)

CHARMETTE: You, Mademoiselle! Ah, what joy. I was worried at the parade. You said to me "till tomorrow."
JULIETTE: I wasn't able to come. And when you came to the house, it was impossible to have a private chat. Still, I was very anxious. Tell me, have you seen him?
CHARMETTE: Who?
JULIETTE: That young man—M. Gontran.
CHARMETTE: The gentleman! Oh, yes! He came here yesterday to see his patient as he calls me. Without him, I would have been crushed. And since that moment he has cared for me so zealously.
JULIETTE: Ah, is he coming today?
CHARMETTE: Hum—I don't know. Still, I think so—
JULIETTE: Charmette, you are my friend—you are devoted to me, aren't you? Listen, I want to see him. I cannot explain to you why at this moment. But bring him to the Hotel d'Orvado. I really must speak to him. Just for a moment—you understand me. This evening.
CHARMETTE: Yes, but—
JULIETTE: Goodbye. You know that I'm being watched and cannot absent myself very long. Till tonight. Both of you come. Here's the key to the small gate.
CHARMETTE: But—
JULIETTE: Later, I will explain it to you. If he hesitates, tell him it's Juliette who's waiting for him.
CHARMETTE: He knows you?
JULIETTE: No!
CHARMETTE: In that case, tell me—
JULIETTE: Till tonight—

(She leaves.)

CHARMETTE (alone): This is singular!

(Polichinelle enters the garret above. He rids himself of his hunchback. He's followed by the Count.)

POLICHINELLE: Take the trouble to sit down.
CHARMETTE (in her room): Why does she want to see him?
COUNT: It's not very easy to get here.
POLICHINELLE: They don't want me at the Louvre, so I rented this place. Oh, less expensive. Not as big as the Tuileries. Let's sit down and chat.
COUNT: Don't be so familiar.
POLICHINELLE: Bah, between no-goods. Besides, it's easier for me.

(Mama Dumont goes into her room.)

MAMA DUMONT: He's already left. He's gone back to vagabonding—wretched child.

(She remains for a moment then disappears.)

POLICHINELLE: I went to Didier's place this morning. He's been solidly at work since he left the Casino at Brest. He's found the track of Marie Dumont who dwells here—you remember her? It was she who rented Didier the apartment on the Rue Soly next to that where the Count de Kerdrel spent such a bad night. In short, he's getting warm. There's no time to lose. You spoke to me of Charmette. I've discovered her, followed her for a week. She dwells in this house—which is why I installed myself here—so as to watch her better.
COUNT: The danger is there. This little kid often comes to the Hotel d'Orvado. She's almost the friend of Juliette, and Juliette knows everything. How she came to know this terrible secret I don't know—but I tell you she knows everything.

POLICHINELLE: The Devil! Little girls are chatterboxes. She must be the one who gossiped—

COUNT: The day before yesterday, after the Parade, Charmette wrote to Juliette. From what she said to me in passing, Charmette was shaken up, jostled in the crowd—and escorted to her home by a young doctor named Gontran. And that name caused Juliette to go pale. We had ourselves met that young man at the Parade, and Juliette was greatly upset. Last night, at the theatre she received a note from an unknown man—doubtless this young savior. Juliette is seeking allies. There's a mystery in it we need to know.

POLICHINELLE: What—we are going to find out if all this is connected to Didier? Well, I, too, have allies. I am going to send Sac-a-Plâtre to Charmette. If our letter's author has come—and he will come, because he can be nothing else but a lover, we'll find out. And perhaps, thanks to the cleverness of Sac-a-Plâtre, we will even have the chicken sent by Juliette.

COUNT: But Didier? How can he live?

POLICHINELLE: He's got his pockets full of gold—which is why we must beware of him. He hid his wealth, the wise-acre, and he's got it back. We must hurry. I'm going to seek out Sac-a-Plâtre. Read the newspapers while waiting for me. The Government's been overturned—they offered me a ministry. But Finance wasn't free, so I refused.

(He gives the Count a newspaper and leaves.)

CHARMETTE (who's finished her lunch): There—and a nice glass of milk to wash down lunch.

(knocking)

CHARMETTE: Who can it be? Suppose it's him? Ah, stupid!

(more knocking. She opens. Gontran appears.)

CHARMETTE: You, Monsieur!

GONTRAN: How is my patient?

CHARMETTE: Just fine, Monsieur.

GONTRAN: I'm delighted—but at the same time allow me to regret it.

CHARMETTE: Why?

GONTRAN: Once the patient is cured, she no longer thinks of her doctor.

CHARMETTE: Oh, Monsieur—what about gratitude?

GONTRAN: That exists only if there is a relapse.

CHARMETTE: You are unfair. I will never forget that you helped me, and that, but for you I would probably have been crushed.

GONTRAN: Go on—why don't you just say you owe me your life. Then I might believe you wouldn't forget me. No more than I can forget you—or stop thinking about you. And what happened to me last night at the theater reminded me of you—

CHARMETTE: And what, or rather who, was that?

GONTRAN: The girl who was with you at the Parade. (Reaction by Charmette) You know her well?

CHARMETTE: Me! (after a silence) Mademoiselle Juliette d'Orvado honors me with her sympathy. Even though we come from different backgrounds she has taken me into her affection. She often gives me work and sometimes I go work with her. (She goes to the window.)

GONTRAN: Ah! (He watches her.) Let me continue my story. (As Juliette makes no objection, he proceeds.) During the intermission—while I was thinking of you—a young working girl brought me a letter...

CHARMETTE: Who sent it to you?

GONTRAN: I don't know.

CHARMETTE: There must have been something concerning me in the letter or you wouldn't mention it to me.

GONTRAN (giving her a letter): Here, read it.

CHARMETTE (reading): "Trust everything Charmette tells you." (She places the letter near her.)

130

GONTRAN: Signed "Juliette." What should I make of all this? Do you think this letter comes from Mademoiselle d'Orvado?

CHARMETTE: Yes, it's from her. I recognize her handwriting.

GONTRAN: She knows me then?

CHARMETTE: Who knows?

GONTRAN: That's impossible. I only came to Paris a week ago.

CHARMETTE: Maybe she knows your family.

GONTRAN: I don't have any.

CHARMETTE: Your mother?

GONTRAN (upset—after a silence): I never knew her.

CHARMETTE: Oh, pardon me.

(Silence. At this moment Polichinelle enters the garret above with Sac-a-Plâtre.)

CHARMETTE: But let's not speak any more of Mademoiselle Juliette—

GONTRAN: Of Mademoiselle Juliette?

CHARMETTE: Isn't that why you came?

GONTRAN: I came to see my patient.

CHARMETTE: Your patient is cured. And if you like, she'll take a convalescent stroll with you.

GONTRAN: That would be nice.

CHARMETTE: I'll take you to the home of Mademoiselle d'Orvado, who has a strong desire to speak to you.

GONTRAN: She told you that?

CHARMETTE: An hour ago.

(They continue to talk in whispers.)

SAC-A-PLÂTRE (in the Garret): A young man in her room?

POLICHINELLE: Yes, I heard him speaking through the door.

SAC-A-PLÂTRE: Ah, I intend to find out—

COUNT: Violence can ruin everything.

POLICHINELLE: Here, go down this rope the masons left. You'll be in front of her window.

SAC-A-PLÂTRE: Yes, that's the thing.

POLICHINELLE: Don't let yourself be seen. And if by chance you see a love letter grab it. The Count will pay you generously.

SAC-A-PLÂTRE: A love letter. I'll snatch it for sure.

(He climbs to the roof and can be seen going down the rope.)

CHARMETTE: Mademoiselle Juliette again. Decidedly, you know more than you intend to tell me.

GONTRAN: No, but if Mademoiselle d'Orvado is the person that I think she is there's a great secret between her and me. You'll soon know it, I swear it.

CHARMETTE: What secret?

SAC-A-PLÂTRE (at the window): So it's true—she's not alone.

CHARMETTE: What's that noise? (turning) Why, it's Sac-a-Plâtre!

SAC-A-PLÂTRE: Yes, it's me. I'm disturbing you from what I see.

CHARMETTE: What are you doing at my window?

SAC-A-PLÂTRE: Me? I stroll over the roofs. Then I heard voices.

CHARMETTE: Come in.

GONTRAN (to Charmette): Isn't he the lad we found at your door when I brought you home the other night—and who looked at me with such curiosity and dislike?

CHARMETTE: Yes.

GONTRAN: Your lover?

CHARMETTE: I don't have lovers—and I don't allow anyone to give himself that title.

GONTRAN: Can you be believed?

CHARMETTE: It's up to you! You are free.

SAC-A-PLÂTRE (taking the letter that Gontran placed near the window): That's done.

GONTRAN: Good evening, Mademoiselle.

CHARMETTE: Yes, till this evening, and remember that Juliette begs you not to miss her rendezvous.

SAC-A-PLÂTRE: A rendezvous. Two home calls in one day. Got to watch this doctor.

(Sac-a-Plâtre and Gontran meet at the door.)

GONTRAN: Monsieur.

SAC-A-PLÂTRE: I prefer to remain near her. I've had the last look.

CHARMETTE: What's this talk of walking on the rooftops?

SAC-A-PLÂTRE: True story. The proof is I'm resuming my stroll.

CHARMETTE: No—I don't want that.

SAC-A-PLÂTRE: That's nice. You are scared I might fall. That's almost love, right?

CHARMETTE: Why, no, I'm not.

SAC-A-PLÂTRE: In the end, maybe it will come. Bye, Charmette.

CHARMETTE: Bye, Sac-a-Plâtre.

SAC-A-PLÂTRE: If he steals her from me I will die of it.

(He leaves.)

CHARMETTE: Sac-a-Plâtre, my lover! Poor M. Gontran. The way he said that to me... But how does Juliette know him? Come-on, I've got work to do, and I'm going to finish it.

(Sac-a-Plâtre enters the garret window.)

POLICHINELLE: Ah, it's you! Come in.

SAC-A-PLÂTRE: It's in the bag!

COUNT: You have the letter?

SAC-A-PLÂTRE: Yes, Hurry, I've got a boyfriend to follow.

POLICHINELLE: Gimme.

SAC-A-PLÂTRE: But where's my honest reward?

COUNT (giving him a gold coin): Here it is.

SAC-A-PLÂTRE: Thanks, my Prince. I'm on my way. (aside) I've got to find out who this character is that Charmette gave a rendezvous to.

POLICHINELLE: We'll see you again?

SAC-A-PLÂTRE: Yes, yes. Soon. Bye

(He leaves hurriedly. The Count reads the letter.)

POLICHINELLE: Well?

COUNT (reading): "Believe all that Charmette tells you." It's in Juliette's handwriting. We must act.

POLICHINELLE: There are two dangers. Juliette and Didier. Let's concern ourselves with Didier.

COUNT: What do you want to do?

POLICHINELLE: Denounce him. I told you already. Write.

(The Count sits at a table and writes.)

POLICHINELLE: "Monsieur the Préfet de Police, a man who calls himself Baron de Lorsay, residing for some time at No. 86, Avenue des Champs-Elysées—I believe I'm doing my social duty by informing you that this man is no other than a wretch by the name of Didier, who escaped a year ago from the Slave Depot at Brest. Signed, A friend of Justice." I'll be surprised if they recognize the signature. Put the address on. M. Louvet, Préfet de Police. I won't be the one to deliver it. I don't care for the neighborhood. It's too damp.

COUNT: Is that all?

POLICHINELLE: For Didier, yes. Now—let's decide about your wife. (They talk.)

CHARMETTE: I'm ready. Let's go.

(knocking)

CHARMETTE: Again!

(She opens, Didier appears.)

DIDIER: Pardon me, Mademoiselle, for disturbing you. I knocked on the side door, but no one answered. Could you tell me at what time I can find Madame Dumont?

CHARMETTE: Madame Dumont is a poor woman who lives on the bounty of several persons. She makes her visits and probably won't return this evening.

DIDIER: I came expressly to offer her my services. Would you be my intermediary and give her this modest gift?

CHARMETTE: A hundred francs. Poor woman—you are bringing her a fortune. Thank you, on her behalf.

DIDIER: You've known her a long time?

CHARMETTE: Yes—she's the one who brought me up.

DIDIER: I don't want to waste your time—but if you would allow me to ask you some questions about Madame Dumont, you would be doing her a service. And me, as well.

CHARMETTE: I'm ready to answer, Monsieur.

DIDIER: Some years ago she owned a furnished house—

CHARMETTE: Yes, rue Soly—

DIDIER: Yes, that's right. When did she leave rue Soly?

CHARMETTE: Oh—a long while ago.

DIDIER: Do you know why she left?

CHARMETTE: A murder was committed in her house. The tenants left and she fell into poverty.

DIDIER: That murder… Do you know anything about it?

CHARMETTE (upset): Yes—she often told me about it. (She hesitates to continue.)

DIDIER: I fear my questions may seem indiscreet to you.

CHARMETTE (very upset): Yes. I was born there.

DIDIER: When was that?

CHARMETTE: In 1816. (She starts to cry.)

DIDIER: I'm sorry to cause you pain. Who was your father?

CHARMETTE: I've never known.

DIDIER: And your mother?

CHARMETTE: No more. She died six months after my birth. Mama Dumont brought me up—I have my mother's portrait. (She points to a picture hanging by the chimney.) There it is.

DIDIER: Helene! (He rushes to it and kisses it.)

CHARMETTE: What's wrong with you, Monsieur?

DIDIER: Nothing, nothing! You are sure this is your mother's portrait?

CHARMETTE: Very sure.

DIDIER: Do you know what happened to your father?

CHARMETTE: Yes.

DIDIER: And you think he was guilty?

CHARMETTE: You actually know—?

DIDIER: Yes. He was unjustly condemned. His life was destroyed. Only you can efface all of his tears.

CHARMETTE (rushing to his arms): Father!

DIDIER: My child! My daughter! None of it matters since I have my daughter. My daughter—my child!

CHARMETTE: Father!

DIDIER: I don't even know your name!

CHARMETTE: Madame Dumont named me Charmette.

DIDIER: Well, Charmette—I'm going to take you away from here.

CHARMETTE: Take me away?

DIDIER: Listen, I'm on the trail of the cowards who ruined me. I have to hide myself because if I were discovered I'd be returned to the Slave Depot. And this time, I'd die of it. Maybe soon, I will succeed, and then des Aiglades and Clotilde—

CHARMETTE: Clotilde d'Orvado?

DIDIER: Yes! You know her?

CHARMETTE: She's my friend Juliette's mother.

DIDIER: And do you go into their Hotel?

CHARMETTE: Often.

DIDIER: Where is it located?

CHARMETTE: Rue de Lille.

DIDIER: Listen, at all costs, I must get into this Hotel d'Orvado and see the Countess. It's a question of avenging your father, and rehabilitating myself.

CHARMETTE: Courage, father. There are two of us to avenge you.

POLICHINELLE: And now to the home of your wife. At all cost, we must get back your letters.
COUNT: Yes, our safety depends on it. But that young girl—
POLICHINELLE: Charmette! I'll take care of her. We should go. I'll see if the street is free. Now's the time to be cautious.

(He leaves. Meanwhile, Gontran appears at Charmette's door.)

GONTRAN: I beg your pardon, but you told me to return.
CHARMETTE: Him!
DIDIER: Who is this young man?
CHARMETTE: A friend. He rescued me in the crowd.
DIDIER (coming forward and extending his hand): Monsieur.
GONTRAN (recognizing him): Ah! The man from Brest. The murderer!
CHARMETTE (rushing to protect her father): My father!
GONTRAN: Your father!
DIDIER: I recognize you. It's thanks to you I reached Paris. You can shake my hand without fear. I'm unlucky, but I'm an honest man.
CHARMETTE: Oh—I swear it!
DIDIER: I am going to tell you everything.
(They talk low.)

POLICHINELLE (going to the garret excitedly): Now we're in for it. I was going down to see if we could go out without being seen. I heard voices from Charmette's room. I peeked through the keyhole on the landing. And who did I see but Didier!
COUNT: Didier!
POLICHINELLE: Yes, Didier! He's here! He knows her. He's got a popinjay there, too. No doubt it's Gontran. It's very suspicious.

COUNT: I say the time has come to act. Unless we do, we are lost.

SAC-A-PLÂTRE: He's come back, the scumbag. Decidedly, he's a lover.

POLICHINELLE: Come in, kid, quick. I need you!

GONTRAN (to Didier) I trust you, Monsieur—and my life and my arm are yours.

DIDIER: Be calm. We shall succeed, my daughter and I. Let the monsters come. I am strong now. It's for her and for you that I intend to avenge myself.

POLICHINELLE: Here, Sac-a-Plâtre. This letter goes to the Prefecture de Police. In one hour, Didier will be arrested. He can move in. They will be all warmed up—waiting for him.

DIDIER
My dear children…

CURTAIN

SCENE V

THE HOTEL D'ORVADO
The room between the bedrooms of Juliette and Countess Clotilde.
AT RISE, Juliette is alone leaning on the window sill.

JULIETTE: When's he going to come? Oh, I really want to see him, to speak to him.

(The Countess emerges from her bedroom.)

CLOTILDE: What are you doing there? Juliette! Juliette!

(Juliette recoils)

CLOTILDE: Why are you avoiding me? What's wrong?

JULIETTE (bitterly): Nothing!

CLOTILDE (taking her by the hand and making her sit down) Look—come here. For some time you've been sad—dreamy. What do you want? What are you lacking?

JULIETTE: Nothing.

CLOTILDE: At your age, the pain can only be passing! Look, answer me. Have you something to reproach me with?

JULIETTE: Have I ever complained?

CLOTILDE: Never—it's true. But I can see plainly you are suffering, that you are unhappy. Still, I have no other wish but for your happiness. (Juliette recoils.) You act as if you are afraid of me? Talk, say something, will you? Oh, I'm crazy—I should have guessed it sooner. At eighteen, it's quite natural—you're in love. Ah, don't lie, don't blush—and tell me his name. That's really it, isn't it? I've figured it out.

JULIETTE: Maybe.

CLOTILDE (pulling Juliette to her): Come on, tell me his name.

JULIETTE: No.

CLOTILDE: Why?

JULIETTE: Because the one I love bears a name you couldn't hear without shivering.

CLOTILDE: What are you saying?

JULIETTE (getting loose from her mother): Leave me alone. Your kisses burn me. Your tenderness revolts my heart. I feel I am going mad.

CLOTILDE: Juliette, I am your mother. I order you to speak.

CLOTILDE: You insist! Well, I'm in love with the son of the Count de Kerdrel.

CLOTILDE: The son of the Count de Kerdrel.

JULIETTE: Yes, the son of the man you had murdered!

CLOTILDE: Ah, shut up, you wretched girl, shut up!

JULIETTE: No. you wanted me to speak and I shall speak. Well, one night I saw on your table—papers, letters. I don't know what fatal curiosity made me peruse them—and in those letters I read your guilt and my misfortune.

CLOTILDE: God!

JULIETTE: I understood everything—even what I didn't want to know. My mother was an infamous accessory to murder.

CLOTILDE: Juliette…

JULIETTE: After that I wanted to make up for your sin. I wanted to find the son of your victim. And I succeeded in discovering him. For the last three years, I've been protecting him. I even felt I loved him without knowing him. And after I saw him, I loved him even more.

CLOTILDE: You've seen him?

JULIETTE: Yes.—Now, I'm at the end of my strength. I want to leave. I'm suffocating in this cursed house. I am afraid. All I think about is punishing the guilty. I'm going to reveal everything to Gontran.

CLOTILDE: But the ones who are truly guilty are your father and your mother. No one will believe you. The evidence, those letters, I have them. I can deny them. I can destroy them—

(The Countess stops, stares at Juliette, then rushes to her room. She soon returns.)

CLOTILDE: Juliette, I beg you, give me back those letters. We will flee, your father and I. We will disappear together. He's the one responsible for all this. Don't give me up. Pity your mother.

JULIETTE: My mother, you? Why, a mother loves her child. Did you ever love me? No. And I no longer know you.

CLOTILDE: You refuse to give me back those letters?

JULIETTE: I do!

CLOTILDE: Fine. I am going to tell your father. Beware of what may happen. His rage is terrible.

JULIETTE: I'm not afraid of you or him.

CLOTILDE: That's what we are going to see.

(The Countess leaves hurriedly. Juliette goes to her room.)

JULIETTE: Charmette, are you there?

CHARMETTE (peeping her head in): Yes, and Monsieur Gontran, too.
JULIETTE: Fine.

(She goes into her room. Polichinelle comes out of the opposite room)

POLICHINELLE: Damn it! I'm learning nice things. Luckily, I am here. Ah, I don't want to go back to sea baths. So we are going to laugh now, my little angels.

(The Count and the Countess enter without seeing Polichinelle.)

CLOTILDE: She knows everything.
COUNT: The wretched child!
CLOTILDE: She's read your letters, robbed me of them. We are lost.
COUNT: Not necessarily.

(He heads towards Juliette's room, but is barred by Polichinelle.)

POLICHINELLE: A moment of your time. I don't work for nothing. Ah, you have a fine opinion of your friends.
COUNT: What do you mean?
POLICHINELLE: I mean that if I were not here, you might be on your way to some sea port somewhere—Brest or Toulon. But, as I don't wish to travel, I watch.
COUNT: Explain yourself.
CLOTILDE: We're in a hurry!
POLICHINELLE: Never mind. I am calm. And when I am calm, all goes well.

(A gunshot is heard.)

POLICHINELLE: There! That's it.

CLOTILDE: What does this mean?

POLICHINELLE: It means that Gontran was with your daughter and that he has run off with those incriminating letters that your daughter just gave him.

CLOTILDE: We're lost!

POLICHINELLE: Not at all! I had the garden guarded. That's how I do things. Now go back to your rooms. It's spring. The birds are singing, sparrows are making their nests. Leave it to me.

(The Count and the Countess go into their room. Rougeot the Younger and a servant carry in Gontran who is wounded.)

ROUGEOT: Where should we put him?

POLICHINELLE (indicating the couch): There. What about the girl?

ROUGEOT: She's fainted. Steel-Throat is taking care of her.

POLICHINELLE: We've got to get her, too. (He searches Gontran.) Where are those letter? Not here. Not there. He doesn't have them. Have I done all this work for nothing?

GONTRAN (moaning): It hurts.

POLICHINELLE: That doesn't matter. But the letters—where are they? Give them to me, and I will save you.

GONTRAN: Who are you?

POLICHINELLE: My name wouldn't mean anything to you. But, don't worry. Just tell me where the letters are that Juliette gave to you. Answer me!

GONTRAN: I no longer have them!

POLICHINELLE: Damn! (very softly) That's a shame. It would have been useful to have them.

GONTRAN: For what purpose?

POLICHINELLE: For a number of things. The innocence of Didier, perhaps. Tell me where they are—and I promise you that, once I have them in my possession, your life will be as precious to me as my own.

GONTRAN: It hurts.

POLICHINELLE: Talk, will you!

GONTRAN: Charmette! (He faints.)

POLICHINELLE: Ah! So, Charmette has them. Then everything's fine. She's been caught, too. Only, we must hurry. I am going to tell the Count and the Countess that all is saved. But this nice young man—Bah! It will all work out.

(He leaves. Didier appears, followed by two servants. He runs to Gontran and puts his head on his chest.)

DIDIER: He will live. My friends, take this man to my place, and give him all the cares his condition requires.

(The two servants carry Gontran away.)

DIDIER: I've been able to snatch my daughter from the hands of those wretches. Now for the others! (He stretches out on the couch.)

(The Countess returns.)

CLOTILDE: Polichinelle said the wretch was here. Oh, there he is. (She goes to the couch.)

DIDIER (rising abruptly): Hello, Countess!

CLOTILDE (recoiling, shocked): Didier!

DIDIER: Yes, Didier, your husband. The man who gave you everything, love devotion, riches and to whom, in exchange for all that, all you gave was infamy.

CLOTILDE: I still cannot believe it.

DIDIER: I understand. You thought I was dead. Well, what do you want, sometimes the dead do return.

(The Countess heads towards her room. Didier bars her way.)

DIDIER: I've come to settle a score with you. Since I am your husband, I have that right.

CLOTILDE: Didier, you don't know how much I've suffered.

DIDIER: What about me—fifteen years in the galleys!

CLOTILDE: I've felt so much remorse. I wanted to return to you, but he always prevented me. Didier, save me!

DIDIER: Too late!

CLOTILDE: You are right. My sins are numerous. But remember our love. All those beautiful dreams we had. We will love each other again.

DIDIER (aside): Ah, demon! (aloud, ironic) The Countess d'Orvado in the arms of a galley slave!

CLOTILDE: Ah, you're right. I hate you!

DIDIER: Good! I like you better this way.

CLOTILDE (rushing to a bell): But I am mistress here. This time you won't get away alive!

DIDIER (trying to stop her): Wretch!

CLOTILDE (struggling): Help! Help!

(Juliette comes out of her room.)

JULIETTE: Mother?

CLOTILDE: Juliette, protect your mother. It's him! Didier, the galley slave.

JULIETTE: Him! Here! (to Didier) Flee, Monsieur. This house is cursed. Here—this way, and you will be saved.

(Didier goes into Juliette's room.)

CLOTILDE: What are you doing, Juliette?

JULIETTE: I'm saving him.

CLOTILDE: You, wretched girl!

JULIETTE: I don't intend to let you commit another crime.

(The Count rushes in followed by servants.)

COUNT: That noise! What's wrong?

JULIETTE (very calm): Nothing! It's my mother—she's ill.

CLOTILDE (to the Count): It's Didier! He was here!

CURTAIN

ACT IV
SCENE V

POLICHINELLE'S GARRET
Same as Act III, Scene IV.
AT RISE, Gervaise, a young woman, is taking care of Mama Dumont.

GERVAISE: Here, Mama, drink this it will warm you up.

(Mama Dumont, rises, supported by Gervaise, drinks and falls back.)

GERVAISE: Poor Mama Dumont, it's really over. And your scoundrel of a son isn't here.
MAMA DUMONT: Sac-a-Plâtre! He'll never come.
GERVAISE: Why, yes—yes indeed, he's going to come. Come on, sleep easy, Mama. Be good. Sleep. I'm going to go find him.
MAMA DUMONT: My son! He wants to kill me.
GERVAISE: Now delirium has seized her. Where to find that little no-good?

(She leaves. Sac-a-Plâtre enters Charmette's room.)

SAC-A-PLÂTRE: She's not here. I must find those letters. Polichinelle says that if the Police find them on her, she'll be lost. (opening drawers) Nothing. Where could they be? Ah, I want to see my mother. Her room is next door. (He opens the door.) Ah, I don't see her. She's not here—yes, she is—she's asleep.
MAMA DUMONT (waking): What do you want?
SAC-A-PLÂTRE: Why, it's me, Mama. I came to kiss you.
MAMA DUMONT: I don't know you.

SAC-A-PLÂTRE: C'mon, it's me—your son.

MAMA DUMONT: My son! I have no son—nor a husband. I want to die in peace. Leave me be.

SAC-A-PLÂTRE: Don't talk like that, Mama. You've got a fever, I'm going to get you a doctor.

MAMA DUMONT: Leave me alone. He wants to kill me. Help! Sac-a-Plâtre, protect me. (She falls back in her bed.)

SAC-A-PLÂTRE: She doesn't recognize me. Mama, don't die, I beg you. It's me! (calling) Gervaise! Gervaise!

MAMA DUMONT: Help! Help!

(Gervaise returns.)

SAC-A-PLÂTRE: Ah, Gervaise—quick—she's dying. Go for a doctor, quick.

GERVAISE: He came this morning. He said it's the end.

SAC-A-PLÂTRE: The end. And I left her alone. Oh, Mama! Answer me.

(Mama Dumont rises slowly, hangs on his neck, then suddenly pushes him away.)

MAMA DUMONT: You! Why should I kiss you? I don't know you. I want my son. I don't want to die alone. He abandoned me. (to Sac-a-Plâtre) Go away! Go away! Ah, I recognize you—ungrateful son. No. no! (changing suddenly) Let me see you. Let me kiss you. I love you all the same.

(She falls back, dead.)

SAC-A-PLÂTRE: Mama! Mama! Dead! Mother is dead! Ah, Mama, Mama, forgive me.

(Sac-a-Plâtre weeps by the bedside. Gervaise places a cross and holy water on the table then leaves. Polichinelle appears and enters Charmette's room)

POLICHINELLE: No one! And where is Sac-a-Plâtre? Lazy lad! None of these people know how to work. (Looking about he sees Sac-a-Plâtre through the open door.) What are you doing, instead of searching for those letters?

SAC-A-PLÂTRE: Look—my old lady.

POLICHINELLE: Who is it?

SAC-A-PLÂTRE: She's my mother.

POLICHINELLE: Your mother—?

SAC-A-PLÂTRE: Yes. And she's dead.

POLICHINELLE: So you actually had a mother. It seems to me I had one, too. Greetings, old lady. I can't stay here.

(He goes back to Charmette's room. The Count appears and enters the room by the main door.)

COUNT: Well?

POLICHINELLE: Nothing. Charmette hasn't returned.

COUNT: I saw her get out of a carriage in which her father remained—and I got here ahead of her. She'll be here in two minutes.

POLICHINELLE: This time, we've got her. Return to my place and let's meet this evening at the place Maubert. But quick, because the Louvet administration received one little chickadee denouncing Didier—in a quarter of an hour, the escapee will be caught.

(They leave.)

SAC-A-PLÂTRE: Poor old lady. So much love, so much work. And this is all that remains of her. Now you are on high, you can see my heart and how much I loved you. (He weeps.)

(Charmette enters, and goes to her room.)

CHARMETTE: Come on, a last goodbye to my little room. My father is waiting for me below. He gave me some money.

I'm finally going to be able to assuage the poverty of Mama Dumont—who's been so nice to me.

SAC-A-PLÂTRE: Noises in her place?

(He opens the door, Gervaise returns.)

SAC-A-PLÂTRE: Stay put, Gervaise—so she won't be all alone.

(He enters Charmette's room.)

SAC-A-PLÂTRE: Excuse me, Charmette, for coming in this way.

CHARMETTE: Ah, it's you, Sac-a-Plâtre.

SAC-A-PLÂTRE: Yes, it's me. Well, my old lady is dead.

CHARMETTE: Mama Dumont! Dead!

SAC-A-PLÂTRE: Yes—it's over.

CHARMETTE: Oh, my poor dear Mama Dumont—just when I was going to be able to make her happy.

SAC-A-PLÂTRE: She forgave me. What's going to become of me? Here I am now, all alone.

CHARMETTE (offering her hand): Well—and what about me?

SAC-A-PLÂTRE: Really, Charmette, you are offering me your hand? Ah, what can I do to prove to you?

CHARMETTE: First of all, you must work and not be such a bad character.

SAC-A-PLÂTRE: Oh, I swear to you. And I will watch over you. First of all, Polichinelle was here just now. Beware of him. I heard him talking of the Police. Saying the house was surrounded.

CHARMETTE: Really? Then take these letters and guard them carefully. (she gives him letters.) And don't let anyone have them. My father's life is in your hands.

SAC-A-PLÂTRE: You found your father?

CHARMETTE: Yes.

SAC-A-PLÂTRE: Goodness. And me, I lost my mother.

(She kisses him.)

SAC-A-PLÂTRE: Ah, don't worry. My life is yours.

(Didier enters.)

DIDIER: Charmette, the Police are pursuing me. I've been denounced. I'm lost if they discover me.
CHARMETTE: Where to hide you? Sac-a-Plâtre, this is my father.
SAC-A-PLÂTRE: Your father! Oh, come, Monsieur, come! I'll hide you!
CHARMETTE: Oh, thank you!

(They go quickly into the room. Charmette closes and bolts the door.)

SAC-A-PLÂTRE: That's my poor old mother, Monsieur, who just died Death doesn't scare you, right?

(Didier hides behind the sick bed.)

SAC-A-PLÂTRE: They won't look for you there.

POLICE OFFICER (outside): Open in the name of the law!
CHARMETTE: Come in, Officers. What do you want?

(Two policemen enters.)

POLICE OFFICER: We're searching for an escaped galley slave who has taken refuge in this house.
CHARMETTE: An escapee? Look, the room is not large.

(They look around.)

POLICE OFFICER: Where's this door lead?

CHARMETTE: To the room of a poor man who's just lost his mother.
POLICE OFFICER: Let's see.

(He opens the door and sees Sac-a-Plâtre kneeling before the bed. The Cop enters followed by his colleague; they remove their hats, check the body, then withdraw. Sac-a-Plâtre shuts the door behind them.)

CHARMETTE: You see, Messieurs, I told you the truth.

(Polichinelle enters hurriedly, followed by the Count.)

POLICHINELLE: Is it Didier you are looking for? I just saw him fleeing over the roof.
POLICE OFFICERS: Fleeing!
POLICHINELLE: Hold on. Follow this gentleman who's going to lead you.
COUNT: Come with me.

(They rush out.)

CHARMETTE (after a silence): Thank you, Monsieur. By deceiving those men, you've saved my father.
POLICHINELLE (rushing her and gagging her): Not really. And now I've got to get my hands on these the letters.

(Two men enter, throw a blanket over Charmette and carry her off. She struggles but is unable to scream.)

COUNT (appearing on the roof, followed by the cops): Come on, this way!

(He points to a window. The Cops run to the next roof and disappear.)

SAC-A-PLÂTRE: I don't hear anything. Charmette! Charmette!

DIDIER: She doesn't reply.

SAC-A-PLÂTRE: Maybe they haven't gone yet. (after a silence) Hold on. I'm going to open the door very softly.

(He opens the door and looks around.)

SAC-A-PLÂTRE: No one! She's no longer here.

DIDIER: Where can she have gone?

SAC-A-PLÂTRE: Gone! Chairs overturned... Polichinelle must be behind this.

DIDIER: Polichinelle!

SAC-A-PLÂTRE: He was here a short while ago.

DIDIER: My child—in the power of that man!

SAC-A-PLÂTRE: I know where to find him. At the house of Papa Misere, Place Maubert.

DIDIER: Come on! Let's go.

SAC-A-PLÂTRE: Wait. Let me kiss my poor old mother one last time. (He goes into his mother's room.) And now, Mother, I swear to you to become an honest man.

CURTAIN

ACT V

SCENE VI

THE SHOWER OF GOLD

A large dark room. On one side a counter. Tables on all sides. A stairway at the back on one side. A Judas on the other.

AT RISE, Rougeot the Younger is seated behind a table. All the hunchbacks surround him. It's a sitting of the Hunchback Council. Uproar, shouting. "Let him speak." "No! No!" "Let him speak!"

PAPA MISERE: Silence! As head of this establishment, I direct the arguments. Speak, Rougeot!

ROUGEOT (dressed as a hunchback): Messieurs, dear colleagues, you've all seen the instructions our families have given us.

SOME: Right! Right!

ROUGEOT: There's a proverb. Nasty like a hunchback. Our illustrious President, Monsieur Polichinelle, who wisely made me his lieutenant, has charged me with reuniting you this evening on a matter of importance—and before he comes to preside, you will allow me to make my little speech.

SOME: No! No!

OTHERS: Yes! Yes!

PAPA MISERE: Silence! Bunch of brawlers.

(The group quiets down.)

ROUGEOT (looking at his watch): The boss will be here any minute. I forego my speech. Papa Misere, you can serve a round. The boss will pay.

ALL OF THE HUNCHBACKS: Long live the Lieutenant!

(The hunchbacks disperse, drink, smoke and grumble.)

ROUGEOT: Papa Misere, give us a deck of cards. Not the one that's marked.

(Sac-a-Plâtre and Didier enter and sit at an empty table.)

SAC-A-PLÂTRE (pointing to Didier): He's a novice.
DIDIER: You are sure Polichinelle is going to come?
SAC-A-PLÂTRE: Yes. There's a sitting of the Council to decide the operations of the week.
DIDIER: What about Charmette?
SAC-A-PLÂTRE: Calm down. I know Polichinelle. He carried her off thinking she had the letters. Furious, because he didn't find them on her, he'll avenge himself by bringing her here.
DIDIER: To do what?
SAC-A-PLÂTRE: Heck—for them!
DIDIER: Horror!
SAC-A-PLÂTRE: Not a word or we are lost. While no one pays attention, we will climb up there, and we will see all. We must save Charmette or die. You've got some gold?
DIDIER: My pockets are full.
SAC-A-PLÂTRE: Fine. No one's looking. Follow me without being seen.

(They climb up the stairway slowly and disappear.)

STEEL-THROAT: You cheated.
ROUGEOT: No! It was you!
STEEL-THROAT: I say it was you!
PAPA MISERE: Shut up, down there!
STEEL-THROAT: Rougeot stole from me.
PAPA MISERE: It would be the first time anything like that's happened here.
ROUGEOT: You are going to take that back or I'll fix your hump back for you.

153

STEEL-THROAT: You've been spoiling for a fight for a long time. Well—come and get it.

ROUGEOT: Yes, I intend to finish it. (He pulls his knife.) The rest of you pull the tables back.

PAPA MISERE: Stop!

ROUGEOT: Don't meddle, old man. I intend to skewer him.

(All the gamblers pull back the tables and stand on them to watch the fight.)

GAMBLER: Be bold, Rougeot!

2nd GAMBLER: Have no fear, Steel-Throat!

(They maneuver back and forth. Finally, Steel-Throat is wounded.)

STEEL-THROAT: Shit!

GAMBLER: Bravo, Rougeot!

(The fight continues. Suddenly, Polichinelle enters, followed by two men carrying in Charmette, gagged. They deposit her in a chair)

POLICHINELLE: Well, well, what's this—having fun—without me. Put your knives away, Musketeers.

BRIN D'AMOUR: Rougeot stabbed Steel-Throat.

2nd GAMBLER: Because he insulted him.

POLICHINELLE: Now that's enough. I'll settle things here. For the moment—honor to the ladies. I'm bringing you a Viscountess.

ALL: A woman!

(A man removes her gag.)

ROUGEOT: Now there's a Duchess.

STEEL-THROAT (clutching his wounded arm): This is Madame Polichinelle.

154

POLICHINELLE: Don't touch her.

CHARMETTE: Ah—where am I?

ROUGEOT: She's wild—the bird.

POLICHINELLE: Come on, Papa Misere—a glass—and some liqueur for the ladies.

(Brin d'Amour goes to Charmette and offers her a glass. She recoils. He insists. She throws it in his face.)

CHARMETTE: Wretch!

(Everyone laughs.)

ROUGEOT: No luck, Brin d'Amour.

(Polichinelle goes to Charmette; she recoils.)

POLICHINELLE: Don't be afraid. Listen, young lady. Those letters from the Countess d'Orvado—

CHARMETTE: I don't have them.

POLICHINELLE: I know that perfectly well. I searched you carefully. Now, tell me where they are and I'll go get them. If not—

CHARMETTE: If not—?

POLICHINELLE: If not—well, I love to be blunt. You will have to pay us damages. A smile, a kiss, and more.

CHARMETTE: Wretch!

POLICHINELLE: Ah, no rhetoric! Yes or no? Right, Messieurs?

ALL: Yes! Yes!

CHARMETTE: I am lost and no one to help me.

POLICHINELLE: Have you made a decision? Look—where are the letters?

CHARMETTE: I don't know.

POLICHINELLE: Enough! I don't like wasting time.

(He goes toward her in a threatening way. She backs away towards a table with a knife on it and grabs it.)

CHARMETTE: Well—come on, wretch!
POLICHINELLE: Take it easy—
CHARMETTE: Cowards! Cowards! Are you afraid of my knife? Cowards! This knife scares you. The letters are in a safe place. You'll never get them..
POLICHINELLE: Let's get this over with.
ALL: Yes—yes!

(A man sneaks behind Charmette and disarms her.)

CHARMETTE: Help me! Help me!

(Suddenly, a gold piece falls from the Judas.)

ROUGEOT: What's that?

(Two more fall. The men release Charmette and rush to pick up the gold.)

POLICHINELLE: It's raining gold.

(Sac-à-Plâtre appears on the stairs and grabs Charmette.)

SAC-À-PLÂTRE: Come, Charmette—just in time!

(He leads her out without being seen. The gold continues to fall. The men begin to fight over it.)

POLICHINELLE: What's it mean? Where's it coming from?
ROUGEOT (pointing to the Judas): From there!
POLICHINELLE: There must be a banker there!

(The men rush toward the stairs. Didier appears.)

DIDIER (throwing more coins): All yours, my friends! I bring you fortune.

ALL: Fortune!

DIDIER: Yes—if you listen and obey me!

POLICHINELLE: No—don't listen to him! He's not to be trusted.

OTHERS: Yes! Yes!

DIDIER: You are my former comrades in the galleys. You can count on the word of convict number 217.

ALL: Yes! He's right! Speak, Didier!

DIDIER: You see this gold? I've got plenty more. I will give you as much as you like. But you must all be with me.

ALL: Yes! Yes!

DIDIER (pointing to Polichinelle): Well—grab this man! I'll pay you what you like.

POLICHINELLE: What? Would you betray me?

STEEL-THROAT: Can you give us more gold than he's got? No? Well, we'll hold you.

ALL: Hear! Hear!

POLICHINELLE (to the men holding him): Release me!

DIDIER: Tomorrow, I will give you even more gold. You will be rich. Tie him up!

POLICHINELLE: Cowards, traitors! I'll be even with you!

DIDIER: Don't listen to him!

STEEL-THROAT: Now—what must we do?

DIDIER: Take him to my place.

STEEL-THROAT: And then?

DIDIER: Do you know the Hotel d'Orvado?

STEEL-THROAT: Polichinelle took me there once. Nice place.

DIDIER: You must carry off the Countess and bring her, too.

BRIN D'AMOUR: Carry off a woman—that's my specialty.

DIDIER: The rest is mine. I'll pay you what you want!

STEEL-THROAT: Long live Number 217

ALL: Long live Number 217! Good health to Didier!

CURTAIN

SCENE VIII

DINNER WITH THE GALLEY SLAVES
A large dining room. Doors on both sides. A large table, brilliantly lit.
AT RISE, Two lackeys bring in the Countess, bow to her and leave.

CLOTILDE: Where am I? Into what power have I fallen? What to do? Hark! Someone's coming.

(The Count enters.)

COUNT: All is lost! Ah! There you are!
CLOTILDE: Why are you here? How did you learn I was here?
COUNT: A note from Polichinelle telling me you'd been brought here. I've just come from the Prefecture of Police where I denounced Didier.
CLOTILDE: Oh!
COUNT: Then I rushed here. The doors of this hotel were wide open. The lackeys said the Baron was expecting you. So I came here.
CLOTILDE: The Baron de Lorsay. It's Didier! We are lost!
COUNT: No. We need to be bold. He's a galley slave who's broken free. The law is for us. He'll go back to the galleys.
CLOTILDE: My God, I'm afraid.
COUNT: The Police are surrounding this house. We have nothing to fear. No one can prevent our departure. Come!

(They head toward the back. The door opens and Rougeot the Younger, dressed as a galley slave, enters and sits at the table.)

CLOTILDE (recoiling): A galley slave.
COUNT: Come on, will you! Fear nothing.

(Steel-Throat enters, similarly dressed, and sits at the table. Brin d'Amour and others block the exits.)

CLOTILDE: What does this mean?

(Didier enters, similarly dressed.)

DIDIER: I'm going to tell you.
COUNT: Didier!
CLOTILDE: You!
DIDIER: Yes, me—
CLOTILDE: That costume?
DIDIER: It's the one you gave me.
COUNT: Who are these men?
DIDIER: They are my companions—and yours!
COUNT: Mine!?
DIDIER: Yes—bandits, murderers, like you.
COUNT: Monsieur!
DIDIER: For fifteen years, they were my brothers, my friends. Before leaving them I want to present my wife to them. Your hand, Countess. (She recoils) You hesitate, Yet they are worthy of you. Comrades, tell them your exploits. We are family here.
ROUGEOT: I strangled an old woman to steal from her. Old women don't count much—it didn't cost me my head.
STEEL-THROAT: I disemboweled a cashier. That's why they sent me to Brest.
DIDIER: The others will speak later. You see, these gentlemen don't yield to you in any respect. Your hand, Countess—and put a good face on for your guests.
CLOTILDE: I must be going mad.
DIDIER: Ah, I, too. I thought of going mad—for the fifteen years of shame your crime caused me.
COUNT: I'm leaving.
DIDIER: I don't think so.

(At a sign from Didier, three galley slaves grab the Count and drag him away.)

COUNT: Ah, wretches.
CLOTILDE: Mercy!
DIDIER: Why are you asking mercy of me? You ought to ask the Count de Kerdrel. We're still missing one guest.

(Didier gestures and Polichinelle is led in.)

POLICHINELLE: See here, Didier—it's not chic to have me dressed like this. It doesn't suit me. I don't like this fashion.
DIDIER (presenting him): Gentlemen. I present to you Claude Gerfaut, nicknamed Polichinelle, convict number 113.
POLICHINELLE: Present!
DIDIER: Who killed the Count de Kerdrel.
POLICHINELLE: We are *en famille* here. There's nothing to fear. Well, yes, it was me, and the gentleman down there who seems not to recognize me.
COUNT: You dare to say—?
POLICHINELLE: —That you had your hand in the pie, my lord, yes, I do.
COUNT: This wretch lies!
CLOTILDE: No! It's true!
POLICHINELLE: Madame la Comtesse accuses you. You see plainly that you're wrong, sweet pie.
DIDIER: Listen, Polichinelle. I promised to save your life if you told the truth before the judges.
POLICHINELLE: I put it in writing, because I don't like to associate with characters of that sort. Here's my deposition—signed and sealed.
DIDIER: Fine. In an hour you will be free,
COUNT: But what are you planning to do with us?
DIDIER: Why, to punish you as you deserve. To do justice myself. These men are great criminals—but they are devoted to me. They belong to me because I have gold to give them.

I'm turning the Countess over to them as you intended to deliver Charmette.

CLOTILDE: Mercy!

DIDIER: No.

CLOTILDE: Didier—in the name of the love I had for you.

DIDIER: No.

(The galley slaves pull the Countess away.)

CLOTILDE: Ah!

DIDIER: As for this man—let him die in the midst of the most shocking torture. You will have gold, my companions. Go— take these monsters away. I give them to you.

(Charmette enters, followed by Gontran and Juliette.)

CHARMETTE: Father—Juliette.

DIDIER: What's wrong?

GONTRAN: She's heard everything.

CLOTILDE: My daughter!

CHARMETTE: She's unable to bear the pain, the shame.

GONTRAN: Seeing her mother ruined, dishonored—she's gone mad. They're taking her away.

CLOTILDE: Juliette!

(Several police officers led by a Commissioner rush in.)

COMMISSIONER: Didier—Baron de Lorsay, I arrest you in the name of the law.

(Police rush in on all sides.)

COUNT: At last! Monsieur, I'm the one who denounced him. Arrest all these men, too. They are escaped galley slaves.

POLICHINELLE: Ah, you old rascal, what you just did is not nice. We're nabbed, too.

(The slaves assume a menacing posture.)

COMMISSIONER: All resistance is useless.(to his men) Fire on anyone who resists.

DIDIER: Monsieur, I am the victim of a judicial error. (pointing to the Count and the Countess) These are the true murderers of the Count de Kerdrel.

COMMISSIONER: Can you furnish any proof of what you say?

(Sac-à-Plâtre enters, holding a bundle of letters.)

SAC-A-PLÂTRE: Proof. Here's a bundle of them!

ALL: Sac-a-Plâtre!

SAC-A-PLÂTRE: Yes, Sac-a-Plâtre with the letters of the Count and the Countess. All the proofs of M. Didier's innocence are there.

CHARMETTE: Thank you, Sac-a-Plâtre.

SAC-A-PLÂTRE: Here, Charmette—here are the twenty sous I owe you.

POLICHINELLE: Come on—en route to the baths of the sea. My doctor told me truly—I will croak of it.

CURTAIN

Xavier-Henry Aymon de Montépin (b. Apremont, 10 March 1823; d. Paris, 30 April 1902) was a famous popular novelist and journalist. His most famous creation was the best-selling La Porteuse de Pain *[The Bread Peddler], published in* feuilleton *in* Le Petit Journal *between 1884 and 1889. It was then adapted as a 5-act stage play by Jules Dornay, and first performed at the Théâtre de l'Ambigu on 11 January 1889. Later, it became the subject of no less than 5 film adaptations (1906, by Louis Feuillade; 1912, by Georges Denola; 1923, by René Le Somptier; 1934, by René Sti; 1950 and 1963, both by Maurice Cloche) and one television series (1973, by Marcel Camus). Constant Jules Alexandre Lacroix, a.k.a. Jules Dornay (his nom-de-plume) (b. Vineuil, 15 January 1829; d. Joinville-le-Pont, 13 June 1906), was a famous playwright who often collaborated with Montépin to adapt the latter's novels into plays.*

THE BREAD PEDDLER

by Xavier de Montépin & Jules Dornay

CHARACTERS

JACQUES GARAUD a.k.a. PAUL HARMANT
MARIE HARMANT
JEANNE FORTIER a.k.a. MAMA LISON
LUCIE FORTIER
GEORGE DARIER (adult)
LITTLE GEORGE FORTIER (child)
LUCIEN LABROUE
ABBÉ FÉLIX LANGIER
CLARISSE DARIER
ETIENNE COSTEL

OVIDE
BRIGITTE
DOMINIQUE
GERMAIN THE POSTMAN
THE MAYOR OF CHEVRY
BALASSON
RÉTIF
CRI-CRI
TÊTE-EN-BUIS
MARIANNE
CLAIRE
MAMA VERBOIS
LEBRET
MADELEINE
OLD MATHIEU, A NIGHT WATCHMAN
A FISHERMAN
SOSTHENE
A RAG PICKER
GENDARMES, PATRONS, POLICEMEN, FEMALE
PASSERS-BY, etc.

ACT I

SCENE I

THE PRESBYTERY OF CHEVRY
The Garden and Courtyard of the Presbytery. Benches and chairs.
AT RISE, it's daybreak. The garden is empty. Suddenly, coming in furtively, a man appears. He carries a small valise in his hand.

JACQUES: The Presbytery of Chevry. If I am discovered, I still run the risks of being given up. Ah, I'm worn out and day is coming. Where can I find shelter until nightfall? Tomorrow night, I'll be in Paris, the next in Le Havre—two weeks later—in America. (looking around) Where can I sleep without being discovered? (opening a gate) In the hay—that suits me.

(He goes in and closes the gate behind him. Silence. Brigitte opens the blinds in a window, then closes the window and disappears. A moment later, she opens shutters on a lower floor. She puts a milk box on the ground.)

BRIGITTE: The Abbé's in the Church—his sister, Madame Darier, is still sleeping. My fire is lit. Now, for my milk.

(The Abbé Langier opens the gate.)

BRIGITTE: Ah, Monsieur l'Abbé—have you already said Mass?
ABBÉ LANGIER: Yes, Brigitte.
BRIGITTE: Mercy! I'm a bit late.
ABBÉ LANGIER: A little. Has my sister got up?
BRIGITTE: Not yet. I'm going to look for my milk.

(She leaves.)

ABBÉ LANGIER: It's idle for us to be in the middle of September. It's as hot as in mid-July. My flowers are wilting. A bit of water will revive them. (noticing Jacques) There's someone there. A man! Come out, I beg you.

(Jacques emerges, suitcase in hand.)

JACQUES: Please, excuse me, Monsieur l'Abbé.
ABBÉ LANGIER: What are you doing there? Who are you?
JACQUES: I'm not a thief, don't worry.
ABBÉ LANGIER: Your presence in a private enclosure is suspicious?

JACQUES: I was traveling all night. I was worn out, exhausted. I found a breach in the wall. I saw this gate and I pushed it. I wanted to sleep—it's not a crime.

ABBÉ LANGIER: There are inns in Chevry.

JACQUES: I don't have much money and I'm keeping it for food.

ABBÉ LANGIER (studying Jacques): You travel at night, and sleep during the day. if I understand you correctly?

JACQUES: It's easier at night—with the breeze.

ABBÉ LANGIER: One hides more easily, too.

JACQUES: Me, hide! What for? I've done nothing wrong. But if my presence displeases you, I'll find shelter elsewhere.

ABBÉ LANGIER: No. Whoever you may be, you need rest. Rest. (pointing to the stairs) There's a room—a bed—Go in and sleep. When you wake up, you can ask for food. They'll serve you. Afterwards, you can be on your way.

JACQUES: Ah, thank you, Monsieur l'Abbé.

ABBÉ LANGIER: Go! Go!

(Jacques heads for the room.)

JACQUES (aside): Here, until night—I have nothing to fear.

ABBÉ LANGIER: Pull the blinds. You will sleep better.

(Jacques does and disappears.)

ABBÉ LANGIER: Another poor devil whose life is tough. That's all you see. Still, the mason needs to come and close this breach.

(Brigitte appears at the gate with her box of milk.)

BRIGITTE: Should I serve coffee outside?

ABBÉ LANGIER: Yes, indeed, Brigitte, right here. We haven't got time to stay shut up all winter. Let's profit by the good weather.

(The Abbot goes into the enclosure. Brigitte goes into the house. The blinds go up in another room. Clarisse Darier appears as the Abbot returns from the enclosure.)

CLARISSE: Good morning, brother dear.
ABBÉ LANGIER: God keep you, sister. Did you sleep well?
CLARISSE: I had frightful nightmares.
ABBÉ LANGIER: Bad digestion?
CLARISSE: No. The light from the fires we observed in Paris.

(Brigitte brings a platter out and sets a table.)

ABBÉ LANGIER: The newspapers will probably have a story about the fires. Are you coming down?
CLARISSE: In a few minutes.

(She closes the window.)

ABBÉ LANGIER: As for me, I'm going to water the plants.

(He places a sprinkler at the fountain and turns on the nozzle to fill it.)

BRIGITTE: You're not going to wear yourself out again?
ABBÉ LANGIER: But my flowers are thirsty.
BRIGITTE: If we could only eat them!

(She goes into the house.)

ABBÉ LANGIER: What a silly argument. She loves flowers only if they are edible!

(He fills his sprinkler and goes to work. At this moment Etienne appears.)

ETIENNE: Can I come in?

ABBÉ LANGIER (happily surprised): For goodness sakes—you—at Chevry!

ETIENNE (as they embrace): My dear Abbé!

ABBÉ LANGIER: Welcome, my dear child.

ETIENNE: Forgive me for arriving so unexpectedly.

ABBÉ LANGIER: I will forgive you, provided you promise to stay for a long while.

ETIENNE: Two weeks.

ABBÉ LANGIER: Wonderful! (calling) Clarisse! Clarisse! Brigitte!

CLARISSE (off): What?

BRIGITTE (off): What?

ABBÉ LANGIER: Come quick. We've got a visitor!

(The two women appear.)

CLARISSE (stretching her arms): Etienne!

BRIGITTE: Monsieur Costel! Now that's a piece of luck!

CLARISSE: What a pleasant surprise.

BRIGITTE: If you had warned us, we could have prepared your room.

ETIENNE: Then I wouldn't have had the pleasure of surprising you.

BRIGITTE: He's even more handsome than he was six months ago!

ABBÉ LANGIER: Brigitte—don't remain gaping here. Take his bags.

BRIGITTE: Yes, yes. Don't worry about a thing.

CLARISSE: And set another place at the table.

BRIGITTE: Give me all that. I won't break anything. Ah, you are making paintings for us.

(She leaves carrying his bags.)

ABBÉ LANGIER: How many things you must have to tell us, since we last saw you.

ETIENNE: No, my dear Abbé—my life's been calm.

ABBÉ LANGIER: Your work?
ETIENNE: I have worked a lot.
ABBÉ LANGIER: And the results?

(Brigitte returns and sets a place for Etienne.)

ETIENNE: Satisfying from a material point of view, but money's not everything.
ABBÉ LANGIER: You dream of glory—
ETIENNE: If not glory, at least notoriety. I'd like to find an excellent subject for the next salon—and cause a sensation. A simple thing, as you see.

(Brigitte goes back in.)

ABBÉ LANGIER: Maybe you'll find it here.
ETIENNE: I hope so, because your friendship has always brought me luck.

(He shakes the priest's hand. Clarisse enters as does Brigitte with the coffee.

CLARISSE: Let's get started.
ABBÉ LANGIER: Etienne, sit here. Do you still have a good appetite?
ETIENNE: As always.

(Brigitte pours coffee then screams.)

BRIGITTE: Ah, I forgot! My tarts are going to burn!

(She rushes out. Everyone laughs.)

ABBÉ LANGIER (to Etienne): You're turning her head.

(A woman—Jeanne—carrying a child—George—exhausted with fatigue, staggering, appears in the roadway. She stops, supporting herself on one of the pillars of the gate. She rings.)

ETIENNE: A visitor.
ABBÉ LANGIER: The gate is open. Folks who come here know the habits of the house. They enter without ringing.

(The woman rings again, then collapses.)

CLARISSE: Decidedly, she's not from here.

(Brigitte appears with sausages on spits.)

CLARISSE: Brigitte, go see who's ringing.

(Brigitte heads towards the gate. Jacques half opens the blinds to his room. He is worried.)

BRIGITTE: Ah, my God!
JEANNE (in an exhausted voice): Mercy! Help for my child and me.

(Jacques shivers.)

BRIGITTE: Come, come quick!
ABBÉ LANGIER: What's wrong, Brigitte?
BRIGITTE (trying to raise Jeanne): A young woman who needs help.
GEORGE: Mama, where do you hurt?

(Etienne and the Abbot bring in Jeanne. Brigitte holds George in her arm. The child has a cardboard hobby horse.)

BRIGITTE: Sweetheart, go.
JACQUES (watching): A child!

CLARISSE: This poor woman and her child are dying of fatigue.

ABBÉ LANGIER: More likely of hunger. Brigitte, get some fresh milk. And a glass of Burgundy.

(Brigitte gets the milk, Clarisse the wine.)

ETIENNE(looking at Jeanne): What an expressive head.

(Brigitte wets her temples. Jeanne opens her eyes and looks for her child.)

JEANNE: My son—

JACQUES: That voice…

ABBÉ LANGIER: Don't worry—we are going to take good care of him.

JEANNE (sobbing): Oh, thank you, thank you, he's very hungry.

CLARISSE: You are both going to eat. Take this first.

ABBÉ LANGIER: You've come a long way?

GEORGE: Yes—very, very far. I was very tired, but my mother carried me.

CLARISSE: After lunch, you'll sleep, my pretty. You'll both rest.

JEANNE: God bless you for your kindness. What would become of us without you?

JACQUES: Why didn't she want to come with me?

ABBÉ LANGIER: Go with Brigitte. She will take care of you.

GEORGE: I can take my horsey, can't I?

CLARISSE: Yes, my pretty, take him.

BRIGITTE: Your horsey's worn out.

GEORGE: I've got to feed him.

JEANNE (kissing Clarisse's hands): Be blessed!

BRIGITTE: Come, my brave woman. Come, my cherub.

(Brigitte leaves with Jeanne and George.)

JACQUES: Jeanne here—like me. What can have happened down there?

CLARISSE: Poor woman. What can have brought her here?

(Germain the Postman appears and put a paper on the table.)

GERMAIN: Your newspaper. I'm late today. There are no letters.

(Brigitte takes the paper to the Abbot.)

CLARISSE: What do you plan to do for this poor woman?
ABBÉ LANGIER: What we do for all those who come to us for charity—give her some money after she's rested and send her on her way.
ETIENNE: Aren't you going to question her?

JACQUES: Question her?

ABBÉ LANGIER (reading the paper): What for?
ETIENNE: Why, to know more—It seems to me knowing the situation of this poor woman would help you to help her.
ABBÉ LANGIER (laughing): You're right. I'll question her.

(Reaction by Jacques.)

CLARISSE: Well, brother, our two guests—
BRIGITTE: The mother doesn't eat—but the kid— (she goes out) Poor kid!
ABBÉ LANGIER (stupefied): Ah—my God!
ETIENNE: Something interesting?

ABBÉ LANGIER: An abominable crime. Theft, arson, murder.
CLARISSE: Where?
ABBÉ LANGIER: Near here. In Alfortville.

JACQUES: Ah!

ABBÉ LANGIER (reading): Listen. "The factory of the renowned Engineer Jules Labroue no longer exists. An arsonist employing petrol left only ruins, and Labroue himself, returning unexpectedly from a business trip in the middle of the night, was murdered by the arsonist caught in the act. Labroue was not the only victim. His overseer, Jacques Garaud—" (reaction by Jacques) "—through his devotion to duty also met his death in the flames trying to salvage the cash box and the accounting books."

JACQUES: They think I'm dead. That's fine.

ABBÉ LANGIER (reading): "The factory was guarded at night by a woman, Jeanne Fortier. The circumstances accuse this woman. The grocer who sold her the petrol recognized his cans. The motive for the crime was vengeance, because the decision to terminate her was made two days earlier by M. Labroue. The wretched creature has fled with her child…"

(Reaction by Clarisse and Etienne)

JACQUES: She's lost!

ABBÉ LANGIER (reading): "Twenty six years-old, tall, brown hair, pronounced features, large black eyes—complexion, light. Fortier is accompanied by a child of four named George…"
CLARISSE (pointing to the house): Why, that's the very portrait of this wretch.
ETIENNE: There's no doubt about it.

173

CLARISSE: Tired, exhausted—she was fleeing.

ABBÉ LANGIER: Silence, sister. That woman is here in God's house. We mustn't hasten to accuse her. If she is guilty, we will know soon enough.

CLARISSE: Are you going to let her go?

ABBÉ LANGIER: I will not denounce her. I will leave it to the Police to find her. Silence, here she comes.

(Jeanne enters timidly, helped by Brigitte, and followed by George with his toy horse.)

ABBÉ LANGIER (to Jeanne): Come sit with us.

(Jeanne sits.)

GEORGE: Can I play in the garden if I don't touch the flowers?

ABBÉ LANGIER: Of course. Go ahead, child.

(George runs into the garden with his toy horse.)

BRIGITTE: What a sweet little boy.

ABBÉ LANGIER (to Jeanne): You're feeling better, aren't you?

JEANNE: Oh, much better—thanks to you. And before leaving, I'd like to—

ABBÉ LANGIER: To do what, child?

JEANNE: I'd like you to help me find a place in this village— a situation that would provide me a living, and allow me to raise my two children.

ABBÉ LANGIER: You have two children?

JEANNE Yes, Monsieur l'Abbé. A little girl of eleven months, currently at nurse—my little Lucie—and George, who is four.

ABBÉ LANGIER: What about the father of your children?

JEANNE (barely audible): He's dead.

ABBÉ LANGIER: Ah! But why have you come to Chevry to seek work? It is a mere hamlet, and it's difficult to find a situation in this town. Before coming here, weren't you employed?

JEANNE: Yes, I had a job.

ABBÉ LANGIER: You quit it?

JEANNE: No, I got laid off. But not for misconduct.

ABBÉ LANGIER: And you came here, on foot, with your child. Are you absolutely without resources?

JEANNE: Absolutely. I had a little, but I spent it yesterday on food for George.

ABBÉ LANGIER: Before I can recommend you, I must know who you are. Do you have identity papers?

JEANNE: Papers?

ABBÉ LANGIER: Yes. You'll need references. What's your name?

JEANNE (very simply): Jeanne Fortier.

ABBÉ LANGIER: Jeanne Fortier—and you come from Alfortville?

JEANNE (shocked): Ah—you know everything.

ABBÉ LANGIER (grasping her hand): My poor child! I know that you are being pursued, tracked by the Police.

JEANNE: Me? Me? (very naturally) Pursued? But why?

ABBÉ LANGIER: You are accused of having set fire to the factory, and murdered Mr. Labroue.

BRIGITTE: Ah!

JEANNE: That's false! Utterly false! I swear it on the head of my child.

ABBÉ LANGIER: But if you are innocent, why did you flee?

ETIENNE: Yes—why are you fleeing?

JEANNE: Why? Why? Ah, you are right. That gives truth to the accusation. I am fleeing because I'm afraid—but I have proof of my innocence.

JACQUES: My letter—

ABBÉ LANGIER: What's become of this proof?

JEANNE: The fire destroyed it like the rest.

JACQUES: Ah!

ABBÉ LANGIER: How to believe you?

JEANNE: I know it's difficult. My husband was a mechanic working for M. Labroue. I thought life was fine. One day, the machine Pierre was working on exploded. I barely was able to recognize his body.

BRIGITTE: Sweet Jesus!

JEANNE: M. Labroue, to help me, suggested I become the night watchman at his factory. He owed us that. Pierre died working for him. So I accepted. Pierre had a friend in the factory—Jacques, the head supervisor...

(reaction by Jacques.)

ABBÉ LANGIER (attentive): Jacques Garaud?

JEANNE: Yes. Without respect for my sorrow, he declared he loved me. I wouldn't listen to him. I swore on my husband's grave that I would never remarry. He said, "I will make you mine despite yourself."

BRIGITTE: Now there's a brigand!

JEANNE: Without intending to infringe the rules, I bought some petrol to light my room. M. Labroue was furious at this infraction, and told me harshly he was letting me go.

ABBÉ LANGIER: Letting you go!

JEANNE: Jacques Garaud was present. He knew what misery awaited me. He offered me a fortune, which I refused. That evening, I received a letter from him. He said he had an invention worth millions, and asked me to go away with him.

ABBÉ LANGIER: His letter said that?

JEANNE: Yes, and it was dated and signed. I thought it was simply a trick, so I crumpled it up and threw it on the floor where George was playing.

GEORGE (feeding his horse paper): Eat this!

JEANNE: Later, I thought I heard voices. When I opened my door, I saw the factory was on fire. Then I saw M. Labroue fall, dying. Behind him, Jacques Garaud appeared, knife in hand. Only then did I understand his letter. I screamed for help. Jacques put his hand over my mouth and tried to drag me away. I resisted with all my strength. "Have it your way," he yelled. "I used your petrol to light the fire!" And then, he fled. I tried to go back to my room to find the letter, but everything was in flames. Then I lost my head and fled with my son. That's the truth—the whole truth.

ABBÉ LANGIER (casting a glance at Jacque's room—surprised) (aside) The window is open, but the man is no longer there. He fled.

CLARISSE (noticing the Abbé's preoccupation): What's wrong? What's going on?

ABBÉ LANGIER: Nothing, nothing. I thought I heard a noise.

ETIENNE: Poor woman.

CLARISSE: Poor mother.

ABBÉ LANGIER: Yes—poor woman—poor mother… (to Jeanne) I believe you. Yes, I believe you. But explain how Garaud died in the fire.

JEANNE: Him dead? Come on—

ABBÉ LANGIER: The news paper is very explicit on the subject.

JEANNE (terrified): In that case, I'll be condemned.

ABBÉ LANGIER: You must stand fast, my child, ready to answer all questions. Your flight was a terrible mistake. You must go to Paris and prove your innocence.

JEANNE: If I do, they'll separate me from my children.

ABBÉ LANGIER: That's inevitable. Still, you must do it. I won't abandon you. I will accompany you.

CLARISSE: Don't hesitate.

ETIENNE: Think that your description has been posted everywhere and they'll soon come to arrest you.

JEANNE: In this home? In this house of God?

ABBÉ LANGIER: My house is not a sanctuary.

JEANNE (sobbing): But what about my children?

GEORGE: Mom, why are you weeping?
(noises off)
ETIENNE: What's that?

(Brigitte goes to the back)

JEANNE: I'm scared.
BRIGITTE: It's the Mayor with the Police.
JEANNE (hugging George): Ah, we are lost.

(The Mayor enters with Gendarmes.)

CLARISSE: Courage, poor child.
MAYOR: Excuse me for entering your property uninvited, Monsieur l'Abbé, but I am seeking Jeanne Fortier—accused of arson, theft and murder.

(Etienne nabs a crayon and starts sketching.)

JEANNE: That's a lie. I am innocent.
MAYOR: That's not for me to judge. Are you Jeanne Fortier?
JEANNE: Yes, Monsieur.
MAYOR: Then, I arrest you in the name of the law. This is the warrant and it is in order.
GEORGE (hugging his mother): Mama!
GENDARME: Give me the cuffs.
JEANNE: Handcuffs? Oh, no, Monsieur! Please, I don't want that.
ABBÉ LANGIER: Don't resist, Jeanne. You must obey.

(Jeanne bows her head. They cuff her.)

GENDARME: Let's go.
GEORGE: Don't go, Mama!
JEANNE: Don't cry, darling. God will protect us.
GENDARME: Your child cannot follow you.
JEANNE: You can't separate me from my son!

MAYOR: Alas, the warrant only concerns you, my poor woman.

GENDARME: The child will have to go to the State Orphanage until further orders.

JEANNE: To the Orphanage? No, no—you cannot do that. Monsieur l'Abbé, please intercede for me.

ABBÉ LANGIER: I will keep the child with me, Officer. He shan't go to the Orphanage. (to Jeanne) He'll be in good hands, do not worry.

CLARISSE: I once had a child the age of yours. God took him from me. I will take care of him as if he were my own.

JEANNE (in despair): Not to see him again. Never to see him again. Love him, talk to him, tell him about his mother. (To George) They will tell you that your mother is innocent—and that she adores you. Never forget her! Never forget her!

ABBÉ LANGIER: Poor woman, poor child.

JEANNE (to Gendarme): Take me away. I am ready.

GEORGE: Mama—

JEANNE (stopping before the Abbé): Your blessing, please, Father.

(She kneels. Everyone removes their hats.)

ABBÉ LANGIER (doing the sign of the Cross): In the name of God, I bless you.

ETIENNE: I was seeking a subject. I believe I've got it. (He draws rapidly.)

CURTAIN

ACT II
SCENE II

PAUL HARMANT'S HOUSE, TWENTY YEARS LATER
A fashionably furnished room in a bourgeois house.
AT RISE, Lucie is sewing a dress that Marie Harmant has just tried on. Marie coughs frequently.

MARIE (to Lucie): Not much to do. Can you fix this?
LUCIE: If you like, Mademoiselle.
MARIE: Yes, my father's returning from a trip this very morning. We'll probably go out together, and I would like to be able to wear this dress.
LUCIE: That will be easy.
MARIE: Well—work on it and I will keep you company.
LUCIE (beginning to work): It will be finished quickly, Mademoiselle.
MARIE (looking at the dress): You know, I give you my sincere compliments, Lucie. You've got great taste. I've never been able to wear a dress like this before. (She coughs.)
LUCIE (aside): Poor girl, how she suffers!
MARIE: Have you been working for my dressmaker for a long time?
LUCIE: Only fifteen months, Mademoiselle.
MARIE: She seems to love you. I understand she wants you to live in her house.
LUCIE (busy): She told me that, but I don't want to.
MARIE: You still live with your parents?
LUCIE: I haven't got any.
MARIE: Are you an orphan?
LUCIE: A foundling.
MARIE: Why, that's horrible!
LUCIE: I was given the number 9. That's all I know.
MARIE: Poor girl. How old are you?

180

LUCIE: Twenty-three.

MARIE: Clever as you are, why haven't you thought of going into business for yourself?

LUCIE: To do that, I'd need two things I don't have. A clientele, and money.

MARIE: You could find a husband with money—why not think of marrying?

LUCIE: I did think of it—but—

MARIE: What prevents you?

LUCIE: The man I love—and who loves me—has no money. He wants to wait until he has a good job that will allow us to marry.

MARIE: I'll be glad to provide you a small dowry.

LUCIE: Oh, Mademoiselle—

MARIE: On the condition you always work for me.

LUCIE: You are nice and I thank you from the bottom of my heart. (finished) Here it is.

MARIE: So quick! It's perfect. I may need you again. Where do you live?

LUCIE: Quai Conti, Number 8.

MARIE: Isn't that the street of the foundlings' home?

LUCIE: A coincidence.

MARIE: Thank you. Good-bye, Lucie.

(Lucie leaves.)

MARIE (watching her leave): A foundling—and yet she's happy. (a pause) Some loves her. I'd like someone to love me.

(Dominique the butler enters and gives her a card.)

MARIE: Etienne Costel. Ah, show him in.

(Etienne enters, carrying a package.)

MARIE: Thank you for having answered my call.

ETIENNE: Good morning, Mademoiselle. How are you feeling today?

MARIE (coughing): I'm still coughing. Look, sit down and let's chat. (seeing his package) What's that you've got there? A picture?

ETIENNE: No, a toy horse.

MARIE: You are taking on pupils?

ETIENNE: It's an accessory. I'm taking it to the home of George Darier.

MARIE: My father's attorney? He plays horsey?

ETIENNE (sadly): It's a relic.

MARIE: A souvenir? What's it for?

ETIENNE: It finishes a painting I began twenty years ago.

MARIE: No doubt you found the picture in the back of your studio, covered with grime that you won't let anyone see?

ETIENNE: Precisely.

MARIE: Why did you hide it like this?

ETIENNE: I'm not hiding it. I'm not showing it, that's all.

MARIE: What's the subject of the picture?

ETIENNE: It's hard to explain. A work of my youth. But let's talk about you. I haven't asked you why you wanted me to come.

MARIE: I want to create a surprise for my father.

ETIENNE: Your portrait?

MARIE: If you would do it, yes.

ETIENNE: We can start whenever you like. Your father is still traveling?

MARIE: He'll be back in an hour.

ETIENNE: Then you can introduce me to him. I'd love to shake the hand of the great American Industrialist.

MARIE: My father is French Burgundian.

ETIENNE: Really? I used to know a Harmant family whose son was educated at the Chicago school.

MARIE: That's my father.

ETIENNE: Ah! People said he was dead.

MARIE: Dead! His prolonged stay in America must have given rise to that rumor.

ETIENNE: And now he's decided to return to France?
MARIE: To please me and to supervise the factory he built in Courbevoie. It's unparalleled in the whole world.
ETIENNE: So they say.

(Dominique returns.)

DOMINIQUE: M. Darier.
MARIE: Show him in.
ETIENNE: George? For goodness sakes!

(Dominique leaves. George enters.)

MARIE: Now this is an unexpected visit.
GEORGE: Ah, Mademoiselle—Etienne ?
MARIE : Come in, come in.
GEORGE: I'm coming to solicit your all-powerful protection.
MARIE: You are asking me for my protection—you?
GEORGE: Not for myself—but for one of my friends. With you, Mademoiselle, success is certain.
MARIE: What's it all about?
GEORGE: I'd like to place one of my school friends as supervisor at your father's factory.
ETIENNE: Without knowing him, I am sure that George's protégé ought to deserve consideration.
GEORGE: I affirm his merits.
MARIE: My father is arriving today. I promise to speak to him. You can tell your friend he can count on me.
GEORGE: You can tell him yourself.
MARIE: Tell him myself?
GEORGE: Yes. I took the liberty of bringing him with me. May I introduce him to you?
MARIE: Why, certainly.
GEORGE (going to the door): Lucien, come in.

(Marie reacts uneasily to this name. Lucien enters.)

GEORGE: Here's the friend I was telling you about.

LUCIEN: Mademoiselle, George told me how kind you are.

MARIE: I'll see to it you are the first to see my father. I don't usually meddle in my father's business, but for you— (meaningfully) I will do so with pleasure.

LUCIEN: I thank you from the bottom of my heart. I was seized with depression.

MARIE: You have only friends here. You shall wait until I've spoken to my father. (She coughs.)

ETIENNE: That's what I call striking while the iron is hot.

MARIE: I need to know your full name, Monsieur.

LUCIEN: Lucien Labroue.

ETIENNE: Might you be the son of Jules Labroue—an engineer in Alfortville—?

LUCIEN: Who was murdered some twenty years ago. Yes, Monsieur, I am his son.

MARIE: Murdered! Your father was murdered? (She coughs.)

(Dominique returns.)

DOMINIQUE: Mademoiselle—your father.

MARIE: Ah, here's my father. Don't tell him I've been coughing a lot. He'd be worried—unnecessarily. (to Lucien) M. Labroue, go in there.

LUCIEN (as he leaves): Mademoiselle, I have faith in you.

(Lucien goes into a side room she indicates. Then, Paul Harmant, or rather Jacques Garaud, as we knew him, dressed entirely in grey, appears. Marie rushes to him.)

MARIE: Ah, my dear father!

PAUL: My dear child. My beloved. Dear, dear daughter! (to the two men) Pardon me, Messieurs, for having neglected you for my child! She's all my happiness, you see.

(He shakes George's hand and bows to Etienne.)

MARIE: This is a friend, father, M. Etienne Costel, whom I've often written you about.

PAUL (extending his hand): Thank you, Monsieur, for having been helpful to Marie in her artistic fantasies. I'm pleased to meet you and to shake your hand.

ETIENNE: A thousand thanks.

PAUL (to Marie): These gentlemen will dine with us, won't they?

MARIE: I won't forgive them if they refuse. Excuse me now, but I need to speak to my father.

(The two men move away.)

PAUL: What's this all about?

MARIE: Imagine I have a fantasy.

PAUL: You do—and often.

MARIE: But this one's not like the others. Promise me you will grant me what I'm going to ask of you. (She coughs.)

PAUL (hugging her): Have I ever refused you anything?

MARIE: It's true. Well, my fantasy is this. There's a man I would like to recommend to you as your top supervisor in your new factory.

PAUL: You've taken someone under your wing?

MARIE: Yes. You told me before you left, you'd need a new supervisor.

PAUL: I said so and I repeat it.

MARIE: Someone on whom you could count like yourself.

PAUL: Where did you get this wonderful man?

MARIE: You'll never find a better one. Never!

PAUL: What passion!

MARIE: I've only seen him once, but I've judged him. He needs a situation worthy of his merits. You'll do it, won't you?

PAUL: We'll see. First, I've got to be certain he's qualified. I'll write him to come and see me.

MARIE: No need to write.

PAUL: Why's that?

MARIE (pointing to the side room): He's in there.

PAUL: So this is simply a conspiracy.

MARIE (to Lucien): Come in, Monsieur. My father's waiting for you.

(Lucien returns.)

PAUL (to Lucien): You've been recommended to me by my daughter. But still, I must ask you some questions first.

LUCIEN: That's very fair, Monsieur.

MARIE: Thank you, father. I'll leave you with this gentleman.

(She moves away.)

PAUL: Are you a graduate of a School of Engineering?

LUCIEN: Yes, Monsieur. With honors, too.

PAUL: It's superfluous to ask you if you are a competent draftsman?

LUCIEN: If I wasn't, I wouldn't have dared to present myself to you.

PAUL: Are you a Parisian?

LUCIEN: Yes, I was born in Alfortville.

PAUL (intrigued): Alfortville?

LUCIEN: Yes, my father owned an important factory there.

PAUL: What's your name?

LUCIEN: Lucien Labroue.

PAUL (shocked): Lucien Labroue... (more resolutely) I think I knew your father. I had business relations with him. His name was Jules Labroue, wasn't it?

LUCIEN: That's right, Monsieur.

PAUL: You must understand my emotion... Meeting... a man who is the son of someone... whose work I...

LUCIEN: Ah, so you knew of my father's death?

PAUL: Murdered in his factory—in a fire, yes... Started by a woman... The night watchman...

LUCIEN: Ah, but I believe that Jeanne Fortier was innocent.

(Etienne barges in.)

ETIENNE: Do you have proof of that?

LUCIEN: No, Monsieur—but I've studied the transcript of the trial extensively.

ETIENNE: She was found guilty.

LUCIEN: What does that prove?

ETIENNE: I was present at the trial.

LUCIEN: And you concluded?

ETIENNE: That the accused might have been guilty.

LUCIEN: What do you mean—might have been? You wouldn't dare to say she was guilty.

ETIENNE: The crushing charges seemed to be borne out by the evidence.

PAUL: M. Costel is right. I recall that.

LUCIEN: The evidence was ambiguous. Someone else had an interest in the death of my father.

(George joins the conversation.)

GEORGE: Someone else?

LUCIEN: Yes. Since you were present at the trial, Monsieur, you must recall what Jeanne Fortier alleged in her defense.

ETIENNE: Perfectly. According to her, the foreman at the factory pursued her with love, and coveted your father's fortune—this man's name was Jacques Garaud. You see, my memory is good.

PAUL (somber): Indeed.

ETIENNE: She claimed that Garaud had written her a letter which proved he was premeditating his crime—but she was unable to produce that letter.

PAUL: A clumsy defense.

GEORGE: Inadmissible.

LUCIEN: Yet, Jeanne wasn't lying. Rest assured, the letter was real and the foreman, Jacques Garaud, was the real thief, arsonist and murderer.

PAUL: I thought they said he died in the fire—a victim of his devotion.

LUCIEN: Nothing is less certain. I don't believe that man is dead.

ETIENNE: The Abbé Langier didn't believe it either.

GEORGE (to Lucien): Do you know if Jeanne Fortier is still alive today?

LUCIEN: I don't know, but I will try to find out. Because she's the only person who can help me avenge my father's death.

ETIENNE: After twenty years!

GEORGE: There's a statute of limitations.

LUCIEN: There's no statute of limitations for a son. If I meet Jacques Garaud, I won't be asking justice from the law.

(A silence.)

PAUL (after an internal conflict): I grant you the position you're seeking. You'll be my new supervisor.

LUCIEN: Ah, thank you, Monsieur! (he takes his hands,)

GEORGE: Now that's a decision that does you honor.

PAUL (feverishly): You will be like my second self. You will choose your own designers. Don't waste a minute. I want the factory to be operating in three days. You can use my house as your office until then. I may have need of you at any time. For the same reason, you ought to stay here in my home.

LUCIEN: As you like, Monsieur.

PAUL: Stay for lunch. Then, we'll go together to inspect the construction site at Courbevoie.

LUCIEN: How can I ever thank you, Monsieur?

(Marie returns.)

PAUL (seeing her): You must thank my daughter and your good friend George. (To Marie) Well, darling, are you satisfied?

MARIE (joyfully): Oh, yes, very satisfied. More than you think. (hugs her father)

ETIENNE (to George): She's really smitten.

PAUL: Calm down. By the way, M. Labroue will lunch with us.

(Dominique returns.)

DOMINIQUE: Monsieur—
PAUL: What?
DOMINIQUE: There's a man who has a manner I can't quite describe who insists on seeing you.
PAUL: See me? Why?
DOMINIQUE: Urgent business, he claims. He wrote his name. (hands him a card)
PAUL (reading—shaken): Ovide! What does he want? (aloud) He's a very able worker I hired in Lyon. I'm going to receive him. Marie, take these people to the salon. I'll be with you momentarily.
MARIE: Come, gentlemen, come—
ETIENNE (to George): Your friend will soon be the master here.

(They follow Marie out. Ovide enters introduced by Dominique.)

OVIDE: Monsieur Harmant, I have the honor of—

(After Dominique leaves, his attitude changes completely,)

OVIDE: How ya doin, ya old top?
PAUL: You! Here, and in such condition!
OVIDE: What's up, my prince? Is it a conspiracy?
PAUL: Keep it down. Why are you here?
OVIDE: I'm down and out.
PAUL: I left you nine months ago with $40,000 dollars and an operation worth millions.
OVIDE: It's a sad turn of events.
PAUL: Let me guess: gambling again?
OVIDE: A bad streak at poker.

PAUL: And what have you come to do in Paris?

OVIDE: I was hoping you'd have a place for your dear cousin Ovide—who loves you so much.

PAUL: Impossible.

OVIDE: Why not?

PAUL: Because I don't want you around. Your presence would be a permanent danger to me.

OVIDE: I don't see that at all.

PAUL: But I do. Is it my fault that you couldn't keep the fortune I left you? If you are ruined, so much the worse for you.

OVIDE: Don't be stupid. What you did before, you must do again. If you helped me in the past, it was because you had to—and couldn't get out of it. You took my cousin's name and his identity, even though he died overseas.

PAUL: Shut up!

OVIDE: You, Jacques Garaud, the former foreman to Jules Labroue, who was murdered.

PAUL: Will you shut up!

OVIDE: So you took the identity of my late, lamented cousin whose passport I gave you. All is well—fine by me. But I kept his death certificate. In short, I can ruin you. You bought my silence with hush money, old top, but I'd earned it.

PAUL: Damn you!

OVIDE: Look, don't be silly. It's true, I'm blackmailing you, but I've never asked for much, and you've got plenty. If you'll help me, I'll try not to gamble. I've really been your friend—and I've no desire to ruin you—because without you, I'm in trouble if I fall on hard times again. Besides, a guy like me can always be of use to you, "cousin"—of use in many ways.

PAUL (struck): Of use to me?

OVIDE: Ah-ha! I've touched a nerve.

PAUL: Yes, because I'm threatened.

OVIDE: Threatened by whom?

PAUL (low): Lucien Labroue.

OVIDE: The son of—?

190

PAUL: Yes. I don't know why, but that young man is convinced that Jacques Garaud isn't dead. He wants to see Jeanne Fortier. He wants to avenge his father.

OVIDE: Hold on—

PAUL: And bad luck led him to me—

OVIDE: What does this kid do?

PAUL: He's an engineer like his father—and so, to keep an eye on him, I've hired him as my new supervisor.

OVIDE: Well—that was a smart move. You shout all is lost when all is well. Are you a man to take advice?

PAUL: What kind of advice?

OVIDE: Good advice, old boy. If you want to keep him quiet, even if he sniffs out the truth, marry him to your daughter.

PAUL: Him!

OVIDE: Why not? He won't be able to denounce his father-in-law. Think about it. You'll see I'm right. You see, I'm useful already. You can't leave me in the lurch.

PAUL: OK! So I won't. How much do you want?

OVIDE: I leave that to your generosity.

PAUL: How about twelve thousand francs?

OVIDE: It's a tad modest, but I'm not greedy. Give me a little advance so I can renew my wardrobe, and a find a place to stay.

PAUL: Fine. I'll give you three thousand francs now to set yourself up. And I'll give you a comfortable pension—as long as I live.

OVIDE: Trust me to keep you alive as long as possible.

PAUL: But you must obey me absolutely.

OVIDE: I ask for nothing else—

PAUL: In that case come along!

OVIDE: I'm with you. (aside) What luck to have such a "cousin"!

CURTAIN

191

SCENE III

A LARGE WINE SHOP
Table, chairs, gas lighting. Servants and diners come and go.

BALASSON: Marianne!
MARIANNE: Here I am, Papa Balasson. What do you want?
BALASSON: Bring me a plate of today's ragout.
MARIANNE: Right away.
RÉTIF: I'll have a tankard of beer and a slice of veal.
MARIANNE: Coming!

(Tête-en-buis and Cri-Cri enter carrying bread in their arms. Claire stands behind the counter.)

BALASSON (seeing Cri-Cri): Heavens, speaking of veal—there's the calf's head!
CRI-CRI (grimacing at him): Heh—you, old monkey.
RÉTIF: Look, don't get riled up. Come sit over here!
CRI-CRI: Screw it! (to Tête-en-Buis who hasn't said a word) What are you eating?
TÊTE-EN-BUIS (stupidly): Dunno.
CRI-CRI: That's not a dish on the menu.
TÊTE-EN-BUIS: It's all the same to me.
CRI-CRI: How about a slice of meatpie? And to say I'm forced to pilot such a dumb-bell! (To Marianne who is now serving Balasson) Marianne—a slice of pie.
CLAIRE: There isn't any left.
CRI-CRI: How about an American Lobster?
CLAIRE: There's none of that either.
CRI-CRI: In that case, a pork-chop?
CLAIRE: A pork-chop coming up!

(She goes into the kitchen.)

CRI-CRI (shouting): Make that two pork chops!

TÊTE-EN-BUIS: Ha, ha.
CRI-CRI: Don't laugh like that, will you! When he bawls like that, you see his big heart.

(They laugh.)

TÊTE-EN-BUIS: Ha, ha.
CRI-CRI: Look at me—shut your mouth. Sit down and cut your bread.

(Tête-en-Buis sits.)

CRI-CRI: A good lad—but so lazy. (to Marianne) Say there, Marianne—
MARIANNE: What, M. Cri-Cri?
CRI-CRI: I'll take you to the dance on Saturday, if it suits you.
MARIANNE: You—with a head like yours?
CRI-CRI: I'll wear my curly wig.
MARIANNE: And for pants?
CRI-CRI: I never leave home without 'em!
MARIANNE: That tonsure looks stupid.
CRI-CRI: I'm stupid? That's possible. But my father was witty.
MARIANNE: You'd have done well to inherit it.
CRI-CRI: Papa remarried.
MARIANNE: No wonder—

(She heads towards the counter. Suddenly, Jeanne appears, hesitant to enter.)

JEANNE: All these people...
MARIANNE: Come in, come in, Madame. There's plenty of room!
CRI-CRI: There's always place for the ladies at the baker's counter.
RÉTIF: Claire—bring me some cheese!

CRI-CRI: And a bottle of red.

MARIANNE (escorting Jeanne to a table): Sit here, you'll be fine.

JEANNE: Thank you, Mademoiselle.

MARIANNE: Our customers are a bit rowdy—but they're good lads. What'll you have?

JEANNE: A bouillon and a slice of beef.

MARIANNE: With two sous of bread?

JEANNE: Yes.

MARIANNE: Coming up.

JEANNE (aside): My last hope has vanished, like all the others. I succeeded in escaping, to find my children, but I can't find any trace of them. In Joigny, the nurse of my little Lucie is dead, and I haven't been able to find any traces of her. At Chevry, the Abbé Langier is dead. His sister, too, is dead. What happened to my George? Is he dead, too? Ah, it's too much! It's too much!

CLAIRE (serving): Two pork chops.

TÊTE-EN-BUIS: Here!

CRI-CRI (to Tête-en-Buis): Let's share, my boy.

TÊTE-EN-BUIS: Ha, ha.

JEANNE: I cannot go to the Police. That would be my ruin. They'd put me back in prison. All doors are closed to me. All that remains for me to do is die.

(Tête-en-Buis coughs.)

CRI-CRI: Mind your manners. Eat properly.

TÊTE-EN-BUIS: I choked.

MARIANNE (serving Jeanne): Your bouillon, Madame.

JEANNE: Thank you!

RÉTIF: A cocktail.

CLAIRE: Coming up!

TÊTE-EN-BUIS: Claire—some mustard!

CLAIRE: Here it is!

(Mama Verbois enters, bread under her arms.)

MAMA VERBOIS: Evening, everybody.

ALL: Evening, Madame Verbois!

MAMA VERBOIS: What news?

CRI-CRI: What news? If you want to know, go ask Claire.

MAMA VERBOIS: What happened to Monsieur Lebret?

CRI-CRI: The cops just administered a clubbing to him (laughing) Ah, gang, I didn't tell you that. The smoke went to my head.

MAMA VERBOIS: What on Earth for?

TÊTE-EN-BUIS: Dunno, but, I saw these monkeys kicking his ass hard. Ha, ha.

CRI-CRI: Say that without laughing. You're too ugly when you laugh.

BALASSON: What we need is more bread peddlers.

TÊTE-EN-BUIS: Yeah. Some nice bread peddlers.

BALASSON: That's all—nothing less, nothing more.

MAMA VERBOIS: It's not so easy.

CRI-CRI: Good bread peddlers are like white blackbirds, these days.

MAMA VERBOIS: Especially in this season.

RÉTIF: We've had four different ones in two weeks.

TÊTE-EN-BUIS: The best was Madame Martin.

CRI-CRI: Except she's in the hospital now.

TÊTE-EN-BUIS: A woman who's present herself at this moment would do good business—she'd be sure of earning four francs fifty per day.

CRI-CRI: Plus, two pounds of bread.

JEANNE (listening intently): It would be a living...

CRI-CRI: If you know someone, gang, you could recommend her.

ALL: Yes. Yes.

RÉTIF: I'll think about it.

JEANNE: Oh, if I could go looking for my children.

CRI-CRI (to Tête-en-Buis): Eat your bread, too, will you—not just the meat.

MAMA VERBOIS (to Claire): I'll have my usual.

TÊTE-EN-BUIS: Claire—some mustard!

CLAIRE: Here you go!

(Lucien appears with a set of drawings under his arms.)

CRI-CRI (seeing Lucien, rising): Ah, Monsieur Lucien, good evening.
LUCIEN: Good evening, Cri-Cri.
CRI-CRI: Coming for dinner as usual?
LUCIEN: My God, yes.
CRI-CRI: The menu isn't too bad tonight. (sits down)
MARIANNE (noticing Lucien): Ah, it's you, Monsieur Lucien. We didn't see you yesterday.
LUCIEN: I ate in town.

(Ovide, dressed like a baker, shows up outside and looks in.)

OVIDE: Ah, there he is.

(He enters quietly and listens.)

MARIANNE: Do you want some food right away?
LUCIEN: No, I'm waiting for Mademoiselle Lucie.
OVIDE (aside): Ah, ha!
JEANNE (hearing the name Lucie, she becomes attentive): Lucie—?
MARIANNE: Your girl friend?
LUCIEN: My fiancée. She'll be my wife.
OVIDE: Oh-oh.
MARIANNE: She's nice enough for that.
LUCIEN: Today's our day.
MARIANNE: It's true. Every Tuesday, a private little dinner. Oh, these love-birds!
LUCIEN: We'll never forget you girls giving us credit in hard times.
CRI-CRI: Despite customers with naked arms! That's really nice, Monsieur Lucien.
MARIANNE (taking a menu): Choose your dish. (She goes to the back.)

OVIDE: My cousin told me to find out what he does, where he goes. I shan't lose sight of you, my lad.

(He sits. Lucie appears with a green bag. Ovide reads a menu while observing them.)

CRI-CRI: Ah, here's Mademoiselle Lucie!

(Marianne comes back.)

JEANNE (musing): Lucie... Could she be...?
LUCIE: Good evening, Cri-Cri, good evening, Marianne!
LUCIEN: I was waiting for you, my darling Lucie.
JEANNE (looking at Lucie): My daughter would be her age!
LUCIEN: Yesterday, I came back late, and this morning, I went out before six.
LUCIE: Without slipping a note under my door to tell me the result of your interview.
LUCIEN: I will tell you as we eat.
LUCIE: I really didn't want to come.

(They go into an adjoining room, followed by Marianne. Ovide watches them attentively.)

JEANNE: My kids would have looked like that...
OVIDE: A private room. This could be a problem for me. I must find out about that girl.
CRI-CRI (to Claire): Who's that character over there, watching Lucien so closely? Real nasty mug, look at him, will you!
CLAIRE: I don't know him.
CRI-CRI: He's sure not one of us. Go ask him what he wants.
CLAIRE (to Ovide): Would you like some dinner?
OVIDE: I won't hide from you that I sure would.
CRI-CRI (aside): Groan!
CLAIRE: Are you a baker?
OVIDE: A baker? Ah, yes, I like baking.
CRI-CRI (aside): That's not an honest reply.

CLAIRE: No doubt you've come to find a job in Paris. If you want to stay in this neighborhood, I recommend this house.

OVIDE: That's understood, girl, that's understood.

CLAIRE: So what will you have?

OVIDE: Let's see.... Coq-au vin, cheese, café.

TÊTE-EN-BUIS (speechless): Ha, ha, ha.

CLAIRE: Wine?

OVIDE: A jug of Beaune—and a napkin.

CRI-CRI (aside): And a napkin! This guy's a banker. He's paying for an ambassador's banquet. It's not clear. I don't like that fellow.

TÊTE-EN-BUIS: Me, too. (to Claire) Claire—some mustard!

CLAIRE: Not again! I already brought you two pots.

TÊTE-EN-BUIS: So? I like mustard. Taste is free.

CRI-CRI: He's going to get stomach rot.

LUCIE: They'd be paying you 18,000 franc per year. Why, that's a fortune!

LUCIEN: Our fortune seems secure. My wife won't have to work.

LUCIE: And this Monsieur Harmant is going to employ you?

LUCIEN: You know him?

LUCIE: No, but I know his daughter. My employer is her dressmaker.

MARIANNE (now serving Ovide): There you are!

MAMA VERBOIS: My brandy, Marianne.

MARIANNE: Coming up!

CRI-CRI (to Rétif) : Give me a cigarette, Rétif. I left mine at home.

RÉTIF: Here you go.

JEANNE (aside): I'm going to give it a try...

MAMA VERBOIS: Hey, Cri-Cri.

CRI-CRI : What's up, Mama Verbois?

MAMA VERBOIS: Remember your bet about that woman, Jeanne Fortier?

(Ovide picks up his ears, Lucien shivers, and Jeanne reacts fearfully.)

LUCIEN: Jeanne Fortier…

(Lucie wants to say something, but Lucien silences her with a gesture. Cri-Cri searches his memory.)

MAMA VERBOIS: You know, the woman who's escaped from prison.
JEANNE (aside): My God!
CRI-CRI: Can't say I recall the name.
BALASSON: Don't pretend to forget now, my lad. You bet she'd be recaptured within a week.
OVIDE (aside): Jeanne Fortier escaped!
MAMA VERBOIS : And I bet she wouldn't! I remember her from when I was a midwife in Alfortville some twenty years ago, at the time of all her crimes.
JEANNE (aside): If this woman were to recognize me…
MAMA VERBOIS: My sister was the grocer who sold her the petrol with which she burned down that factory. Look, did you make a bet or didn't you?
ALL: Yeah, he made the bet! We remember!
CRI-CRI: Well, yes, I bet. No need to noise it about like that.
MAMA VERBOIS: Well—you lost.
CRI-CRI: What proves that?
MAMA VERBOIS: The newspaper. (pointing to an article) She's still at large, nearly three weeks later.
JEANNE (shivering): Oh, my god!
MAMA VERBOIS: There it is, my boy.

LUCIEN: So Jeanne Fortier is still alive…

ALL: He lost! He lost!
OVIDE (mocking): And when one loses, one pays.
CRI-CRI: Not to you, anyway, I don't know you.
OVIDE: Oh-oh! The Monsieur is annoyed because he lost.

CRI-CRI: I don't like wise-guys who displease me. And you're one of those.

OVIDE: Your mug displeases me, too—wise guy.

CRI-CRI: I lost, I'll pay. Marianne, a round for the house on me. Except for this Gentleman. I'll pay.

MARIANNE: Coming up!

CRI-CRI (noticing Lucien and Lucie): Ah, Mademoiselle Lucie, you are here. A glass of anisette? You, too, Monsieur Lucien?

LUCIEN: Yes, Cri-Cri, I'll click glasses with you—but to wish that Jeanne Fortier escapes recapture, so I can find myself face to face with her some day.

(Jeanne looks at Lucien with terror.)

CRI-CRI: You—?

LUCIEN: Yes, I, Lucien Labroue.

ALL: Lucien Labroue!

LUCIEN: The son of the man who was murdered.

JEANNE (aside): His son! Jules' son!

CRI-CRI: Now that's something, for goodness sakes!

LUCIE: She must have suffered greatly, but she deserves little pity.

(Jeanne reacts emotionally.)

LUCIEN: I wish I were certain of that.

JEANNE (aside): I can tell him something.

OVIDE (aside): The young man has a girl-friend to whom he's promised marriage. Jeanne Fortier's escaped from prison. Well, I haven't wasted my evening. (he looks at the paper.)

JEANNE (aside): I've got to get work to stay in Paris to find my children, and to prove my innocence. If they reject me, or discover me—time enough to kill myself then. Courage! (turning to Cri-Cri) Excuse me, Monsieur?

CRI-CRI: What can I do for you, Mama?

JEANNE: You were saying just now that your boss needed a bread seller.

CRI-CRI: Were you thinking of offering your services?

JEANNE: Yes.

CRI-CRI: You're in this business?

JEANNE: No—But I need the work.

CRI-CRI: It's tiring work.

JEANNE: I'm strong. Do you think your boss will take me?

CRI-CRI: Oh, I'll answer for that. He's been looking for someone everywhere. This evening, if you like, I'll speak to him.

JEANNE: I beg you—

(Lebret enters.)

LEBRET: Hello everyone!

CRI-CRI: Speak of the Devil!

LEBRET: Claire! A carafe of Beaujolais.

CLAIRE: Coming up!

CRI-CRI: Monsieur Lebret—

LEBRET: Ah, is it you, Cri-Cri? What is it?

CRI-CRI: Sorry to disturb you, but I think I've found a new bread carrier for you.

LEBRET: That'd be nice.

CRI-CRI (pointing to Jeanne): This lady needs work. She seems strong and intelligent. She could start tomorrow morning.

(Jeanne nods.)

CRI-CRI: Right, mama?

JEANNE: Yes, willingly—

LEBRET: I ask nothing better. But it's not a job for lazybones. If you still want the job, show up at daybreak at the Lyonnaise Bakery, Number 15, Rue Dauphine.

CRI-CRI: Thanks, Boss.

JEANNE: Oh, thank you, Monsieur.

LEBRET: Till tomorrow then.

TÊTE-EN-BUIS: You must learn the different types of bread.

JEANNE: Are there a lot?

CRI-CRI: There's a catalogue. I will give it all to you in writing, Mama. By the way—what is your name?

JEANNE (after a slight hesitation): Lise Perrin.

CRI-CRI: We'll call you Mama Lison. Let me introduce you to the others. Attention!

ALL: What is it?

CRI-CRI: I have the honor of presenting my new protégée to you—Madame Lison, the new bread peddler of the famous Lebret Lyonnaise Bakery!

ALL: Long live, Mama Lison!

JEANNE (choked up): Thank you, thank you, my friend.

LEBRET: Give her a brandy.

JEANNE (coming to herself): Oh—you've saved my life.

MARIANNE: Cri-Cri—this round's on you.

CRI-CRI: Well, that's for the bet I lost on Jeanne Fortier, I'll drink to the health of Mama Lison—our new bread peddler.

OVIDE: I'm in it, too, young man. I'll pay my share.

CRI-CRI: Come on, lads—to the health of Mama Lison!

(They all drink to Lison and come round to congratulate her.)

C U R T A I N

ACT III
SCENE IV

THE TWO LOFTS

The Fifth Floor of Number 8, Quai Bourbon.

The insides of two garrets can be seen, each lit by a window from the back. Each has a door to another room. The garret at the left is furnished by a couturier with mannequins. The garret on the right is in disorder.

AT RISE, Jeanne is in the garret on the right. The door is open. She seems to be waiting for Cri-Cri, who appears at the top of the stairs with a trunk. Jeanne is wearing the traditional costume of a bread peddler.

CRI-CRI: Son of a gun, the stairs leading to your apartment are steep, Mama Lison.

JEANNE: Yes, aren't they? Hold on while I help you.

(She helps him to put the trunk down.)

CRI-CRI: Oof! There it is. Need to put on a light.

(At this moment, Tête-en-Buis appears carrying various objects; he trips, and sprawls on the landing, breaking some dishes.)

TÊTE-EN-BUIS: Ah!

CRI-CRI : Watch it. (going into the corridor) Imbecile.

TÊTE-EN-BUIS (looking at the shards) Lots of plates broken.

JEANNE: It's nothing. You aren't hurt?

TÊTE-EN-BUIS (laughing): Me? Ah, no.

CRI-CRI: Don't laugh and pick up the shards.

TÊTE-EN-BUIS: Where to put them?

CRI-CRI: Where to put them? Sell them to the grocer to make candles! (Tête-en-Buis laughs.) Let's get going. Beat it, and bring back the rest of the things that are in the carriage.

(Tête-en-Buis picks up the mess. Cri-Cri goes into Jeanne's garret.)

CRI-CRI: Well, how's your new lodging, Mama Lison? It used to belong to Monsieur Lucien Labroue.
JEANNE: Yes, it's very nice.
CRI-CRI: It's quite a hike to the bakery.
JEANNE: I'll be happy here.
CRI-CRI: That's still a crazy idea. Why here, and not closer to work?
JEANNE: Here, I have my little neighbor, to whom I've taken a liking.
CRI-CRI: Ah yes, Mademoiselle Lucie, Monsieur Lucien's fiancée.
JEANNE: He had to leave here to be near his boss—and I profited by it.
CRI-CRI: It's up to you. (looking around) But these trunks aren't yours?
JEANNE: No—they belong to Monsieur Lucien. He'll be back to get them today.
CRI-CRI: Today? He's coming today? Then I'll tell him of a discovery I've made for him.
TÊTE-EN-BUIS (appearing with some chairs): Here's all that's left.
CRI-CRI (ridding him of them): At least you didn't break anything this time.
TÊTE-EN-BUIS: Nah, they're made of wood.
CRI-CRI: You'd be capable of that. But let's be on our way. Gossiping is just adding to the carriage fee. We'll go bring your bed, Madame Lison.
TÊTE-EN-BUIS (laughing): Ha, ha, ha.
CRI-CRI: Let's move.

(They leave.)

JEANNE (alone): Yes, I'm happy—to live near her—she, who reminds me of my daughter. I'd like to tell her, but I must take care not to betray myself. Until I can prove my innocence, I must remain Lise Perrin.

(Lucie appears. Seeing the door half open she sticks her head in.)

LUCIE: Ah, there you are, Mama Lison?
JEANNE: Yes, I'm almost completely moved in. I brought you your bread. (She gives her bread.)
LUCIE: Thanks, Mama. So you'll start living here tonight?
JEANNE: Yes, and I'm really happy about it.
LUCIE: Me, too. I've only known you a month and I love you with all my heart.
JEANNE: Dear sweetie.
LUCIE: I just got some work from my boss. Lots of work to do, and I'm expecting Lucien, who I haven't seen for a week.
JEANNE: A week?
LUCIE: His job takes all his time. He lives so far away now. I'll see you soon, Mama Lison.
JEANNE: I was wondering if you would like to make a dress for me?
LUCIE: Why, sure. Come to my place and I'll take your measurements.

(She goes into her garret, and rids herself of the packages she was carrying.)

LUCIE: Are you coming, Mama?
JEANNE: Yes, dear child.

(She goes without locking the door to her garret.)

LUCIE: I'll make you something very flirty. You wait and see.

JEANNE: I know that you are a fairy.

(Lucie begins taking Jeanne's measurements, writing them down as they chat.)

JEANNE: Have you done this sort of work for a long while?

LUCIE: Soon it will be six years.

JEANNE: Did you apprentice in Paris?

LUCIE: No, first in the orphanage.

JEANNE: You were raised in an orphanage?

LUCIE: Yes, Mama Lison.

JEANNE: Which one?

LUCIE: The one for foundlings.

JEANNE: In Paris.

LUCIE: Yes, on Quai Conti.

JEANNE: A long time ago?

LUCIE: Twenty years ago.

JEANNE: Ah! How old are you?

LUCIE: From what they told me, I must be twenty-three.

JEANNE: Do you know anything of your parents?

LUCIE: Nothing.

JEANNE: But the orphanage must know?

LUCIE: Probably, but that wasn't a reason to tell me.

JEANNE: Why's that?

LUCIE: They protect the privacy of those who relinquish the child.

JEANNE: And if you asked to know?

LUCIE: They wouldn't tell me.

JEANNE: And your name—

LUCIE: I was abandoned on Saint Lucie's day. Doubtless that's why I was given this name.

(She writes down her measurements. Jeanne shows disappointment but says nothing. Lucien appears and raps.)

LUCIE: Ah, here's Lucien.

LUCIEN: Hello, Lucie!

LUCIE: Finally, after a week—you don't hug your friend?

LUCIEN (hugging her): Darling Lucie—(offering his hand to Jeanne) Hello, Mama Lison.

JEANNE: Hello, Lucien.

LUCIEN (to Jeanne): I'm going to ride you of my books.

LUCIE: Not now, I suppose?

LUCIEN: During the afternoon.

LUCIE: You won't give them all to me?

LUCIEN: I'd like to—

LUCIE: I'll put my work off until tomorrow. I'll go get food and prepare dinner. Mama, you will dine with us?

JEANNE: Really?

LUCIEN: Yes, please, Mama Lison.

JEANNE: Well, then I accept.

LUCIEN: I'll pack my books.

(He goes into the room at the right. Lucie sighs.)

LUCIE: Ah.

JEANNE: What's the matter?

LUCIE: Nothing, Mama, nothing. It seems to me that Lucien is no longer the same with me.

JEANNE: That's pure childishness. He loves you and thinks only of you.

LUCIE: But if he doesn't—I'll die.

JEANNE: Chase away thoughts like that. Think only of living to be happy.

(Jeanne heads towards her apartment where Lucien is packing, and enters.)

JEANNE: Would you like me to help you, M. Labroue?

LUCIEN: No need, Mama Lison.

(Cri-Cri appears on the landing with more stuff.)

CRI-CRI: Mama Lison—

JEANNE: What?

CRI-CRI: Open up.

JEANNE: You should have made two trips.

CRI-CRI (putting things down): Ah, Monsieur Lucien! Hello!

LUCIEN: Hello, Cri-Cri.

CRI-CRI: I'm really glad to see you! Mama Lison, go to the shop quick. I just saw the boss—his wife is sick and he needs you.

JEANNE: Ah, the poor woman.

CRI-CRI: I'll finish unpacking the carriage, and I'll put everything in order for you. Your key will be with Mademoiselle Lucie.

JEANNE: I'm on my way, Cri-Cri. Bye, Monsieur Lucien I hope I won't be long.

CRI-CRI: Get going for God's sake! Oh, these women have to jabber—

(Jeanne goes out. Cri-Cri locks the door behind her.)

CRI-CRI: Now that we are alone...

LUCIEN: What, Cri-Cri?

CRI-CRI: I'm going to tell you.

(George appears and knocks.)

CRI-CRI: Ah! Now who's interrupting us?

(He opens the door.)

LUCIEN (seeing George): George! You, here!

GEORGE: I hadn't heard from you in two weeks. So I came here to see you.

LUCIEN: I moved out two weeks ago. I came back today to remove some things I'd left behind.

CRI-CRI: Well, I've got some news for you. You're being followed.

LUCIEN: Me?

CRI-CRI: Yes. You and Mademoiselle Lucie.

LUCIEN: You're crazy, Cri-Cri.

CRI-CRI: Not at all. You remember that character that came to the Baker's Dinner some time ago? Well, it's him who's following you. And he dresses in disguise. I've seen him. Tête-en-Buis has seen him. He's probably here again today. (goes to window) There he is! Decked out like a peddler of rings and necklaces.

LUCIEN: It's true. (looking) Yes, it's him.

CRI-CRI: I should blacken his eye.

LUCIEN (deeply puzzled): Who would have an interest in Lucie or me?

GEORGE: Why would anyone do that?

CRI-CRI: Why? Well, he must know. Ah, he's beating it. He's stopping a carriage. I don't like the looks of that creep at all.

LUCIEN: If you meet him again, follow him. Find out where he lives, or where he's going—then tell me or M. Darier.

CRI-CRI: If I ever spot him again, don't worry, I'll follow him and I'll find out where this bird has his perch.

(Cri-Cri bows and leaves.)

GEORGE: Why didn't you give me news of your new address?

LUCIEN: I was going to write to you today of my impending departure.

GEORGE: Your departure?

LUCIEN: Yes, in a month. I'm being sent to Belgrade to install some machinery.

GEORGE: You're still happy—?

LUCIEN: No.

GEORGE: Why not?

LUCIEN: I'm in a difficult situation.

GEORGE: Why?

LUCIEN: My employer is offering to put me in charge of building a factory in Alfortville—a huge one.

GEORGE: That seems like a great opportunity.

LUCIEN: Magnificent, indeed. But based on an impossible condition.

GEORGE: What do you mean, impossible?

LUCIEN: That of becoming his son-in-law.

GEORGE: That's refusing a fortune.

LUCIEN: Yes, but I love Lucie.

GEORGE: Did you tell Harmant?

LUCIEN: Yes, it was my duty.

GEORGE: And does Mademoiselle Harmant, apparently so suddenly smitten with you, know her father's plans?

LUCIEN: I'm certain he acted at her instigation.

GEORGE: You're going to break her heart.

LUCIEN: The alternative is to break Lucie's.

GEORGE: Poor Lucien.

(George and Lucien go out. After a while, Ovide, a bit breathless, climbs the stairs.)

OVIDE: Yikes! 107 steps! (reading the sign) Here's the bird's cage. Let's have a look. (knocking at the door) Mademoiselle Lucie, please?

LUCIE: That's me, Monsieur.

OVIDE: I've been directed by M. Paul Harmant—

LUCIE: Paul Harmant?

OVIDE: To ask if you are at home. Are you at home?

LUCIE: That's plain to see, Monsieur.

OVIDE: I'm going to telephone him.

LUCIE (straightening up her room): M. Harmant—in my room.

OVIDE (shouting down the stairwell): She's here. No mistake.

(Paul can be heard climbing up. He goes into Lucie's room.)

LUCIE: You, Monsieur—in my home.

PAUL: Yes, child, I need to chat with you.
LUCIE: Please have a seat.

(Ovide goes back down the stairs.)

PAUL: I'm here on behalf of my daughter.
LUCIE (bewildered): Monsieur—
PAUL: First, let me ask you some questions—
LUCIE: By all means.
PAUL: Have you been living here long?
LUCIE: Around two years.
PAUL: Isn't your neighbor a man who works for me?
LUCIE: Yes. Lucien Labroue. (Paul nods) My fiancé. Thanks to Mademoiselle Marie and you, we can realize our dream and get married.
PAUL: I'm coming to ask you to forget that dream, To give up your plans to marry Lucien.
LUCIE: Ah—Mademoiselle Marie loves Lucien…
PAUL: In a word, yes. She's crazy about him. You know her health is not good. You must forgive her, Lucie. She loved him as soon as she saw him.. She was unaware you were his fiancée. I'm asking you to give him up, Lucie—and I'll make you rich.
LUCIE: What are you proposing?
PAUL: You will leave France. Lucien will never see you again and he will marry Marie.
LUCIE: Leave France?
PAUL: So Marie can feel calm and safe.
LUCIE: To save your daughter, I should break my heart. And you're offering me money?
PAUL: A small fortune.
LUCIE: And you imagine for a moment that I will accept?
PAUL: Why would you refuse?
LUCIE: Why? Because I love Lucien. I love him. If your daughter loves him too, well—let him choose between us. Now, Monsieur, I think we have nothing more to say to each other.

PAUL: Lucie, Marie might die if Paul doesn't love her. Have pity on her! Have pity on me!
LUCIE: Monsieur, I beg you. I have neither the right, nor the will, to dispose of Lucien's heart.
PAUL (wildly): So you refuse?
LUCIE: Yes. I would prefer to die than to give him up.

(Paul takes his face in his hands.)

PAUL: Well—so be it. You'll be sorry! Mark my words!

(He rushes out. She collapses in tears.)

C U R T A I N

SCENE V

SAME AS SCENE II. PAUL HARMANT'S HOUSE
A fashionably furnished room in a bourgeois house.

(Paul enters, reading a letter. He sits down. Then Dominique enters.)

DOMINIQUE: A telegram for you, Monsieur.
PAUL: Ah? Let me see.

(Dominique leaves. Paul reads.)

PAUL: So Lucie is indeed Jeanne Fortier's daughter...

(Marie comes in.)

MARIE: Hello, Papa.
PAUL: Hello, sweetie. I've got good news for you.
MARIE (joyfully): Lucien is coming back?
PAUL: How did you—?

MARIE: No one had to tell me. What other good news could you have for me?

PAUL: His work in Belgrade is finished. He'll be here shortly.

MARIE: Ah, father, I feel better. I'm going to see him again, to see him again.

PAUL: You love him so much?

MARIE: More than anything in the world.

PAUL (smiling): Ingrate!

MARIE: Except you—

PAUL: Dear child.

MARIE: I'm happy—and yet—

PAUL: Yet what?

MARIE: His coming back may bring me new sorrows.

PAUL: Don't be jealous of Lucie. I sent him to Belgrade so he'd forget her.

MARIE: Sometimes I feel criminal. I would kill Lucie. If she were dead, he could no longer love her.

PAUL: Marie, calm down.

MARIE : How? I love Lucien. I want him to be mine. I especially don't want him to be with anyone else. It would kill me. I would die!

PAUL: Calm down. I swear to you, Lucien will be your husband.

MARIE: And he will love me?

PAUL: And he will love you.

MARIE: My sweet Papa!

PAUL: Come what may, this marriage must take place.

(Dominique returns.)

DOMINIQUE: Monsieur Labroue.

(Dominique leaves. Lucien enters. Marie shivers with emotion.)

PAUL: My dear friend.

LUCIEN: Monsieur—Mademoiselle. Are you feeling well? (aside) God—how she has changed.

MARIE (with effort): I'm fine. Never better. I'm happy to see you again, M. Labroue.

LUCIEN (taking her hand): Me, too. I'm very happy to see you. Very happy.

MARIE: For true?

LUCIEN: For true. I swear it.

MARIE: Then you won't leave us this evening?

LUCIEN: Mademoiselle, I—

MARIE: You accept my invitation.

LUCIEN (reluctantly): Well, yes, certainly, Mademoiselle.

MARIE: It's agreed then—we'll keep you here. I'll give you a short time to do your business. Till soon.

(She leaves.)

LUCIEN: Allow me—

PAUL: Later. First of all, allow me to thank you.

LUCIEN: For what?

PAUL: For your kindness to Marie. Her situation is serious, but not hopeless. Her life is in your hands— (Lucien looks shocked.) Jealousy is aggravating her illness. She'll die if you reject her. Don't you have any pity?

(Marie reappears, but draws back and listens to the conversation without being seen.)

LUCIEN: It pains me to cause you pain. But would you break your solemn oath?

PAUL (a bit wildly): What do you want me to say? All I know is that my daughter is everything for me, and that her life is at stake.

LUCIEN: To save her, must I kill the one I love?

PAUL: The one you love is unworthy of you.

LUCIEN: Don't say that!

PAUL: Do you know who this Lucie is?

LUCIEN: Certainly. A foundling. There's no shame in that. The parents who abandoned her should be considered culpable.

PAUL: Agreed. But do you know who they are?

LUCIEN: Whoever they may be, their actions cannot soil Lucie.

PAUL: Not even if they were criminals? Murderers?

LUCIEN: What are you talking about?

PAUL: Even if the blood shed was that of your father? Would you marry the daughter of Jeanne Fortier?

MARIE (gasping): Ah!

LUCIEN : Don't slander her, Monsieur! I want proof!

(Ovide enters.)

OVIDE: Take a look at these, M. Labroue. Here's the record—a certified copy from the Foundlings' Hospital giving the name of the mother. The nurse gave up the child after Jeanne Fortier was convicted.

LUCIEN (reading, then crushed): Ah, it's true—Lucie is the daughter of Jeanne Fortier!

OVIDE: There's no doubt about it.

PAUL: Jeanne Fortier—who murdered your father.

LUCIEN: I've never believed that—

PAUL: Perhaps, but unless she is exonerated, Jeanne Fortier is still considered guilty. And all the world will— indeed does— believe she's your father's murderer.

LUCIEN: My God, my God—

PAUL: It's infamous for the son of the victim to marry the daughter of the murderer. Give up a marriage that no one will forgive you for, and save Marie, save my daughter.

(Marie appears, staggering.)

ALL: Marie!

MARIE: You cannot love that girl.

215

LUCIEN: Don't ask anything of me. Live for your father who loves you.
MARIE: Lucien!
LUCIEN: Wait for me to forget—if I can.

(Lucien rushes out.)

MARIE (in despair): Ah, he still loves her. He will always love her.

(Dominique returns.)

DOMINIQUE: Mademoiselle.
PAUL: What is it?
DOMINIQUE: Mademoiselle's dressmaker is here.

(Lucie appears carrying a package.)

PAUL: What audacity.
LUCIE: Mademoiselle, they sent me—
MARIE (wildly): Make her leave and never let her come back again!
LUCIE (stupefied): Mademoiselle!
MARIE: And I'll unmask you everywhere—everywhere! Leave, leave! I'm kicking you out! (she faints.)
PAUL: Marie! My daughter, my poor child!
OVIDE: Dad had it right—kids in the family. They're the rub!

CURTAIN

SCENE VI

THE BAKERY LEBRET
The inside of a bakery. Rows of bread of different sorts. A counter. The gas lighting is lit.
AT RISE, Jeanne is behind the counter—looking at some court papers. Tête-en-Buis is next to her.

JEANNE: These are official papers—court papers.

TÊTE-EN-BUIS: There's a name on the envelope.

JEANNE: Yes. Maître Darier, attorney-at-law.

TÊTE-EN-BUIS: He's a friend of Lucien.

JEANNE: He must have lost them.

TÊTE-EN-BUIS: What are you going to do with them, Mama Lison?

JEANNE: Tomorrow morning, on my route, I'll take them back to him.

TÊTE-EN-BUIS: Time to close up.

(Mama Verbois enters.)

JEANNE: Hello, Mama Verbois!

MAMA VERBOIS: Hello, everybody.

(Tête-en-Buis is slowly closing the shutters outside.)

MAMA VERBOIS: Are you in charge tonight, Lison?

JEANNE: Yes, Mama Verbois.

MAMA VERBOIS : Then, would you weigh me out two pounds of *boulou*?[9]

JEANNE (cutting the bread and weighing it): Monsieur Lebret went to see his Mother-in-law.

MAMA VERBOIS: Ah, you're on a new footing here, since the death of his wife.

JEANNE: Well, I do all I can to be useful to him.

MAMA VERBOIS: I bet! Thank you, Lison! Bye!

(She leaves.)

TÊTE-EN-BUIS: Time to put out the lights, Mama Lison.

JEANNE: Yes. Go ahead.

---

[9] *Boulou* is an enriched Challah-style *bread* studded with fruit, nuts and seeds, and scented with orange and anise.

(Cri-Cri enters.)

CRI-CRI: Good evening, Mama Lison!
JEANNE: Good evening, Cri-Cri.
CRI-CRI: Where's the Boss.
JEANNE: He's not here.
CRI-CRI: Bah!

(He leaves with Tête-en-Buis. Jeanne starts to do her accounting, when Lucien enters.)

JEANNE: Monsieur Lucien—back in Paris ! (she hurries to him.)
LUCIEN: Yes, I'm back
JEANNE: Ah, how happy Lucie will be.
LUCIEN: Lucie—
JEANNE: What's wrong?
LUCIEN (weeping in despair): Ah, Madame Perrin, it's horrible.
JEANNE: What's it all about? Is it about Lucie?
LUCIEN: Yes.
JEANNE: Your coldness shocks me. I'm afraid you'll tell me you don't love Lucie anymore.
LUCIEN: Something has happened. It's possible—it's likely I'll never be able to see her again.
JEANNE: You can't be speaking seriously. That would be monstrous.
LUCIEN: It may be—honor would force me to do it.
JEANNE: Honor demands that you keep your word—and you swore to marry her.
LUCIEN: Suppose an insurmountable barrier exists between us?
JEANNE: What are you talking about?
LUCIEN: I love Lucie as much today as I ever loved her—but—
JEANNE: But what—?
LUCIEN: She's the daughter of—

218

JEANNE: No one knows who—

LUCIEN: I cannot marry the daughter of the woman convicted of my father's murder.

JEANNE: What are you talking about? Lucie is the daughter of—

LUCIEN: Of Jeanne Fortier.

JEANNE: Lucie! Lucie! (she chokes.)

LUCIEN: Mama Lison—what's wrong with you?

JEANNE: Proof—proof—have you got proof?

LUCIEN: Yes.

JEANNE: Show me! Show me!

LUCIEN: Here— (he hands her the report)

JEANNE (reading avidly): So be it! But is she responsible for the crimes of her mother?

LUCIEN: No—not at all. But I cannot marry the daughter of the woman who killed my father.

JEANNE (despite herself): That's false.

LUCIEN: What do you mean?

JEANNE: You believe that Jeanne is innocent?

LUCIEN: Yes, I think so. I still think so.

JEANNE: Well?

LUCIEN: My belief is not evidence. Until Jeanne Fortier's name is cleared—I simply cannot marry Lucie.

JEANNE: But you will marry the daughter of a millionaire. And you come to me—you want me to tell Lucie, right?

LUCIEN: The crime her mother was convicted of—creates an abyss between us—

JEANNE: Shame on you, M. Labroue. Don't count on me to do your dirty work!

LUCIEN: Mama Lison!

JEANNE: Go away! Go away, M. Labroue. Yes, I will see Lucie.

LUCIEN: Thank you, thank you.

(He leaves crushed.)

JEANNE: What to do? What to do? God give me strength!

219

(Lucie knocks at the door.)

LUCIE: Mama Lison!

JEANNE (opening) : Ah, it's you, my child.

LUCIE: Have you seen, Lucien?

JEANNE: Isn't he out of town?

LUCIE: No—he's back. He doesn't love me anymore. He doesn't want to see me.

JEANNE: Lucie, my child. You mustn't despair.

LUCIE: He hasn't come. To see me because he loves her—and she kicked me out.

JEANNE: You must be strong, my daughter.

LUCIE: : Lucien was my entire family—my future! Now, I have nothing.

JEANNE: Lucie! Lucie!

LUCIE: This will kill me. But, before dying, I want to see him. I want to know why—I'll go ask him.

JEANNE: No, no, Lucie—don't do that.

LUCIE: Why? Lucien knew that I was a foundling—it didn't matter before—why does it matter now? He's got to tell me!

JEANNE: No, don't see him, Lucie, don't see him.

LUCIE (thinking about it): You know—you know why he's abandoning me—don't you?

JEANNE: Don't try to learn his secret.

LUCIE: So you do know!

JEANNE: Yes.

LUCIE: You've seen Lucien.

JEANNE: Yes.

LUCIE: Are you going to tell me? Say something!

JEANNE: Your marriage with Lucien is impossible.

LUCIE: Why?

JEANNE: Because—before becoming his wife, you would have to prove your mother's innocence.

LUCIE: What crime did she commit?

JEANNE: She was convicted of—

LUCIE: Of—?

220

JEANNE: —Of murdering Lucien's father.

LUCIE: Well—that explains everything. (she bows her head.)

JEANNE (with unspeakable rage): And these devils will not be punished? No, no—it shall not be. I will defend you.

LUCIE: How?

JEANNE: We shall consult a lawyer. Ah, why not M. Darier?

LUCIE: Lucien's friend?

JEANNE: What difference does it make. Mama Lison loves you as if she were your own mother. And she will defend you as if you were her own daughter! And weak as she is, she will be strong enough to save you.

(They embrace, weeping)

CURTAIN

ACT IV

SCENE VII

GEORGE DARIER'S OFFICE

An attorney's office. Desk, chairs. A diploma framed on the wall. A door leading to the secretary's office; another leading to George Darier's apartment.

AT RISE, Madeleine, George's Secretary, is letting Etienne Costel into the office.

MADELEINE: M. Darier will be with you shortly.
ETIENNE: Thank you. (he sits down)

(George comes in from the apartment.)

GEORGE: Ah, my tutor—Pardon me for not being here to receive you. I had to get a case postponed because I lost the file.
ETIENNE: Probably, just mislaid—

(Madeleine returns.)

MADELEINE: M. Labroue is here.

(George and Etienne exchange a surprised look.)

GEORGE: Show him in.

(Lucien enters. Madeleine closes the door behind him.)

GEORGE: Finally, you're back in Paris!
ETIENNE: What a sad look. It looks as if your absence hasn't been good to you.
LUCIEN: Say rather, my return.

ETIENNE: Your return?

GEORGE: Is this about Marie Harmant's grand passion for you? And your love for Lucie?

LUCIEN: I can no longer love Lucie.

GEORGE: Then you've accepted Harmant's offer?

LUCIEN: I've accepted nothing. I love Lucie with all my heart—but my duty is no longer to her. There's a crime separating us.

GEORGE: What are you talking about?

LUCIEN (in despair): Lucie is the daughter of Jeanne Fortier!

ETIENNE: Her daughter? Are you sure of that?

LUCIEN: I've seen proof.

ETIENNE: Who gave it to you?

LUCIEN: Paul Harmant.

(reaction of surprise)

ETIENNE: Where'd he get this proof?

LUCIEN: From the Joigny City Hall.

ETIENNE: And how did he know to look there?

LUCIEN: He must have asked that Monsieur Ovide, a cousin of his—who returned from America a few months ago. He's the one who went there.

ETIENNE: What does it mean?

LUCIEN: I don't know. I've lost my head. All I know is that I love Lucie, but I have no right to do so. How can I marry the daughter of the woman convicted of murdering my father?

GEORGE: Of course—you cannot. Be a man—don't you agree, Etienne?

ETIENNE: Not at all. Chance brought you together. Chance may yet prove the innocence of Jeanne Fortier.

GEORGE: But what if it doesn't?

LUCIEN: Yes. What to do in that case?

ETIENNE: You must buy time by letting Paul Harmant believe that one day you'll marry his daughter. Meanwhile, you must search for Jacques Garaud.

LUCIEN: How will I do that?

ETIENNE: Do you know what your father's invention was?

LUCIEN: My aunt told me he was hoping to win a large fortune with a new machine to make unbreakable glass.

(Cri-Cri knocks and opens the door, looking in.)

CRI-CRI: May I come in?
GEORGE: Cri-Cri? Of course!

(Cri-Cri enters.)

CRI-CRI: Hello, everybody.
LUCIEN: Something new?
CRI-CRI: Would I come if there wasn't? You were followed yesterday, after you got off the train, by that same character I warned you about. I'd taken a friend to the station, and was smoking a cigarette after his train left when your train pulled in. I saw you get off and was about to greet you, when I noticed that bird behind you. I followed him. He followed you to where you were staying—then he went off. I kept following him. He wound up at the hotel of engineer Paul Harmant.
ETIENNE: Lucien! Go see Mademoiselle Marie, and tell her you accept her father's offer.
LUCIEN: But—
ETIENNE: Don't question me. Obey blindly. Just remember that I promise you that Lucie will be your wife. I give you my word on it. You, Cri-Cri—get back on the trail of that man.
CRI-CRI: Don't worry.
ETIENNE: Go—both of you!
LUCIEN: Come, Cri-Cri.

(Cri-Cri and Lucien leave.)

GEORGE: What's your plan?
ETIENNE: I'm looking for the murderer of Jules Labroue.
GEORGE: So you think Jeanne Fortier is not guilty?
ETIENNE: I'm convinced of it.
GEORGE: Well, who do you accuse then?

ETIENNE: I'm not accusing anyone—yet. I'm looking for a trail—and all roads are good. Pray God that I succeed!
GEORGE (puzzled): And that's why you advised Lucien to accept Harmant's offer?
ETIENNE: Perhaps.

(Madeleine enters.)\

GEORGE: What is it now, Madeleine?
MADELEINE: There's a woman who'd like to consult you.
GEORGE: Let's not make her wait.

(Jeanne enters; Madeleine closes the door.)

GEORGE: You want to speak to me, Madame?
JEANNE: Yes, Maître.
GEORGE: Please have a seat and tell me what brought you here?
ETIENNE (aside): She looks familiar.
JEANNE (sitting): Did you lose some documents yesterday?
GEORGE: Why, yes! Could you have found them?
JEANNE: Yes, Maître. Place Dauphine. (giving him papers.) Here they are—make sure nothing's missing.

(George takes the papers and examines them.)

ETIENNE (aside): It's Jeanne Fortier!
GEORGE: Everything's here, Madame. I hope you'll accept the promised reward?
JEANNE: No, Maître, I will accept nothing. These papers are yours. I found them—it's my duty to return them.
GEORGE: Then I won't insist. But, if I can help you in any way, now or in the future, I'll gladly do so.
JEANNE: In that case, Maître, I'll take the liberty of asking you for some advice.
GEORGE: By all means. Speak.

JEANNE: Can one, without violating the law, reproach a child for the crimes of a parent?

GEORGE: Could you be more specific?

JEANNE: Suppose a baby was placed in n orphanage after one of her parents was convicted of a crime. She grew up without anyone revealing to her the crime of her parent. She worked honestly as a seamstress. She met a young man and they fell in love, and were going to get married.

GEORGE: I see. Go on.

JEANNE: A rich woman fell in love with the young man. In order to break off the engagement, they told the young man she is the daughter of the person who killed your father. In addition, they made this known to her employer who promptly fired her.

GEORGE: Is it true?

JEANNE (slowly): Yes, Maître.

GEORGE: Unless it was false, there's no defamation. But— it's a very nasty business.

JEANNE: There is nothing can be done about it?

GEORGE: Alas, no—nothing can be done about it.

JEANNE: Ah! She will die. The poor child is not responsible for her mother's past—and besides, the mother was innocent.

GEORGE: Who are we talking about?

JEANNE: Lucie Fortier.

ETIENNE and GEORGE: Ah!

GEORGE (looking at Jeanne): You've known Lucie a long time?

JEANNE (slowly): No, Maître.

GEORGE: You are Lise Perrin, right?

JEANNE: Yes. And I love Lucie like my daughter. Please, save her!

(Madeleine enters.)

MADELEINE (announcing): M. Paul Harmant.

GEORGE (to Jeanne): You must ask him to let the child you love live.

226

(Paul enters; Madeleine closes the door.)

PAUL: Hello, George! I've brought you all the necessary papers to draft the marriage contract.

JEANNE: Ah, pity, Monsieur!

PAUL: Who is this woman? What do you want with me?

GEORGE: This poor lady is named Lise Perrin. She has a deep maternal affection for a young woman who is dying of despair, and came to ask me to intercede with you on her behalf.

JEANNE: Yes, Monsieur. Please, save her!

PAUL (recognizing her): Ah!

ETIENNE (aside): He seems to recognize her.

PAUL (coldly): Don't intercede with me. I don't understand what this is about.

GEORGE: It's about Lucie Fortier.

ETIENNE (aside): But she doesn't recognize him.

JEANNE: Louise is a poor creature who isn't responsible for the crime imputed to her mother. You've taken the man she loves from her, for your daughter. And if that weren't enough, your daughter kicked her out of the dress shop where she works. You are killing her. What has she done to you? It's a great injustice, Monsieur. Don't allow it!

PAUL (violently): What can I do about it? Is it my fault that this Lucie is the daughter of a convicted murderess?

JEANNE: So all you can do is offer a new insult?

PAUL: I simply did my duty—by preventing Lucien from marrying the daughter of the woman convicted of murdering his father. Actually, he's still free to do so, if he so wishes. But I can see who you are now... You are not Lise Perrin, you are Jeanne Fortier, who's escaped from prison!

(Paul starts to leave.)

GEORGE: This woman is Lise Perrin, I know her. But even if she were Jeanne Fortier, she is under my protection. She entered here freely, and she will leave here freely. Come, Madame, you may go without fear.

(Jeanne seizes his hand and kisses it. Then she leaves.)

ETIENNE: I believe George is right.
PAUL (controlling himself): He's right. A hundred times, right. (offering his hand) Shake!
ETIENNE (still holding Paul's hand, aside): I've got you now—and yet I have no proof. But patience...

CURTAIN

SCENE VIII

RUE GIT-LE-COEUR
As seen from the corner of the Rue Hirondelle.
AT RISE, Cri-Cri and Tête-en-Buis are advancing cautiously.
Old Mathieu, a night watchman, is asleep behind a window.

CRI-CRI (seeing a police patrol): There's a patrol. Stop here!

(He and Tête-en-Buis stop.)

CRI-CRI: They're coming this way. Let's go back!

(They vanish into the Rue Hirondelle. Two policemen enter.
)
1st POLICEMAN (noticing the night watchman asleep): Heavens! He's sleeping. If that's how he watches the work.
2nd POLICEMAN: Let him sleep. That's not our job.

(They go off; Cri-Cri and Tête-en-Buis reappear.)

CRI-CRI: They've gone. We mustn't lose a minute.
TÊTE-EN-BUIS: Where's the house?
CRI-CRI: That one! (pointing)

TÊTE-EN-BUIS: Can you open the door?

CRI-CRI: Yes, I've got a pass key.

TÊTE-EN-BUIS: Suppose there's someone in there?

CRI-CRI: Can't be. I checked. The man who lives here left. We've got time for a visit.

TÊTE-EN-BUIS: But—

CRI-CRI: But what? Are you going to get cold feet? We've got to find the papers that will save the day.

TÊTE-EN-BUIS: Let's go then. (he laughs.) I hear someone.

(Cri-Cri goes to the door.)

CRI-CRI: Sonofabitch! He's back. In a different get up.

TÊTE-EN-BUIS: He must have forgotten his handkerchief.

CRI-CRI: Keep your mouth shut.

(Ovide goes in. Once inside, he lights a candle.)

CRI-CRI: He's staying put, the swine.

(They remain watching.)

OVIDE: He'll be here. He's usually punctual.

(Paul appears at the corner of the Rue Hirondelle and goes to Ovide's door.)

CRI-CRI: Who's that?

OVIDE: Come in.

(Paul goes in. The two policemen return on their rounds.)

OVIDE: No use for words, right? You haven't changed your mind?

PAUL: No—the woman has got to go.

OVIDE: Agreed. She cannot be allowed to destroy our peace and quiet. In a few hours, she'll no longer be a nuisance.

PAUL: How will you do it?

OVIDE: A piece of bad luck. A house in repair. The scaffolding collapses, and unluckily, three hundred kilos will fall on the head of Jeanne Fortier. (takes lantern) Come.

(He opens the window.)

OVIDE: See that house? You see the scaffolding?

PAUL: Are you sure she passes by in the street every morning?

OVIDE: Yes, rolling her cart with her bread. Her path never varies. She stops at the same time at the same place every day.

(He shuts the window and the blinds.)

PAUL: But who will unhook the scaffolding?

OVIDE: I will. For the last week, I've become a sort of helper to the painters who are restoring the façade and I've got a key to the chicken coop.

PAUL: The house is completely uninhabited?

OVIDE: Completely on weekends, and today is Sunday.

PAUL: And the scaffolding will collapse?

OVIDE: Everything is ready. All that's necessary is to pull a simple rope and the whole thing will fall on her.

PAUL: At what time does she pass by?

OVIDE: Five-ten.

PAUL: What do I have to do?

OVIDE: You stay here and watch from this window—raising the curtain a little—and watch for her. As soon as you see her—let the curtain drop. From where I will be, I cannot see her—but I can see you. When she's underneath, I'll release the scaffolding.

PAUL: But the Police will search the place for the cause of the accident.

OVIDE: Let them. Not to worry. There are two exits. I will enter and leave by the Rue Hirondelle. You can leave here without the least risk. It's three-thirty now. Let's go get some food! There's plenty of time.

(They leave.)

TÊTE-EN-BUIS: We're going to get moldy eavesdropping.
CRI-CRI: Shut up, will you!
TÊTE-EN-BUIS: My feet are freezing.

(Ovide and Paul reappear on the first floor. Ovide blows out the candle, and they leave, locking the door.)

TÊTE-EN-BUIS: They're leaving.
CRI-CRI: Both of them.

OVIDE: This way.

(Ovide and Paul leave by way of the Rue Hirondelle.)

TÊTE-EN-BUIS: They're gone.
CRI-CRI: Let's go to work. Keep watch while I open the door. (starts using keys.) I think I've got one.
TÊTE-EN-BUIS: Hurry-up!
CRI-CRI: Ah, this one works. Open, Sesame! Enter, Milord, and lock the door behind you.

(They go in.)

CRI-CRI: Quick—a light.
TÊTE-EN-BUIS: There! (lighting the candles Ovide left) That's done.
CRI-CRI: Give me this one. (takes a candle)
TÊTE-EN-BUIS: Now what?
CRI-CRI: You go through the furniture down here. I'll do the room above. Grab every letter you can find and don't miss one.
TÊTE-EN-BUIS: Count on me.

CRI-CRI: Get to it.

(He leaves. Tête-en-Buis starts going through drawers.)

(A Fisherman with fishing gear enters from the Rue Hirondelle, stops at a nearby house. The two policemen walk back and forth.)

FISHERMAN: Hey, Mathieu, are you still snoring?
MATHIEU (opening the window): What? I heard you.
FISHERMAN: It's past 4 o'clock.
MATHIEU: Ah. I'll be down.
FISHERMAN: I'll wait.

TÊTE-EN-BUIS: A pair of boots. I haven't found a thing.
CRI-CRI (upstairs, searching): There's got to be something.

(In the street, a Ragpicker appears, a sack on his back.)

RAGPICKER: There's nothing to be found here.
FISHERMAN: You can be sure of that.
RAGPICKER: Ah, Paris is ruined. The sewer wins. Everything goes in the sewer! Bad luck.

(The Ragpicker leaves. Day begins to come.)

1st POLICEMAN: Night's over, Mathieu!
MATHIEU: As today is Sunday, I'm going home, and get some sleep.
2nd POLICEMAN: Good-bye.

(Mathieu and the Fisherman leave in one direction. The policemen continue to stroll the other way. A wine shop opens. Windows go up. Cri-Cri is still upstairs, and Tête-en-Buis on the ground floor.)

TÊTE-EN-BUIS: Nothing. I haven't found a thing..

232

CRI-CRI: Not a single slip of paper. Not one.

(Ovide returns with Paul. Ovide goes to the house opposite and enters. He can be seen. Paul goes to the door of Ovide's house. Tête-en-Buis starts towards the other room.)

TÊTE-EN-BUIS: Let's see in the other room.

(Cri-Cri continues to look with increasing frustration.)

TÊTE-EN-BUIS (stopping suddenly): Huh! I think someone's at the front door. (snuffing his candle) We're smoked.

(Paul enters the ground floor. Ovide appears on the landing of the house opposite.)

OVIDE: Now to work.

CRI-CRI: Ah, some letters—a bill fold. I've got some files.
TÊTE-EN-BUIS: Cri-Cri.
CRI-CRI : What?
TÊTE-EN-BUIS: Someone's in the house. We've been caught.
CRI-CRI: Caught? Just when I found what we need.
TÊTE-EN-BUIS: How to escape?
CRI-CRI: There's a loft. Silence! Just follow me. We'll go out by the roof.

(They vanish. Paul appears with a candle.)

PAUL: I thought I'd heard somebody walking upstairs. I'll go and check.

(He heads upstairs. Cri-Cri appears in the loft with Tête-en-Buis.)

CRI-CRI: A fire escape. That's one way out.

TÊTE-EN-BUIS: That way?
CRI-CRI: No choice. Let's go!

(Paul opens the window. Two women pass by, looking at the scaffolding.)

1st WOMAN: These masons will never finish it seems.
2nd WOMAN: The more they work the less complete it seems. And this is not work for Sunday.

PAUL (looking at his watch): Five o'clock. She'll be here soon!

(He puts out his candle and raises the curtain. At the other end of the street, Jeanne Fortier appears, rolling her bread cart in front of her. She stops at several houses to deliver bread.)

JEANNE: You need eight parcels today?
3rd WOMAN: Yes, Mama Lison.

PAUL: There she is. It's her! Finally!

(Jeanne comes on her route. Several persons emerge from their houses. Jeanne pushes her cart slowly.)

MAMA VERBOIS (emerging from a house): Madame Perrin, Madame Perrin. You are forgetting me today!
JEANNE: It's true. For goodness sake! Here, Madame Verbois. (Jeanne gives her bread.)
MAMA VERBOIS: Thank you!

(She disappears. Cri-Cri and Tête-en-Buis appear near the house Ovide is in.)

CRI-CRI (to Tête-en-Buis): Get on the sidewalk. Go one way, I'll go the other.

(He meets Jeanne under the scaffold.)

CRI-CRI: Ah, Mama Lison, we were going to collide.
JEANNE: Cri-Cri!

(Paul let the curtain fall. The scaffolding collapses loudly. Two screams. Then yelling. Jeanne is hit in the face by a corner of the scaffolding, and Cri-Cri is trapped under it.)

SEVERAL VOICES: Help! An accident! Call a doctor!

(Ovide appears on the landing of the house. Windows fill with people.)

OVIDE: That's the way one pays the bills.
CRI-CRI (noticing Ovide): A man in the house! And he's fleeing by the rue Hirondelle.

(The two policemen appear and rush to the rue Hirondelle. General reaction.)

VOICES: Arrest him! Arrest him!
(Tumult)

                                        CURTAIN

ACT V

SCENE IX

PAUL HARMANT'S OFFICE
Doors in the back and at the sides.
AT RISE, Paul is seated behind his desk. Dominique enters, bringing newspapers.

DOMINIQUE: These are the evening papers, Monsieur.
PAUL: No letters?
DOMINIQUE: None.
PAUL: Telegrams?
DOMINIQUE: No, Monsieur.
PAUL: Fine.

(Dominique leaves. Paul goes through his papers.)

PAUL: Still no word.

(Dominique returns.)

PAUL: What is it Dominique.
DOMINIQUE: A woman wishes to speak to you.
PAUL: What's her name?
DOMINIQUE: All she'll say is that she's coming on behalf of someone bringing news of Rue Git-le-Coeur.
PAUL (thinking about it then deciding): Show her in.

(Dominique returns with Jeanne, then goes out closing the door behind him. Paul looks up and sees Jeanne.)

PAUL (despite himself): Jeanne!

JEANNE: Yes, it's me! I didn't recognize you before at Maî-
tre Darier's, but today, I do! There's no doubt you attempted
to kill me at the Rue Git-le-Coeur.
PAUL: Wretched woman!
JEANNE: You are Jacques Garaud! You never expected to see
me alive again. God didn't wish it.
PAUL: You are crazy.
JEANNE: Crazy! Yes—I've been away. But I recovered my
reason. I've come to demand an account from you for all I've
suffered for the last twenty years, Jacques Garaud.
PAUL: I repeat, you are crazy, Lise Perrin.
JEANNE: I'm not Lise Perrin. I'm Jeanne Fortier—convicted
of crimes you committed.
PAUL: Another word, and I'll ring to have you thrown out.
JEANNE: Go ahead and ring. If you do, I'll tell your servants
who you really are.
PAUL: Shut up!
JEANNE: I will not shut up! I came here so the Police can
arrest us together! Once caught, you'll be forced to admit you
are the true author of the murder and arson at Alfortville.

(Marie enters.)

MARIE: Father, what's going on?
PAUL (crazed): Marie—Go away! This woman is mad. She's
totally insane!
MARIE: Then call the servants—have her thrown out.
JEANNE: I'm waiting.
MARIE (to Jeanne): What do you want?
JEANNE: That they arrest this man with me, and let justice be
done.
MARIE: You must call, father. (Jeanne laughs mockingly.)
Why don't you call?
JEANNE: Because he's afraid.
MARIE: Well, I'm not—I'll ring.
PAUL (stopping her): No—no—don't call them—don't ring.
MARIE: But why?

JEANNE: Because he doesn't want it known that Paul Harmant is really Jacques Garaud—thief, arsonist—and murderer!

PAUL: Ah, shut up! Have pity for my daughter!

JEANNE: Did you have pity? Pity for my children? Let your daughter learn who her father really is!

PAUL: Ah, shut up! Shut up—or else…!

MARIE (getting between them): I want to hear her speak. Violence resolves nothing. If she lies, she'll pay for it.

PAUL (shaking): Marie!

MARIE (to Jeanne): Speak!

JEANNE: Twenty years ago, this man stole, committed arson, and murder. And made it believed that he died heroically—and let me be convicted in his place. He assumed a false name and married your mother.

PAUL: Shut up! Shut up, will you!

MARIE: Speak—I insist on it.

JEANNE: He made an immense fortune in America and returned to France while I agonized in prison. But I escaped. I wanted to find my children. Then, luck caused him to find the son of his victim—Lucien Labroue—whom he wanted you to marry.

MARIE: Ah!

JEANNE: But Lucien loves my daughter, and to tear this love from his heart, your father had the audacity to tell her: "The woman you love is the daughter of the woman who killed your father."

MARIE (recoiling): Justify yourself, father.

JEANNE: Come on, Jacques Garaud, tell your daughter the truth.

(Paul rushes on Jeanne and starts to strangle her.)

PAUL: Ah, wretch!

(Marie screams and rushes out.)

PAUL (pushing Jeanne towards a door): You are here, in my home. No one can hear you. You attacked me. You threatened me, and I defended myself. You are going to die! Die, Jeanne Fortier, die!

(Jeanne faints. Paul pushes her body into the other room.)

PAUL: My name is Paul Harmant, not Jacques Garaud. Proof to the contrary no longer exists.

(Etienne and Cri-Cri enter.)

ETIENNE: You are mistaken, Monsieur, it does.
PAUL (staggering): Ah!
ETIENNE: It exists, and here it is. It's the death certificate of Paul Harmant—who died in Chalons twenty-five years ago.
CRI-CRI: Taken by me from your cousin's house on the Rue Git-le-Coeur
PAUL: Ah!
CRI-CRI: That scaffolding gave me a good bump on the head. Luckily my skull is hard to break.
ETIENNE: Sit down, Monsieur.
PAUL: But—
ETIENNE (glaring at him): M. Paul Harmant—it's a question of an object, ridiculous in itself, a child's toy...
PAUL: I don't understand.
ETIENNE: I'm going to help you.
PAUL: Well?
ETIENNE: Your lawyer turns 25 today—George Darier.
PAUL: Happy birthday to him. So?
ETIENNE: I have the mission of revealing to him that his name isn't George Darier, but actually George Fortier. (Paul reacts) The cardboard horse broke up, but strangely, it contained a letter. Jeanne Fortier told us at the time that she had a letter from you, Jacques Garaud, confessing your intentions—which she thought she had lost in the fire. She so testified at her trial. Of course, no one believed her—but apparently Little

George found it and put it inside his rocking horse. Let me read it. "My dear Jeanne, I've got the fortune I was promising you. Tomorrow, I will be master of an invention worth millions—and for now, I have 200,000 francs—"

PAUL: Ah—

ETIENNE: Come on, Jacques, the hour has come to settle the score with those you've destroyed.

PAUL (crazed): Well—what do you want? Say it! Say it! I'll do anything. Only—protect my daughter.

ETIENNE: Write what I'm going to dictate.

PAUL (taking a pen): I'm ready.

ETIENNE (dictating): "I, Jacques Garaud, in the presence of Etienne Costel and Benjamin Laurent…"

CRI-CRI: A.k.a. Cri-Cri—that's my nickname—

ETIENNE: "…I hereby confess that on the 6th of September 1861, I wrote the letter signed in my name—hereto attached."

PAUL: You want me to write a confession?

(Marie appears in the doorway, staggering)

PAUL: But with that confession, you could ruin my daughter. I won't write it.

MARIE: Write it father.

ALL: Ah!

PAUL: Why? They intend to dishonor you.

MARIE (almost dying): You will write what they dictate, father. Return honor, money, everything…

(Paul is dominated by his daughter.)

ETIENNE (dictating): "I confess to having stolen 200,000 francs from Jules Labroue…"

PAUL: No! No!

MARIE: Write, father, unless you want me to take the pen and write in your place. Write so I can die without reproach.

ETIENNE (dictating): "I further confess to having stolen the plans and formulas invented by my employer, M. Jules

Labroue, for a new type of unbreakable glass—and to having murdered him after having set fire to his factory…".

MARIE: Oh!

ETIENNE: "finally, I also confess to having tried to murder Jeanne Fortier…"

PAUL: That's false.

JEANNE (appearing in the doorway): No! It's true!

PAUL: Her! Alive!

JEANNE: You tried to strangle me.

CRI-CRI: Mama Lison!

JEANNE: Right here, just now.

MARIE: Now sign!

PAUL (in despair): Ah! (he signs)

MARIE (taking the paper): Here's proof of your innocence, Madame.

(The doors open on all sides. Enter the Police, Lucien Labroue, Lucie, George, Tête-en-Buis, and Ovide in hand-cuffs.)

GEORGE and LUCIE (going to Jeanne): Mother!

JEANNE: My children! (She presses them to her heart.)

OVIDE (to Paul): What do you want, old sport. I bit the bullet. They forced it out of me, the swine!

MARIE (going to Lucie): Lucie, I did you wrong. And yet, I'm not a bad person. What do you want? I loved him so much. Forgive me, I'm dying. (She dies.)

PAUL: Dead! Marie! My daughter's dead. I can die now!

CRI-CRI: (pointing to Jeanne, George, Lucie and Etienne): Now that's what's called a nest of honest men.

TÊTE-EN-BUIS: That's for sure.

CURTAIN

Screenplays

Mike Baron. *The Iron Triangle*
Emma Bull & Will Shetterly. *War for the Oaks*
Emma Bull & Will Shetterly. *Nightspeeder*
Gerry Conway & Roy Thomas. *Doc Dynamo*
Steve Englehart. *Majorca*
James Hudnall. *The Devastator*
Jean-Marc & Randy Lofficier. *Royal Flush*
Jean-Marc & Randy Lofficier based on Marc Agapit. *Despair*
Jean-Marc & Randy Lofficier inspired by Joël Houssin. *City*
Andrew Paquette. *Peripheral Vision*
Robert L. Robinson, Jr. based on a character created by Arthur
Bernède & Louis Feuillade. *Judex*
Roy Thomas, Janis Hendler & L. Sprague de Camp. *Rivers of
Time*

Non-Fiction

Stephen R. Bissette. *Blur 1*
Stephen R. Bissette. *Blur 2*
Stephen R. Bissette. *Blur 3*
Stephen R. Bissette. *Blur 4*
Stephen R. Bissette. *Blur 5*
Stephen R. Bissette. *Green Mountain Cinema*
Stephen R. Bissette. *Teen Angels & New Mutants*
Win Scott Eckert. *Crossovers: A Secret Chronology of the
World* (2 Vols.)
Georges Grison. *The Heads That Fell in Paris*
Jean-Marc & Randy Lofficier. *Shadowmen: Heroes & Villains
of French Pulp Fiction*
Jean-Marc & Randy Lofficier. *Shadowmen 2: Heroes & Vil-
lains of French Comics*
Randy Lofficier. Over Here: *An American Expat in the South
of France*
Brian Stableford. *The Plurality of Imaginary Worlds*